Dreams, Interrupted

The St. Louis Sisters Series, Book Two

Holly Gilliatt

Turquoise Morning, LLC
P.O. Box 43958
Louisville, KY 40253-0958

DREAMS, INTERRUPTED
Copyright © 2014, Holly Gilliatt
Trade Paperback ISBN: 978-1-62237-361-1

Editor, Judy Alter
Cover Art Design by Calliope-Designs.com
Stock Art by ThinkStockPhotos.com

Digital Release, July, 2014
Trade Paperback Release, December, 2014

DEDICATION

For Angie and Kara—and your five little miracles.

DREAMS, INTERRUPTED

*Maybe having dreams and getting what you wish for
is all a load of crap.*

It took Karen years to let the walls she'd built up finally start to crumble down. She was never one to hope and dream, and now she remembered why. It was just setting herself up for disappointment. She'd never considered herself mother material, but after marrying the one man in her life who had never let her down, she started to think having a baby was a splendid idea…if only she could get pregnant.

One of her best friends, Jayne, was the poster child for dreams with the wonderful family she'd always imagined. Perennially cheerful, Jayne believed in happily-ever-afters, looked for rainbows, and Karen figured she could probably conjure a butterfly on demand. But while Jayne plastered a smile on her face, she was drowning in a sea of diapers and domesticity.

Claudia, with support from her friends, had managed the role of single mother after her divorce with her usual grace. Scarred from the breakup she never saw coming, she submersed herself in raising her daughter and was content to stay away from men and the potential for another broken heart. Or was she….

Dreams, Interrupted is a story of three best friends that ride the often bumpy road of their dreams together—potholes and all.

4

Chapter One

Something strange started happening to Karen a year earlier. When she first noticed it, she wouldn't allow herself to acknowledge it. But after a few weeks, she couldn't ignore it anymore.

Shit.

It was happening. The whole mothering instinct, maternal craving thing she never thought she had.

Well, she did. And those feelings wouldn't back down.

It was probably Rick's fault. Ever since they'd gotten married, she was unreasonably happy. Like, to the point of being a happily-ever-after. It was something she'd never believed in, and quite frankly, always made fun of. Her friend Jayne was all about romance and true love and all of that crap.

Not Karen. But what a difference the perfect man could make. For her, Rick was that man. Caring, tender but never overbearing or too mushy. She didn't deal well with mush. He gave her space but was there when she needed him to close the gap. And he was fun and, *damn*, so hot.

She'd never ever forget the way he looked on their wedding day. Much to the dismay of her BFFs Jayne and Claudia, there was no way she was going to have a big ceremony with a poufy dress in a church. Nope. Karen was no fucking Cinderella.

So instead it was a beach in Punta Cana in the Dominican. Just her mom, her brother and sister-in-law, Rick's parents and brother, Claudia, and Jayne with her then-boyfriend Josh. All the people in the world that mattered to her, and no people she had to pretend to like for the occasion. And no poufy dress.

She and Rick were barefoot for the ceremony on the beach. The sun was just beginning to set. She walked down the tiki torch-lined aisle to the gentle ukulele sounds of Israel Kamakawiwo'ole's *Somewhere Over the Rainbow/What a Wonderful World,* which was about as sentimental as she would allow. Her brother Jonathan, who looked like a male version of Karen with his blond hair and hazel eyes, walked her down the aisle. She missed her dad, but even her cynical heart felt like he might be with her there in spirit.

As she approached Rick, her heart filled with that enormous, overwhelming love she thought she'd never experience. But with Rick, it was there. Always there. His shoulder-length wavy dark brown—nearly black—locks looked perfect in the tropical setting against his white linen shirt and tan linen pants without a wrinkle in them. Poor guy must not have sat down for an hour.

And his eyes. Those intense, gentle dark, dark eyes that saw Karen with all of her flaws and loved her anyway. She actually teared up for a moment. Though she would have never admitted that to anyone. But seeing the look of love in his eyes as she approached the man she would spend her life with...well, that was enough to bring out the emotions in even Karen.

Then the next five years flew by and she couldn't believe how happy, how comfortable they were. Oh sure, there were arguments and they drove each other nuts from time to time. But nothing big and nothing that ever dragged on for long. Just the usual "Why can't you ever put your dirty clothes in the hamper?" and "Karen, why on earth does it take you so long to get ready?" irritations.

So it was springtime, just a couple of months before their fifth anniversary when it started to happen. The way suddenly, everywhere she went, Karen noticed babies. Everywhere. And instead of a passing, "Oh, isn't that a cute baby" thought, she felt drawn to them. Walked up to them, smiled, made silly faces, asked their moms how old they were.

What the hell was wrong with her?

If she wanted to play with a baby, she could go to Jayne's house whenever she wanted. She was a baby-making machine. Jayne had only been married for four years and already had two kids. And if Karen was being honest with herself, she did go to Jayne's more than she used to. She was always offering to pick her up before they went out for a girls' night instead of just meeting her somewhere. And yes, she was sure to suck in that unbelievably delicious powdery baby scent and hold the baby longer than necessary.

She'd tried to tell herself it was a momentary lapse in judgment and perhaps even a mid-life crisis. *Can you have a midlife crisis when you're only thirty-three?* As usual, Karen kept the feelings to herself and didn't dare say anything out loud. Because then maybe it would sound more real outside of her own head.

And she didn't really want one of those crying, messy, unpredictable miniature humans, did she? She liked her life the way it was. She and Rick were both into music and loved going to concerts and hearing live bands at local clubs, even on weeknights. He was an artist, and they were often at local showings or spent a whole day at the St. Louis Art Museum seeing the latest exhibits. Their time was their own. They planned last-minute trips to Chicago for long weekends when the airfare dropped low and went on at least two weeklong trips each year, usually one to a beach and the other to some place fun like San Francisco or New York.

How on earth would they ever continue that life with a baby? And they'd never really talked about having kids. They'd probably only had a couple of conversations about it over the course of their seven-year relationship. Karen knew Rick was open to the idea of having kids but said he'd be fine without them, too. He was forty now, and Karen wondered if he was past the point of still being open to the idea.

But why the sudden baby obsession? Was this some cosmic joke? Sure, there were times she had thought about it in the past. Especially when Claudia had her beautiful baby girl while Karen was still in the post-wedding honeymoon glow. But it was a passing thought, akin to "Maybe we should get a puppy."

Which she had resisted until the baby cravings were undeniable. Rick had always liked dogs, and Karen never had one. But she figured maybe a cute little puppy would be just the thing to get rid of those terrifying thoughts of a kid.

Karen and Rick were just a few weeks into being puppy parents when she knew it hadn't done what she'd hoped. Although she loved the dog more than she'd ever anticipated, it didn't fill that annoying *I want a baby* craving she now carried around with her like a summer cold you can't shake.

They were lying in bed one night, Rick watching something on the SyFy channel while Karen dove into the latest David Sedaris book. Maybe reading about an even more dysfunctional family than her own would convince her bringing a child into the world was a bad idea. It was, wasn't it?

Kramer, their spazzy puppy, was curled up between the two of them, entertaining himself by chewing his own nails. What kind of dog does that? He loved gnawing on his claws more than chewing on the bones they bought him. And yes, even though Karen was insistent when they first got him that he would sleep on his dog bed on the floor, she soon realized she couldn't resist his big brown eyes any more than she could Rick's. So it was only a few days before he'd made their bed his own.

She couldn't even be firm with a damn dog. Some mother she would make.

But before she knew what was happening, she said out loud, "Do you ever think we should have a family?"

She could feel Rick stiffen up as he turned to face her. Even Kramer stopped chewing and looked up.

"You mean a baby?" Rick asked, clearly not understanding those words coming from his wife's mouth.

"Well, yeah, they usually come out as babies and get bigger over time." She turned back to her book, her heart pounding. *Why did I even say anything? Oh my God, what is wrong with me?*

He rolled over toward her, putting his arm around her waist. "I always said I would be okay with that."

"I mean, do you want that, or would you just 'be okay' with it?"

"Karen, are you serious about this? Because you always pretty much said you weren't the mothering type." His brows furrowed and his dark eyes searched hers. He looked at her like he wasn't sure who she was. Hell, she wasn't sure who she was.

"I know…but lately…" She sighed. "I've just been thinking about it a lot."

"This is a big decision, a big change for us."

"So you don't want a family?"

"No, that's not what I said." He pulled her tighter. "I would actually love to be a dad. But it was never a deal-breaker for me, and you always seemed opposed to the idea so I made peace with it."

Her heart started pounding harder in her chest. She realized now she had hoped he'd put the kibosh on the whole baby thing by saying he didn't want one and then she could put it to rest and blame it on him. Healthy, she knew. But she'd never been a poster girl for emotional health, so why start being rational now?

He tugged at her stomach. "So what's going on in that pretty little head of yours?"

"I think…I'm thinking that I want one now."

"Really?" She could hear the excitement in his voice. She couldn't resist a smile.

"But Rick, a baby would change everything…."

"Well, sure it would."

"What about all of our trips and lazy Sundays…."

"Gone. But we've enjoyed this life for years. And we can have it again someday. But maybe it's time for a change. Time to create something new together."

Looking up at Rick, she hoped they would have a little boy that looked like him. "You're right." She kissed him, as the yearning for a child grew even stronger, knowing Rick was on board.

"If we're gonna do this, we shouldn't wait too long...I'm not getting any younger. I don't want anyone thinking I'm the kid's grandpa."

Karen laughed. "Are you kidding me? You'd make the hottest grandpa on the planet. You don't look a day over thirty-five."

"Well, now that you've buttered me up, should we try for a baby now?"

"I'm still on the pill, though...."

"But practice makes perfect," he whispered in her ear.

Kramer barked.

"Out, you mongrel," Karen said, picking up the puppy and putting him outside the bedroom. She shut the door. She walked in the bathroom, grabbed her contraceptive pills out of the medicine cabinet and tossed them in the trashcan. Pulling off her top as she walked back into the bedroom and toward Rick's approving eyes, she purred, "Let's practice."

****

So after a year of practice and no results, Karen was getting pissed.

It wasn't supposed to happen like this. You just have unprotected sex and you have a baby. There were plenty of teenagers it worked for. Why not Karen?

I mean, really. If there's one thing Karen knew she was good at, it was sex. How could there not be a baby yet? They'd been copulating like bunnies. And then when she knew she was most fertile, it was at least an everyday if not twice a day occurrence. It was actually starting to feel like a chore. She sensed Rick felt the same way.

What was happening? Who knew too much sex could get boring?

And still nothing. Every month, her period showed up like clockwork. With each passing month, it weighed on her heart a little more. After six months, she went to see her doctor. He assured her there was likely nothing wrong, that it took a lot of couples a year to finally get pregnant.

But they weren't any couple. This was Karen. She had goals and she met them. She didn't have time for things that weren't going according to plan. There wasn't even a baby yet and it was already defying her wishes. Figured. Dreams, hopes—what a load of crap.

She knew she should have left all that feel-good stuff to Jayne. Being optimistic was Jayne's game, and Karen should have known better than to let it rub off on her.

****

"Josh, a little help would be nice," Jayne said with a sigh. She was struggling to put a sock on Emma's chubby little wriggling foot. Meanwhile, Tori was twirling around in nothing but a pink sequined tutu. "Tori, how many times have I asked you to get dressed? Your clothes are on your bed."

"But I have to finish my dance," she said with her usual insistence that came naturally to a three-year-old.

"Come on, Princess Tori," Josh said, walking into the room. "The ballet must wait. We have a birthday party to go to."

"What were you doing?" Jayne asked, looking at Josh with what she knew was exasperation. "I asked for help ten minutes ago. We're going to be late. Again."

"I'm sorry, sweetheart," he said. "I was just caught up in a book. Lost track of time."

His big green eyes did show regret. It was hard to stay angry with him. But it didn't make it any less frustrating. Sometimes she felt like he was her third child. He smiled at Jayne as he grabbed Tori's hand. "Let's get you dressed quick so we don't get in trouble."

"We get to go to Isabelle's party!" Tori announced. "She's gonna be five but I'm only three and a half. I want to be five."

"Yes, but your sister is only eighteen months old."

"Yeah, she's just a baby," Tori said, following Josh down the hall to her room. "*I'm* a big kid."

"That's right, big girl. And big girls get dressed when

their parents tell them to."

"All right, Daddy."

Jayne smiled at their banter as she finally won the toddler sock battle and moved onto sock number two. Emma started chewing on Jayne's hand and when Jayne looked down at her watch, she realized they should have already left the house.

Sighing, she pulled the toddler's teeth off her arm and resumed the sock wrestling, round two.

****

Claudia smiled, looking around the room. Everything looked perfect, just as she had imagined. There were pink and purple paper lanterns hanging from the ceiling—Isabella's favorite colors, of course. The "My Little Pony" theme was tastefully interspersed with pink cloth tablecloths and purple tulips in delicate arrangements on the tables (which were not easy to find in November).

As usual, Claudia made decorative place cards. She used thick, scented paper in a lilac shade with pieces of flower petals ingrained in the paper. She'd pulled out her calligraphy kit and with great care wrote each child's name in fancy script before inserting the cards into delicate little ceramic baskets filled with color-coordinated candy.

She'd made the cake herself, following instructions she'd found on a website. It had taken her about four hours to complete last night, but she was pleased with the outcome. It looked just like Isabella's favorite Little Pony, Twilight Sparkle. She couldn't wait to see what Isabella thought when her dad brought her home.

Just then, the doorbell rang, and Claudia glanced out the front door to see her ex-husband Sam's black BMW parked in the driveway.

"Come on in," she hollered, stepping back from the table she'd been admiring with the cake.

"Mommy!" Isabella yelled as she stormed through the door, with Sam laughing as he followed behind. Soon Isabella was hugging her mom. "Everything is so pretty! Oooh!" She squealed with delight, pointing at the cake and jumping up and down.

"Wow. Claud, that's amazing," he said, leaning over and giving her a quick peck on the cheek. "You got lucky in the mommy department, Bella. She's like Martha Stewart, only way hotter."

Claudia shot him a dirty look but cracked a smile. It had taken a lot of years to get them back to the playful banter stage, but it was nice that they were now in a comfortable place with each other.

"I have the best mommy ever. Wait until my friends see my Twilight Sparkle cake."

"Well thank you," she said, kissing her daughter on the head. "Now take your bag upstairs to your room and put on your birthday dress."

"Okay," she said, scrambling up the old wooden stairs of the refurbished turn-of-the-century home.

"So, Claud, everything does look fantastic as usual."

"Thanks, Sam. And it really helped with you having Isabella at your place last night. I couldn't have gotten everything done with her in the middle of it all."

"Yeah, she can be a little...enthusiastic." They both chuckled, knowing full well their daughter had the energy of at least three five-year-olds. "So we've got an hour until party time. What can I do to help?"

"Well, I need to make the punch and finish getting myself ready."

"Why don't you take care of yourself, and show me the punch recipe and I'll take care of that?"

"That would be perfect." They headed to the kitchen, and Claudia pulled out her red and white checked *Better Homes and Gardens New Cook Book*. Hers was from 1990, given to her by her grandma. After her grandma passed away a few years ago, she inherited her copy from 1959. She often enjoyed pulling recipes from the older edition, which used antiquated cooking terms like oleo, salad oil, and called for a liberal usage of fat in many recipes. The pictures of women cooking in dresses only added to its charm. But today she was using her newer version for her favorite punch recipe, and by using raspberry sherbet, it would fit in with the party's color scheme.

"Think you can handle this?" she asked Sam, passing him the cookbook with the Post-It arrow pointing to the sherbet punch recipe.

"Four ingredients, one of which is water. Yeah, I've got this."

"Great."

"Is the punch bowl still under here?" he asked, opening a cabinet door.

"Yep. I'll be back down in a little bit." She stopped by Isabella's room, asking her to stay in her room and play— so she wouldn't mess up anything downstairs. Isabella complied, playing with, what else? My Little Ponies. Claudia marveled at her daughter's beauty…a perfect blend of both of her parents' features. Their dark hair, Claudia's fair skin and delicate features, Sam's broad smile and full lips. Of course Claudia knew she was biased, but there was no denying she was a pretty girl.

And Claudia's dream come true.

Her whole life she'd wanted to be a mom. Of course she'd never imagined motherhood would only come after the demise of what she thought was the perfect marriage. So as her heart was breaking for the loss of the man she'd loved, her heart also began to soar with the love of a child that was so much greater than what she had ever shared with Sam. It turned out they were better at creating love than making it last.

The first couple of years were difficult. There were hurt feelings, anger, loneliness. But in time, the frost thawed. It was hard not to have a bond with Sam as they both oohed and aahed over their daughter's first steps, first words and all the other milestones parents cherish. So they weren't together as husband and wife. They still had to work together as parents.

And they'd figured out a way to do that. They had somehow become friends again. Sam was always open to that, but he was the one who left, not Claudia. So it took a couple of years for the pain and embarrassment to fade to a dull ache she could, for the most part, suppress.

Claudia changed out of her yoga pants and T-shirt into a pair of slim-fitting jeans and creamy sweater, then pulled her hair into a sleek ponytail that would come in handy during a hectic birthday party for a five-year-old. After applying her make-up, she headed down the hall to check on Isabella.

She was curled up on her bed with Sam snuggled next to her, helping her read a book. They looked so content, so comfortable with each other. And for a moment, Claudia imagined they were a real family, whole.

That dull ache—the one she worked so hard to suppress—rose into her throat as she pushed back tears.

Chapter Two

To Karen, it looked like nothing short of a zoo. A very girly, pink-and-purple zoo.

Maybe she needed to re-think the whole baby thing.

Claudia's normally stunning home had been transformed into a colorful, albeit as classy-as-possible homage to My Little Ponies. And it was *loud*.

Kids ran everywhere, twirling wands and wearing princess crowns that looked way too beautiful to have been store-bought. Karen was sure Claudia had carefully made each one herself. There looked to be about six little girls running around and three little boys, two of them wearing prince crowns and one who looked to be older that had apparently balked at the royal headwear.

"Karen, Rick!" Claudia shouted from across the pony-princess abyss. Her broad smile somehow seemed to be genuine and relaxed. Always the poised hostess.

"How the hell are we ever going to do this crap?" Karen whispered to Rick as she waved to Claudia.

"We will *never* do this," he said, laughing. "Claudia Knight is a domestic superwoman."

"Well, I'm sure as hell not."

"I'm thinking Chuck E. Cheese is more our speed."

"Yeah, or one of those places where the kids jump around in those inflatable things, wear themselves out and fall asleep on the way home. As long as they're not in our house."

Rick laughed and Karen was relieved they were on the same page as she reached out to embrace Claudia in a hug. "Claudia, you never cease to amaze me. This place looks...exactly like I'm sure Isabella wanted it."

Claudia chuckled. "I know pink and purple and ponies

aren't everyone's speed. But it seems to be a hit with the targeted demographic." They shared a warm hug; besides Rick, there was no one else Karen felt closer to in the world than Claudia and Jayne.

"It sure does. Wow—did you make the cake? That's fantastic."

"Yes, thanks," she said, smiling as she began to blush.

Karen rolled her eyes. "I will never live up to you."

"Oh stop, you know celebrations are my thing. I love this stuff. You, however, are the cool, hip Aunt Karen. No one will ever call me the cool aunt."

"Okay, true."

Claudia and Rick hugged, and then Claudia rushed off to greet some parents who had just arrived with yet another over-enthusiastic little girl.

"Hello, Karen," Sam said with a smile, approaching her.

Karen eyed him warily. "Hello, Sam," she said in a tone reminiscent of the famous, "Hello, Newman" from *Seinfeld*.

"I see you're still my biggest fan. Can I take your coats?"

"Sure, man," Rick said, smiling, in an obvious attempt to defrost the mood Karen had created. He pulled off Karen's coat and handed them both to Sam.

"Karen," Rick whispered as Sam walked away. "Will you chill out? It's been years since they split."

"Oh, I'm sorry, I didn't know there was a time limit on loyalty," Karen hissed back.

"I think if Claudia's gotten past it, you can too."

"Everyone knows she's way nicer than me."

Sam returned. "Can you believe she's five years old?"

"No, I can't," Rick said, giving Karen a gentle nudge.

"I guess time flies when you only see your kid on the weekends, huh?" she offered with a sickeningly sweet smile.

Sam sighed. "I see her during the week, too."

"In between all those power dinners and mindless flings, I presume."

Claudia was heading their way. "Karen," she said, shaking her head. "I could tell from across the room that you're stirring up trouble. You have to obey the same rules as the rest of the partygoers. Everyone has to get along and use your nice words and manners."

"Well, shit, I'm certainly at the wrong party then."

"Karen—"

"I'm just joking. I'll play nice, Sam." She smiled at them both. "As nice as I can."

Karen headed to the food table with lavender-colored punch, saying under her breath, "It will be a lot easier if the punch is spiked."

Her suspicion of virgin punch was confirmed as she took a drink, but the frothy concoction was, of course, delicious. She was surveying the controlled melee in the living room as Claudia somehow corralled all the kids to sit down and play Bingo when the front door flew open and a curly-, auburn-haired little girl came running in the room shouting, "I'm here, Isabella! I'm here!"

Standing behind Tori Brandt was her mom, Jayne, with matching auburn hair and looking absolutely overwhelmed and exhausted. Josh followed close behind, holding their dark-haired toddler with huge cheeks and an equally huge smile flanked by her Uncle Gray's dimples. Josh, as always, appeared relaxed and smiled as he waved.

Karen was still not used to this version of Jayne. As Jayne approached, she plastered a smile on her face that a stranger would have bought, but Karen knew better. She missed the genuine Jayne smile, the one full of hope and general optimism.

It had been a while since she'd seen that.

This Jayne looked tired and, although Karen would never say a word about it to Jayne, at least twenty pounds heavier. Gone was the perkiness Karen had grown to love and loath all at the same time. But no one could stay cranky around Jayne's happy attitude. Which was why it was all the more disconcerting to see Jayne faking it.

"Please tell me there's booze in that punch," Jayne said, hugging Karen.

Karen laughed. "No, but it's good." She ladled some

into a pony cup for Jayne and handed it to her.

After taking a healthy swig, Jayne smiled. "That is sooo yummy." Her smile drooped. "So I'm sure it's full of calories and fat."

"I think it's against the rules to count that at a birthday party."

"Yeah, well, tell my body that." Just then, they both noticed Emma climbing onto a chair, reaching for the birthday cake. "Oh no!"

Jayne dashed across the room and managed to grab the toddler…but not before she stuck her hand right in the pony's nose.

"Oh, Emma," she said, looking as if she were about to cry. Claudia was heading over. "Claudia, I am so sorry."

Emma stuffed her hand full of icing into her mouth.

"Don't worry about it," Claudia said, grabbing a napkin and wiping off Emma's hand. "Is that yummy, Emma?"

The little girl nodded her head.

"Please tell me you got a picture of it before she destroyed it," Jayne said quietly.

"Of course. It will look flawless in her birthday scrapbook. Don't look so upset." Claudia headed back to the Bingo game.

Josh approached and Karen was surprised at the anger she saw flash in Jayne's eyes as she looked at him with silent accusations.

"I'm sorry, I just put her down for like one minute…" he began.

"Well, a toddler can get into a lot of trouble in one minute." Jayne shoved Emma back at Josh. "Please keep a close eye on her. I'll be back."

Jayne hurried out of the room, into the kitchen.

Josh looked at Karen with pleading eyes. "I think she's been a little overwhelmed lately. I need to step things up a bit. Can you take Emma? I should probably go talk to her."

"No, I've got this," Karen said, patting him on the back. "Go get princess crowns for your girls out of that hideously perfect basket over there, and I'll go talk to

Jayne."

Josh smiled with appreciation. "Thanks, Karen. She'd probably kill me if I went in there now."

"Possibly."

When Karen reached Jayne in the kitchen, she was standing at the sink, wiping tears from her eyes. She turned at the sound of Karen's footsteps.

"I'm sorry, this isn't like me...."

"Jayne, I'm going to send Rick over one night this week to help Josh with the kids, and we're going to have a girls' night out. I'm sure I can scare Sam into giving Claudia a night off." They both laughed. "I mean, what's it been...three months?"

"Probably."

"Well, it's been too long. We've got to get that bubbly Jayne back and I am never one to turn down a drink."

Sam walked in the kitchen. "Oh, I'm sorry...I didn't mean to interrupt."

"Well, you did, so now you owe me," Karen snapped. "What night this week are you free to watch Isabella so Claudia can get a night out with us girls?"

"Uh...Tuesday?" he said, looking surprised.

"Then Tuesday it is. Can you pick her up from daycare?"

"Yeah, I can manage that."

"See, and Claudia thinks we can't get along." Karen smiled at him as he shook his head with sparks of irritation in his eyes.

****

"Oh, I needed this so badly," Jayne said, putting down the half-empty oversized glass. "Hacienda has the best margaritas in town."

"They're in the running, that's for sure," Karen said, delighting in the combined flavor of tequila and salt.

"Karen," Claudia said, nudging her, "I don't know what you said to Sam so he'd pick up Isabella from daycare today, but he almost seemed scared."

Karen smirked. "We had an understanding." She

dunked a still-warm, greasy, salty chip into the house-made salsa with just the right amount of kick that she loved. The perfect margarita accompaniment. "So, Miss Jayne...what's going on with you? What's wrong?"

"Oh, nothing's wrong," Jayne said, taking another gulp. Karen did notice she looked much more relaxed around her friends and drinks than she had at the party on Saturday.

"At the party I practically saw fire shooting from your eyes at Josh. Normally you two are so snuggly and goo-goo-eyed it makes me nauseous."

Jayne laughed. "It was just a stressful day. Nothing a night out with you two can't fix."

"Amen to that," Claudia said, raising her glass. They tapped their glasses as she said, "To best friends."

"And to designated drivers," Jayne said with a giggle. "Thanks for agreeing to drive us home, Claudia."

"Yep, that's why I'm drinking iced tea."

"Not me!" Jayne said, motioning to the waiter. He came over. "I need another margarita. What about you, Karen?"

Looking down at her half-empty glass, she smiled. "Sure, what the hell? Another for me, too."

After the waiter walked away, Karen started keeping tabs on a guy across the room who seemed to be paying a lot of attention to Claudia. And why wouldn't he? She was gorgeous. He wasn't bad looking, either. *Maybe I should intervene.*

"Earth to Karen," Jayne said, pulling Karen away from Mr. Potential BFF Suitor. "What are you staring at?"

"I wasn't staring," Karen clarified. "I was doing recon."

"What are you talking about?" Claudia asked.

"Okay, casually look at your three o'clock."

Claudia's head whipped around like a recoiling sprinkler.

Karen shook her head. "So much for being casual."

"What am I looking at?"

"The guy in the black golf shirt. Blondish hair."

"What about him?"

"He's been checking you out."

Just then, he turned and looked in their direction. Their heads snapped away as they all appeared to have a sudden fascination with their silverware. Jayne, under the apparent influence of the margaritas she'd downed, started uncontrolled giggling.

"Shhh!" Claudia said, her face turning red.

Karen rolled her eyes but couldn't dare to look in the guy's direction. "You guys are hopeless. Clearly we would have sucked at being Charlie's Angels."

"Claudia," Jayne whispered, "I think Karen's right. He smiled at you."

"There's no way I can look over there now." Claudia stared into the salsa bowl in front of her.

"Well, you don't have to because he's coming this way," Karen said, smiling at the man who seemed to realize he might be the source of their apparent hysterics.

"Oh, jeez," Claudia said, looking up with a terrified, fake smile on her face.

Jayne kept giggling.

"Hello," he said as he reached their table. "I couldn't help but notice this table full of lovely ladies."

Claudia's face turned the color of Kool-Aid Fruit Punch, and it was obvious that she'd lost her ability to speak. So Karen spoke for her. "Why thank you. And although two of us are wearing wedding bands, I notice that you're not."

He smiled, and his straight white teeth and soft lips made him look even more handsome than Karen had detected from across the room. "Sharp eye." He turned to Claudia. "And neither are you."

She cleared her throat. "Uh, no...I'm divorced."

"Aren't we all?" he chuckled, pulling a card out of his pocket. "I don't want to interrupt what appears to be a girls' night. But I'd love to take you out for coffee or lunch sometime." He handed the card to Claudia.

"Well, I...."

"I'm sure she'd love to," Karen interrupted, giving him her biggest smile. "She'll be calling you."

"Okay then." He chuckled, still looking squarely at Claudia. "What's your name?"

"Claudia," she said in a quiet voice, her face still an unrealistic shade of red.

"I look forward to hearing from you, Claudia. Don't leave me hanging." He winked at her and then looked at Jayne and Karen. "Sorry to interrupt. You all have a great night."

"You too, handsome stranger," Jayne said, erupting in giggles again. He walked away.

"Jayne!" Claudia hissed.

"What?" she asked, looking hurt at Claudia's tone.

"Pull it together, you embarrassed me."

"Oh, shit, Claud," Karen said. "Lighten up. We're just having a little fun."

"And I don't need you to throw me out there to guys." Claudia sighed. She actually looked pissed.

"I was just trying to help. He looks like good material." Karen patted Claudia's arm. "And I know it's been a long time."

The waiter brought their plates, overflowing with delectable Mexican fare. Karen knew it was going to cost her at least an extra twenty minutes on the treadmill, but the chicken chimichanga was going to be worth every step.

They were silent for a moment while they began eating. Finally, Claudia broke the silence. "It may have been a long time, but it doesn't mean I'm ready to date yet."

"But it's been more than five years," Karen said gently.

"And I went on a few dates, but I hated it. I'm okay with my life the way it is. Just me and Isabella. That's enough."

"What would it hurt to have a man buy you dinner every now and then?"

Jayne nodded her head. "She's right, you know."

"Because I'm just not ready." Claudia looked down. "I met Sam when I was only nineteen. That's a lot of years to love one man."

"I didn't say you had to fall in love," Karen said,

sticking another gooey bite in her mouth. "Just test the waters every now and then. You never know what might happen."

"Wow, Karen," Jayne said, smiling. "You sound downright encouraging. So unlike you."

"You're drunk, so I had to fill in for you." They all laughed. "Well, Claudia, what does his card say? Is he a garbage man? A masseuse?"

"A doctor," she said, grinning. "And he *was* cute."

"A cute doctor. I'm such a bitch, trying to set my friend up with a hot doc."

"Yes, you are," Claudia said, looking at Karen with a warm smile. "Hey, speaking of doctors, when are you going to see that fertility specialist?"

Karen stiffened. She hated sharing personal stuff. Especially when it was something that made her feel like a failure.

"Apparently he's so popular that he had a three-month waiting list. I don't get in to see him until next month." She swallowed. "We will have been trying for fifteen months by then."

"Who knows—maybe you'll be pregnant before then," Jayne said with her usual bubbly enthusiasm.

"Maybe," Karen said, although even her usual pessimism was giving way to a deeper funk. She didn't mention she'd thought she might actually be pregnant earlier in the day, until a mid-afternoon bathroom break told her otherwise.

Look where hope had gotten her. Just another date with a tampon.

"Enough baby bullshit," Karen said, stuffing more chimichanga in her mouth. Maybe if she ate enough for two, her body would reconsider and make a second human.

"We can talk about it if you want," Claudia said, and the compassion in her eyes was enough to even make Karen's heart feel grateful. The fact was she probably did need to talk about it. It was all she could think about these days.

But Karen wasn't a talker; she was a doer. So she'd

made the appointment, continued regular sexual relations with Rick whether they were sick of it or not, and read up on whatever she could regarding increasing fertility. Rick had switched from boxer briefs to boxers, she was taking her temperature and using ovulation predictors...whatever was in her power, she was doing it.

The problem was she felt completely powerless. Which was something Karen Gordon wasn't used to.

****

How Karen had found herself shopping for a home in the suburbs was beyond her. She and Rick had lived together in a cool loft space in the eclectic Central West End neighborhood for the past several years...and now she was in suburbia hell. All for a baby. This baby that didn't even exist yet was really screwing everything up.

And yet, somehow, Karen was happy about it. She actually was.

She never thought she'd look forward to swapping out her stylish high-heeled boots and perfectly sculpted designer jeans while shopping in her neighborhood on a Sunday afternoon, for yoga pants and tennis shoes to push a stroller to the park. But she found herself dreaming of comfortable attire and baby slobber. Hormones—powerful stuff.

And now, with a baby in mind, their loft just wouldn't do. Although Karen loved their neighborhood with its historic buildings, unique shops and artistic vibe—she wanted something different for her child. Well, that is, the child she was going to have. Someday. If it would just happen.

Living in a loft meant no backyard, no swing set, and stairs to climb with a stroller and diaper bag and all the other accoutrements a little person required. And she knew she was jumping ahead here, but she had to consider schools. Their loft was within St. Louis city limits, and it was no secret the city's schools were sub-par. Karen was way too progressive and liberal to consider sending her child to a Catholic or other religious school, and other private schools were ridiculously expensive. She believed in public education, just not in her neighborhood.

So she'd been scouring the real estate sites online, trying to find what she was looking for. She'd enlisted the friend of a friend who was a realtor, once she'd summed up the courage. Rick knew she was scouting for their new digs, but they agreed she wouldn't drag him through the house-hunting trenches until she found something she liked.

And of course she'd found plenty she liked, but not in their price range. She really wanted to live in one of the older suburban areas that had unique, beautiful old homes and massive tree-lined streets. Where the arts were revered and everyone knew their neighbors' names. Kirkwood, Webster Groves...one of those charming towns that had character and a days-gone-by feel.

Apparently that warm-and-fuzzy feeling came with quite a price tag. For fifty-thousand dollars more than their loft was worth, all they could get in those neighborhoods were homes with less square footage than they already had and a house that could only be called a fixer-upper. If she wanted to live in one of those neighborhoods, either they'd be living in a very old cracker box or they'd have to win the lottery.

Since neither of those ideas seemed to suit her, she had branched out into newer (and in Karen's mind) even more suburban-like areas. Soccer mom havens. PTO enclaves. Even though she could literally feel the city-dwelling vibes seeping out of her pores, she was excited. As she followed Joe, the realtor, into the Chesterfield subdivision, there were kids everywhere. Riding their bikes, running around in fenced-in manicured yards with SUV's parked in the driveways. It was an older neighborhood that seemed less cookie-cutter than the other ones they'd been to. This seemed to have a little more character.

They pulled into the driveway of a home that was well maintained. It was a story-and-a-half house with good-sized trees in the front yard and a welcoming front entrance. She knew from the paperwork Joe had given her the house was almost forty years old, but it didn't look like the typical Midwestern house from the seventies; it had almost an Arts and Crafts style to it.

After Joe showed her around the house, she knew it would be a good fit for them. It had nearly twice the square footage of their loft, three bedrooms (including a main-floor master suite), and a bright, open kitchen that seemed like the perfect heart of a family home. The main floor boasted gleaming hardwood instead of the usual carpet. It would need some updating; Karen didn't like the old style of the cabinets and the bathroom fixtures. But it certainly had some potential.

Joe was talking about low-E windows and the new furnace when she looked outside the breakfast room doors, which led to a deck. Outside was a large, flat backyard filled with trees. A tire swing hung from an old tree, and Karen had a sudden vision of Rick building a tree house in that great big oak. Emotion swelled in her throat. She could really picture them here. A family.

Her heart was pounding. She was excited and terrified all at the same time. She was so thrilled at the thought of starting a family and creating a whole new chapter of her life. But she was also afraid of losing the hip, cosmopolitan, urban side of herself. Would she have anything in common with the women in this neighborhood? Would they all be in scrapbooking and Bunko clubs, listening to light pop music and swapping diet tricks? Would they just sit around and gab about the school fundraiser while their kids were on a playdate? What if her artistic, graphic-designer Rick had nothing in common with the other husbands who she assumed were all hunters and ultra-conservatives who quoted Rush Limbaugh?

Could they fit in here? Could they swap art galleries for little league? Cosmopolitan cafés for McDonald's? Funky boutiques for Gymboree?

Karen almost felt as if she couldn't breathe. She was so close to a turning point in her life, and it was something she knew she truly wanted. But she was afraid of losing herself.

Of losing her identity and becoming like the bland, uniform houses she'd seen earlier in the day. She wanted to retain her individuality and keep some of the Karen she'd grown to be the past thirty-four years.

"So what do you think?" Joe asked, pulling her back to the present.

"I think it's got potential." She composed herself, though her mind was still swimming. "Definite potential."

"Do you want to put in an offer?"

"No, not yet. This is a big step. I need to think about it and talk things over with Rick."

"That's fine. Why don't we go and you can give me a call tomorrow when you're ready to talk?"

"Perfect." They walked outside and Karen twisted her bright purple scarf around her neck, trying to insulate against the wind that had picked up. It was turning colder by the day. As she opened her car door, she saw two men with a double stroller on the sidewalk, coming closer to her.

They smiled and she gave a small wave.

"Are you going to buy it?" one of the men asked. He was tall and thin, with a shaved head and round glasses. His cheeks were rosy in the cold air.

She stepped away from the car and headed toward them. Her baby-craving heart noticed there was an African-American baby and an Asian toddler in the stroller. "I'm considering it. Any neighborhood advice you can give me?"

"Watch out for the gays," the other guy piped up with a smirk and chuckle. He was shorter and had a thick head of brown hair with blonde tips.

"I'll be sure to do that." Karen laughed. "Are they a real problem around here?"

"Well, besides us there's a house with *lesbians*," he said in a conspiratorial whisper.

"Oh, stop it, Anthony," said his partner. "I'm Gabe, by the way." He held out his long, thin hand and they shook.

"Nice to meet you, Gabe," she said, smiling. Karen turned to the shorter man and shook his hand. "And you're Anthony. I'm Karen."

"So nice to meet you, Karen," Anthony said with a wink. He might have been short in stature but she could see he was tall on trouble.

"Who are these cuties?" she asked, kneeling down to see the kids.

"Simone is our big girl, and Colton is our little man."

Karen smiled at them as they stared at her, both wide-eyed. Colton had the chubbiest cheeks she'd ever seen with huge, dark eyes that matched the color of his cocoa skin. His sister had little bows around the shiny black pigtails peeking out from under her hood, and she gave Karen a tentative smile.

"They are adorable. How old are they?"

"Two years and seven months," Gabe said, looking very much the proud papa. He adjusted his glasses. "So do you have kids?"

"Not yet," Karen said, trying to act nonchalant.

"You're not a lesbian, are you?" Anthony asked, a twinkle in his eyes.

Gabe shook his head. "Anthony! Karen, I apologize for him. He's my third child, I swear."

Karen grinned. "I don't mind a bit. And no, I'm not a lesbian. Not that I wouldn't be a damn good one." She met Anthony's gaze, and they both laughed.

"Ooh, I like you," he said. "I bet you're fun."

Gabe interjected. "Please just promise that if you buy this house, you'll get rid of those hideous cabinets."

"Yeah," Karen agreed, "they would definitely have to go."

"Unless, of course," Anthony said, "you enjoy reliving the seventies every morning when you get coffee."

"No thank you."

"And to answer your earlier question about the neighborhood, it's good. Quiet but with some fun people around. Lots of kids, a few older people. Pretty much young families, white-collar workers. Most of the moms work, but there are some stay-at-home moms."

"Like me," Gabe said, grinning. His tall, thin frame,

bald head and round glasses reminded Karen of Mr. Mackey, the school counselor on *South Park*.

"And he's the neighborhood gossip," Anthony said with a chuckle.

"Well, hell, I'm here all the time. I see people come and go all day, so I just keep tabs on things."

Anthony snickered. "Code words for gossip."

"You're just jealous because you have to go to work every day."

"Trust me, honey, I love our kids, but there's no way I would want to stay with them all day."

"Shhh, Simone can understand what you're saying."

Karen was cracking up at the two of them.

"Simone," Anthony said, bending in front of the stroller with his blond-tipped hair, "Daddy loves you."

"So do you know anything about the schools?" Karen asked.

"They're supposed to be great," Gabe said, rubbing his bald head. "The parents around here are really pleased. Of course we won't know ourselves for three more years, but Parkway schools are rated very high."

"Yeah, that's one reason I was looking in this area."

"So, Karen," Anthony said, crossing his arms. "Whaddya think? We've got an African-American son and an Asian daughter...do you think our next one should be Latino or Middle-Eastern to complete our United Colors of Benetton ad?"

"Jesus, Anthony," Gabe said with a sigh. "We just met her. She probably thinks we're out of our minds."

Anthony put his hand on her arm. "Am I scaring you, Karen?"

"Hell no. Takes a lot more than that to scare this broad."

"See?" Anthony turned to Gabe. "I told you she looks fun."

"You have no idea," Karen said with a wink. Both men laughed, their breath visible in the frigid air. "It was so nice to meet you both, but it's getting cold out here."

"Yeah, we need to get the kids inside," Gabe said.

"Which house is yours?" Karen asked.

"Two doors down," Anthony said, pointing to a two-story home with elaborate landscaping.

Karen started heading back to her car. "Well, you never know, we might become neighbors."

"That would be delish," Anthony said as Gabe started pushing the stroller. "Simone, tell Miss Karen good-bye."

"Bye-bye," the little girl said, with a wave of her chubby hand. Karen waved back as she climbed into her car.

A sense of relief flooded over Karen. Maybe suburbia wasn't the vanilla, boring, uninspired land she'd imagined it to be. Maybe she was being a snob and had been making false assumptions. As she backed down the driveway of the house she hoped to call their home, she smiled to herself. The house was perfect, and nothing made her feel more at home than a fantastic gay couple. There was definite hope for the neighborhood!

****

Jayne was so glad they'd decided to take the kids to cut down their own Christmas tree. She loved the holiday season and nothing said Christmas more than a tree. Growing up, one of her favorite traditions was going to Eckert's Orchard to pick out their tree and cut it down. It never really mattered what the tree looked like; to Jayne it was always the perfect tree because they had gotten it themselves.

Of course, taking a three-year-old and a toddler didn't exactly create the Hallmark moment she'd envisioned. She did that a lot—set unrealistic expectations for events that couldn't ever truly measure up. But Jayne, the eternal optimist, just knew the next time it would be as wonderful as her heart imagined.

She'd taken dozens of great pictures of the girls in their matching red pea coats, trudging through the fields and gazing at the trees. She took candid shots and then some posed ones in front of the decorative displays on the grounds. Both of the girls were excited; Tori understood what they were doing and had a great time, while little Emma was just along for the ride. She was smiley and happy as usual, always content to take in her surroundings.

Until they were trying to leave. Tori started throwing a fit because she wanted them to buy her some little ornament in the country store. Josh, as always, wanted to buy it for her because no matter how much Jayne tried to make him understand, he still apparently thought money grew on trees. His teacher's salary and her job in customer service didn't exactly make them well-to-do. Jayne was trying to break the cycle of Tori getting some new toy or gadget every time they went somewhere. It was obvious Tori wasn't too happy about her mommy putting her foot down.

So while Tori was mid-meltdown, Emma started fussing and crying because she was tired and likely figured she might as well add her lungs to the melee. Jayne just put a smile on her bright-red face as she dragged Tori out the door toward the parking lot, kicking and screaming, "It's not fair!" Josh followed right behind with Emma in his arms, crying and flailing about.

So much for treasured family traditions.

But despite the eventual mass hysteria, they did manage to have some fun and she had the pictures to prove it. And Jayne was sure that next year would go better.

They were driving home and the girls had both fallen asleep on the long ride. Thank God. Since there was no way they could have gotten the tree home with either their Honda Civic or Toyota Prius, they had borrowed an SUV from Josh's brother. Gray's SUV was an Infiniti QX80, so he wouldn't allow them to strap the tree to the top of the sixty thousand-dollar vehicle. But since it had a trailer hitch, they rented a twenty-dollar trailer from U-Haul to bring the tree home.

Jayne remembered the smirk on Gray's face when they'd stopped by to pick up the car.

"This sure sounds like a lot of trouble for a Christmas tree, Charlie Brown," he said, chuckling.

"It will be worth it," Jayne said, landing a playful slap on his arm. "It's about making memories."

He grinned at her. "I don't know, Jaynie. All the kids care about are the presents that go under the tree."

"You do not understand the magic of the Christmas season." She shook her head.

"Sure he does," Josh said, slapping Gray on the back. "All it takes is a Best Buy gift card, right, little brother?"

Gray rolled his eyes at the reference to Christmas six years earlier. He and Jayne had been dating at the time, and he'd never lived down the fact he had given her an impersonal and unwanted gift of a fifty-dollar Best Buy gift card, when she had given him a Movado watch worth ten times that. It was less than two months later when Jayne realized Josh was the Brandt brother worth keeping.

With a grin that brought out his charming dimples, Gray countered, "Well, it sure as hell shouldn't require a trailer and a saw."

So as Jayne stretched out in the car that was much more spacious and luxurious than she was used to, she let out a sigh.

"I don't know about you," Josh said, "but I could definitely get used to a car like this. I mean, I know it's bad for the environment and it's ridiculously expensive...but damn, it's nice."

Jayne laughed. "I was just thinking the same thing. But since it costs more than either of us make in a year, we better not get too used to it. We're lucky to pay the mortgage."

"Yeah, I know," he said in a subdued tone. Money was tight; there was no doubt they were living paycheck to paycheck. Josh looked over at her. "That was a crazy day, huh?" She loved that his dark wavy hair was always a mess but somehow suited him to perfection. He looked adorable as always, his bright green eyes sparkling.

"Yeah, but I'm glad that we went, aren't you?"

"Definitely. The girls had a great time." He chuckled. "That is until they fell apart."

Jayne laughed with him. "Oh, God, that was so embarrassing."

Josh just shrugged his shoulders. "They run a business that caters to families. I'm sure they see that kind of scene at least a dozen times a day."

"Yeah, you're probably right." In the background, the local radio station that featured Christmas music all month long was playing Johnny Mathis' classic version of *Winter Wonderland*. Jayne grabbed Josh's hand and squeezed it tight. It wasn't every husband who would put up with listening to Christmas music for weeks on end or drive more than an hour to cut down a tree like one they could have bought two miles from home.

Josh squeezed back and raised her hand to his lips, delighting her with a gentle kiss.

Jayne's heart was full. She knew she was a lucky woman. In the backseat sat two little girls that brought more joy than she ever imagined possible. And holding her hand was the man who taught her the true meaning of selfless, unconditional love. He was more than she'd ever dreamed of, really. Sometimes lately, she'd lost sight of that more than she should. In between working, raising two young children and running the house—it was often easier to get flustered and frustrated with his shortcomings. But a day like today reminded her of how lucky she was.

Sure, Josh could get easily distracted. Give him the right book and it was hard to break him free of that imaginary world. Or ask him to cut the grass and she'd look out and find him helping the next-door neighbor with a project while their fescue continued to grow in the Midwestern sun. And she couldn't count the number of times she'd found him rough-housing with the girls and getting them all riled up—when he was supposed to be putting them down for bed.

But she couldn't entirely blame Josh. The thing was, Jayne realized after their first year together that some of the things she loved most about him were the same things that caused problems between them.

His big heart was probably his greatest asset, and what truly won Jayne over. And his great body and striking green eyes didn't hurt. Yet that big heart also meant he was seemingly always lending a hand or going out of his way for someone in need.

Josh seemed to be the one his friends always relied on to help them when they hired a U-Haul to move. Or fix up the house they just bought. If someone was despondent over a breakup—call Josh, he's a great listener. Need your grass cut because you had foot surgery? Josh would take care of it.

Students always hit Josh's soft spot. If he had a student who was struggling and needed some tutoring or extra help, he'd offer to work late with them. His caring, open attitude often meant that kids who were having other problems— maybe at home or with another student—came to him for advice. So he'd stay late for them, too.

When they were newly married, it was endearing to see his selfless ways. But over time, it started getting old when Jayne was eating meals alone or, worse, when she'd have dinner ready and he'd call at the last minute, saying he was going to be late.

Then they had their own kids, and it was hard to find Josh's friendly neighbor attitude at all endearing. It became a huge deal. Jayne would be at her wits' end at home with two sick kids—snot dripping from their noses, whining because of sore throats and ear aches, clinging to her pant leg while she tried to cook dinner. And where was Josh? Off somewhere, playing Mr. Nice Guy again.

It was hard to argue with someone for helping others. But she tried to get him to understand the old adage, "Charity begins at home." She reminded him he had responsibilities at home, especially now that he was a father.

He was an amazing dad. So much more involved with his kids than most of the other dads she knew. Very hands on: he'd make Play-Dough animals with them, do puppet shows, have tickle marathons. And it's not like he was gone all the time—he was very present. It was just that he wasn't always there when he said he would be, when Jayne was counting on him. When she needed him.

Because the truth was, she was struggling.

Her optimistic vision of motherhood turned out to be...well...wrong. Not that it wasn't great. It was. But it was hard. So much harder than she'd ever planned or dreamed it would be.

Maybe if she had been a stay-at-home mom, she would have felt better about things. It wouldn't have been any less work, or any easier, but it would have all been centered on her family. Being a working mom meant guilt and a precarious juggling act. She felt like no matter what she did, something wasn't getting the attention it deserved.

If she really focused on her job, she felt like she was leaving her kids at daycare for too long and neglecting them. If she tried to leave work earlier or pay some bills online while at work or make personal phone calls to schedule doctor appointments or ask questions about signing up Tori at a dance school—then she felt like she was cheating her employer.

And if she was somehow managing to give her kids quality time at night and on the weekends, and giving one hundred percent at the office...well, that meant her house was in utter disarray. She was finding out what she'd resisted admitting for at least a couple of years. She hated to be pessimistic, but she could no longer ignore the truth.

Having it all was a complete lie.

And Jayne was angry about it. Who had perpetuated that myth, anyway? Who had sold that horrible misconception to women? Was it other women? Was it men who had no clue? Was it the advertising industry that just wanted to sell you more products to try to help you manage the impossible task of having it all? All in an effort to cram more into your day than was humanly possible.

Jayne was disheartened, felt like a failure...and just wanted a nap.

She wasn't a pessimist or jaded, necessarily. Her idealistic heart still believed in true love, miracles, good always winning over evil, and she still looked for the best in everyone. That would never change.

What had changed, though, was her image of herself. Gone was the perky woman with the can-do attitude. Now she felt like a fraud. She had the life she'd always dreamed of. A wonderful, adoring husband; two beautiful, healthy children; a nice (albeit too small) home; and even the perfect, lovable dog. But she was drowning. Drowning in a sea of domesticity, diapers, fur balls on the floor and dishes in the sink. When she should have been grateful, she was often left feeling overwhelmed.

She couldn't bear to talk about it to anyone. Saying it out loud would make her monumental failure seem more real. And it would mean that she had dreamt all those years about a lie.

****

"You're awfully quiet," Josh said, bringing Jayne back to the present as he glanced at her while she fiddled with the seat warmer in Gray's car, wishing she had one in hers.

She smiled at him. "Just enjoying the quiet and the ride with you." On days like today when she spent time with Josh and the kids and made some lasting memories, she was happy. She knew that was what really mattered, and being with them brought her so much joy. It's when she felt like maybe, just maybe, she did have it all.

When they arrived home with the Christmas tree they'd cut down themselves, they woke up their little sleeping angels. As they each pulled a girl out of her car seat, Josh caught Jayne's eye and they shared a smile that said, *Wow, aren't we lucky to have such great kids?*

And they were. Jayne knew that to her very core. So her optimistic heart soared as she followed her incredibly handsome husband into the house, each of them carrying a groggy girl in their arms. They would put up the tree and decorate it while they sipped hot chocolate and played Christmas carols in the background.

But when they walked in the kitchen from the garage, reality set in. Jayne saw the dirty dishes in the sink. Her eyes moved to the mess she'd left on the stove from doing her best to be a Supermom and make a huge, traditional breakfast to start their day. She put Tori down on the ground, and suddenly remembered she hadn't started the washing for the week. As Jayne walked into the hallway to hang up her coat, one glance in the family room showed toys scattered everywhere and the morning paper strewn all over the couch where Josh had been reading it.

Jayne sighed.

"Babe," Josh said, putting his arms around her, "I'm going to drop off the trailer and take the SUV back to Gray."

"Okay," she said, feeling the anxiety start to rise in her chest. "But that shouldn't take too long, right? We need to get dinner going pretty soon and clean up the house."

"Well…" That crooked, sheepish grin on his face was typically not a good sign.

"Well what?"

"I promised Gray I would help him hang some shelves at his place. You know he's completely helpless with anything requiring tools." He kissed her on the nose. "But I'll hurry."

"I'm sure you will," she said, her voice quiet as he dashed out of the kitchen.

As Emma whined, "Momma! Momma!" and put up her arms to be held, Jayne retreated to her new stress coping mechanism: eating.

She intellectually knew that overeating was counter-productive because it meant that she should start working out to get rid of the twenty (or if she was honest with herself, thirty) pounds that had crept up over the last couple of years. And God knew she didn't have any extra time to add a workout routine to her already impossible-to-achieve daily schedule.

But the extra bites made her feel good, for at least a few minutes. It buried the lies deeper inside while she put on her perky smile and pretended to everyone that she had, indeed, gotten everything she'd ever dreamed of and it was perfect.

So while Emma called out to her, Jayne walked to the pantry and turned her back to the girls while she snuck two Oreo cookies and stuffed them in her mouth.

"I'm coming, Emma," she said with a mouthful of dark brown wafers and creamy white filling. She grabbed one more cookie and shoved it in her mouth.

Chapter Three

Karen was pretty sure the monotonous sound of the scraping windshield wipers was saying, "Failure. Failure. Failure."

Rick was driving them home from the fertility clinic, where they'd just had intrauterine insemination, more commonly known as IUI. Or as Karen liked to think of it, shooting Rick's sperm directly into her uterus.

She knew she should be feeling hopeful. This was a better chance at them getting pregnant. But nothing about this whole baby-making escapade was turning out the way she'd imagined, and although Karen was never known for being optimistic and hopeful in general, this experience was bringing her down even more.

Karen had decided to have a baby and expected it to just happen. When it didn't and they went to the fertility doctor, she expected him to figure out the problem, fix it and they'd make a baby. Problem solved, on with her new life's plan.

But the doctor found nothing wrong. There was nothing to fix.

"Unexplained infertility," they called it. So Karen could only believe that it was her fault. Her controlling, stressful demeanor was psyching out her ovaries or eggs or whatever. She'd been doing yoga and taking vitamins and doing what she could to work against her caustic personality that she'd decided was the problem. All to no avail. Still no baby.

And as the wipers taunted her with their grating song of "Failure, failure, failure," she was reminded that it was probable IUI would fail, too. She was stressing out her body and not providing the welcoming environment needed to create life.

The wipers' accusations were starting to get on her nerves, so she turned on the radio, which was tuned to Rick's favorite local classic rock station. The Rolling Stones' *You Can't Always Get What You Want* came blaring out. *You've got to be kidding me,* Karen thought. *Fuck you, Mick Jagger. I don't need your input.* She quickly changed to the soft rock station. Amy Grant's eighties hit *Baby, Baby* came pouring through the speakers.

"Seriously?" Karen muttered under her breath. Rick was fast to change the station. Robin Thicke's infectious *Blurred Lines* played and even Karen couldn't help but feel her mood lift a bit.

"Hey," Rick said in a gentle tone, taking her hand in his. "We might have just made a baby. This could be it. We need to stay positive."

"I know," she said, not daring to look into his intense dark eyes. "I'm just afraid to get my hopes up."

He squeezed her hand. "I know you're scared…I am too. But I'm also excited. This could be the start of our family. Let's focus on that, and if it doesn't happen, well…then we'll go to the next step."

It was easy for Rick to say. She doubted that any of this was his fault. It was hers. Not even considering her bitter, jaded personality, she couldn't stop thinking of her actions when she was just nineteen years old. That was fifteen years ago—a decision made by a scared, young girl. But now, as she struggled with fertility, she wondered if karma was coming back to haunt her.

She was usually so guarded and cautious and careful. But there was one night—just one—where she'd failed to make the guy use a condom. She wasn't on the pill because the ones on the market back then made her sick. So she always made men wear condoms. She was in college and focused on her grades, but she was also becoming a woman and trying with desperation to find love and repair the damage done to her heart by her father when he left them.

Somehow she'd gotten into her psyche that sex equated

with love. If a guy was having sex with her, he was loving her.

Ha. What a fucking joke. She knew that now.

But at nineteen, although she could be objective with her friends and point out their errors in judgment, she wasn't willing or able to turn that same magnifying glass on herself. She might have known on some level that sometimes sex doesn't mean anything but sex.

She wasn't thinking of that, though, when in the heat of the moment in his dirty bedroom in a dirty house that he shared with four other guys...when he said he was out of condoms, she proceeded anyway. It was just *one time*.

Apparently back then she was fertile, and one time was all it took. She thought they were in love...after all, they'd been having sex for a few weeks. When she'd told him she was pregnant, he only got angry. They agreed on an abortion. He stopped taking her calls and a few days later she found an envelope in her mailbox with enough cash to pay for half of the procedure and a note that said, *My half. See you around.*

She didn't break down, she didn't cry. She just felt utter sadness. And when Jayne came to Karen's apartment the night before the procedure was scheduled, Karen was pretty despondent. She wanted to tell someone, and Jayne's earnest face and overall welcoming, big heart was the perfect place to share her troubles.

As she told Jayne, she didn't feel any judgment, just comfort. Love, actually. The love she was seeking from guys was instead coming in the form of friendship from this amazing woman. They'd met a year earlier when she, Jayne and Claudia all ended up working as tellers at a local bank. They were the drive-thru divas and all felt an instant connection. An instant friendship.

So of course Jayne offered to take Karen the next day for the procedure. But Karen was too independent and, quite frankly, too ashamed to share that experience with anyone. It was her mistake, her failure. It was her mess to clean up.

The next day, she realized that her pro-choice views and firm opinions that a fetus was not yet a child and early first-trimester abortions were at such a cellular level that they were okay...suddenly came into question as the sterile, cold procedure was performed.

What if she was wrong? What if those ideals she believed in were just convenient excuses? Her detached emotions instead went into overdrive, and she instantly wondered if she'd made the biggest, most selfish mistake of her life. Over the years, she often thought about what she'd done. Sometimes she convinced herself it was the right thing to do. She was in no shape at that stage in her life to be a parent, and she never heard from the guy again. But it didn't stop her from sometimes thinking, *my baby would have been six this year. I wonder if it was a boy or girl?*

And lately of course, she wondered if that was her one shot at a child and she blew it. And fate or karma or God was punishing her. She tried to tell herself the universe didn't work that way, but what did she know?

She wanted to talk to her friends about her feelings, but that was hard for her. Feelings were private. Guarded. Opening up was so scary.

But she knew she could, if she ever got brave enough. They wouldn't judge. They would just be there for her. Just like Jayne was on that day all those years ago.

When Karen pulled up in front of her apartment building after having the abortion, there was Jayne, bundled up in her cheerful pink coat, sitting on the steps in front of the building waiting for Karen. Tears instantly sprang to Karen's eyes. Maybe that asshole who abandoned her didn't care, but Jayne did.

She knew then that love really was possible, even when you least expected it.

"Whatcha thinking about?" Rick asked, bringing Karen back to the present.

"Oh, nothing," she said, as they pulled up in front of their local Imo's restaurant, famous for its unique St. Louis-style pizza with Provel cheese. "I don't really feel like eating out tonight."

"I know," he said, smiling. "I ordered online while you were checking out at the doctor's office. I just have to run in and get our carryout order."

"You are damn near perfect, you know that, right?"

His dark eyes seemed to smile. "Just remember that the next time I piss you off." He opened the car door and started to climb out.

"Did you order their cheese garlic bread that I love?"

"Of course."

In a few minutes they were getting out of the car in front of their building. Rick somehow managed to balance the pizza and bread, while gently putting his arm around her as they walked up the stairs. For once, she decided she liked it and didn't pull away.

Walking inside their loft, she was quickly met with a reminder of how things were not going as planned. Their place was in disarray—boxes, bubble wrap and tape scattered about. They had bought the house in Chesterfield and started packing.

Karen had hoped to be pregnant by the time they moved in at the end of the year. She touched her belly and wondered if maybe they had just made that happen today. Or would they be moving into a big house, with no baby in sight?

Just when she was considering feeling sorry for herself and moping for the night, their puppy Kramer careened around the corner of the couch and slid across the hardwood floor, stopping only when he stumbled into her feet.

"Well, hello, goofball!" she said, laughing. He wagged his tail with enthusiasm, always pleased to make a grand entrance.

They had gotten him at a shelter, and the vet and Karen's research determined that he was likely a Viszla mixed with something dark brown—maybe a Labrador. To many, he looked like a very skinny chocolate lab with a slightly longer snout. He was a handsome dog, but that's not what won over Karen's heart. It was his happy, goofy, spazzy disposition. Karen could use more of that in her life, especially now.

"Get comfy on the couch," Rick said in what sounded like an order, not a suggestion. "I'll take Kramer out before he has an accident, then we'll veg out in front of the TV and eat."

"Okay." Karen chuckled to herself at his new take-charge attitude. She was usually the one telling him what to do, although he didn't seem to mind.

When he came back in, Rick insisted she stay put while he poured drinks, grabbed plates and napkins and brought the food over to the coffee table. Kramer promptly jumped onto the couch and curled up next to Karen, resting his head on her lap. Probably in an effort to get closer to her dinner, but Karen decided it was because he adored her so much.

Rick had one last surprise up his sleeve; although they'd already packed up their DVDs, he'd left out one of their favorites, *Best in Show*. It was a Christopher Guest-written-and-directed mockumentary about the sometimes fanatical and crazy lives of the competitive dog show circuit. The movie never failed to make them laugh, and now with their own pampered pooch, it hit home even more.

The greasy thin crust pizza and hilarious movie helped take her mind off the obvious. And Karen enjoyed being snuggled between her two favorite boys. She didn't let it happen much, but it felt good—even for Karen—to be taken care of, every now and then.

****

Parking at the Galleria Mall could be ridiculous during the holiday season, but it was a nice mall and a relatively central location in between the girls. So they met up to do some Christmas shopping and squeeze in some BFF time.

Claudia was glad to be out with her friends, and besides, it was Sam's weekend with Isabella. It was nice to have a little down time at home when Isabella was with her dad, but by mid-day on Saturday, Claudia usually just felt lonely and didn't know what to do with herself. Isabella was her whole life now...she felt lost without her.

As they strolled from shop to shop, managing to make some purchases along the way, Claudia noticed that Karen seemed a little quieter than normal and Jayne looked tired. They were having fun, but Claudia had the sense that the world was dragging them down lately. She loved those two women like the sisters she never had, and her deep mothering sense just wanted to see them looking as happy as they used to.

They stopped into St. Louis Bread Company for lunch. The rest of the country knew it as Panera Bread, but in the city where it began, it was still named for its hometown.

"Wow, I'm glad to sit down," Jayne said, as they took a seat in a comfy booth. "And there is nothing better on a winter day than their broccoli-cheddar soup in a bread bowl."

"I know," Claudia said, sitting down next to her. "But don't look at the fat and caloric content."

"Tell me about it." Jayne sighed. "That's why I paired it with a salad and low-fat dressing."

Karen sat across from them. "I just said screw it, and went with the decadent Caesar salad and the turkey sandwich on asiago foccacia."

"Wow," Claudia said with a smile. "Very reckless of the usually restrained Karen Gordon."

"It was either that or hard liquor, but one o'clock in the afternoon seemed a little desperate for that."

"What's wrong?" Jayne asked.

Claudia knew that Karen and Rick would be finding out the results of their IUI soon. She'd wanted to ask about it but knew from experience Karen wouldn't talk unless she wanted to.

Karen didn't say anything right away, instead choosing to dive into the Caesar salad. Finally, as she swallowed the bite she muttered, "Fucking IUI didn't work."

Claudia exchanged a quick glance with Jayne before saying quietly, "I was going to ask but didn't want to bring it up if you weren't ready to talk. I'm so sorry, Karen."

Karen looked away and sighed. "I'm just pissed. You know me, control freak Karen. Always controlling everything. And now this is utterly out of my control." She took another bite and chuckled. "Although I'm pretty sure my anal-retentiveness is actually psyching out my body. I'm probably the one thing keeping it from happening."

"I doubt that," Claudia said, even though she figured Karen might be right.

"So what's next?" Jayne asked. "I'm sure there's something else you can try, right?"

"We could do IUI again. Or move onto IVF, in vitro fertilization. Or just say to hell with it."

"Oh, Karen, don't say that," Jayne pleaded. "It's going to happen for you. I just know it."

Karen rolled her eyes. "I wish I could bottle your optimism and shoot it up like a drug, Miss Jayne."

"Well, until that's medically possible, you'll just have to put up with me."

"Jesus," Karen said with a smirk but then broke into a grin.

"So what do we want to do this year to get together for Christmas?" Claudia asked, wanting to steer the conversation away from what she knew was uncomfortable for Karen.

For six straight years, Claudia and Sam had hosted the annual Knight Christmas get-together for Jayne, Karen and whatever men they were with at the time. It was always fun and something they looked forward to.

But then there was no "Claudia and Sam." And that first Christmas after their divorce, Isabella was only a few weeks old and even Claudia—who her friends called the Midwestern Martha Stewart—wasn't up to hosting a Christmas celebration with a newborn and a broken heart.

So Karen and Rick, newlyweds back then, stepped in and threw a nice, intimate dinner party with just Claudia and the recently engaged Jayne and Josh. Of course it was nothing like the elaborate, fancy affairs Claudia was known for throwing, but it felt fun and unfussy like Karen, and she was a great cook. It was less fanfare, more casual and no frills. And as always with them, it felt like family.

Ever since, they'd done their best to keep up the tradition, but it was becoming more difficult. Between Jayne having babies and Claudia shuffling Isabella back and forth with Sam...they'd skipped a couple of years. And although she knew Jayne and Karen didn't care, Claudia always felt awkward, like a fifth wheel. She wasn't part of a couple, and she had no desire to scrounge up a date.

"I don't mean to be a bitch," Karen said, sitting back in her seat, "but could we do it without the kids this year? Last year was a little nuts."

Jayne shook her head. "That was my kids, sorry."

"You know I love them like my own, but if we want to enjoy a meal with grown-ups, that wasn't exactly my idea of relaxing."

Claudia had to agree. But without Isabella, she'd feel even more out of place with just the adults. "Hey...."

"Hey what?" Jayne asked.

"What would you guys think of doing it with just us girls this year?"

"No kids, no husbands?"

"Yeah."

"Count me in!" Karen said, diving back into her salad, chomping on a crouton.

Jayne clapped her hands. "I have the best idea." She grabbed the phone out of her purse and quickly dialed a number.

Claudia saw the name "Gray Brandt" flash on the screen. Gray was not exactly on their list of favorite people. He might be Jayne's brother-in-law now, but when he and Jayne dated years ago, he had acted like a cad and broke her heart. "How could Gray be involved in a good idea?"

"Shhh," Jayne said, turning the phone on speaker.

"Hey, Jaynie, what's up?" Gray's deep voice answered.

"Hey, Gray, I've got you on speaker so be nice."

"Well, who's the audience? My gorgeous nieces or

knucklehead big brother?"

"Neither. Karen and Claudia."

"Oh." He sounded more subdued. "My biggest fans."

"Always," Karen said, grinning. "Lucky for you Sam flaked out and made you look not so bad."

"Nice to talk to you, too, Karen," he said with a chuckle.

"Hi, Gray," Claudia said.

"Hello."

"So…" Jayne said, taking a breath. "Is there any chance that the three of us could borrow your cabin out at Innsbrook for a girls' sleepover?"

"Can I be there to watch?"

"Gross."

He laughed. "Just kidding. Maybe. Anyway, sure—I don't mind. When do you want it?"

"When aren't you…entertaining someone there?"

"I don't plan on being there until New Year's Eve, when I'm throwing a little bash."

"So really—any time before then?"

"Sure, just let me know when and I'll notify the guards you're coming and get you the alarm code and all of that."

"Oh, thank you so much! We really appreciate it."

"There is one condition."

"What's that?" Jayne asked, looking concerned.

"Karen, you have to ask me pretty please." There was a pause. "And it has to sound nice."

"You are a sadist, Gray Brandt," Karen snarled.

"Well, that's the deal." His smirk was evident through the speakerphone.

Karen rolled her eyes. "Gray, pretty please, can we use your cabin?"

"Oh, wow, that was awesome. I even recorded it." He was laughing so loud Jayne had to turn down the volume.

"You son of a bitch," Karen whispered.

"And," he continued, "it's technically a chalet, not a cabin. Sounds fancier, don'tcha think? Anyway, ladies, it's all yours. Just give me a date when you decide, Jaynie."

"Thanks so much, Gray," Jayne said. She and Claudia gave a cheery good-bye while Karen stewed across the table.

"So what do you guys think?" Jayne asked, her face brightened with the enthusiasm Claudia was used to. "The place is gorgeous, and it can be like old times—just the three of us, lots of food, foo-foo drinks and talking about boys all night."

Claudia laughed. "Sounds perfect."

"Gray is an asshole," Karen said, "but I will take advantage of his *chalet.*"

Jayne pulled up the electronic calendar on her phone. "Let's check our calendars and plan the date."

Claudia was glad to see them both excited. And glad she had dodged the out-of-place feeling she'd been stuck with the past few years. Or worse yet, the thought of finding a date.

A girls' sleepover would be perfect.

Chapter Four

"So why are you so anxious to get away from me?" Josh asked from the bedroom doorway as Jayne hurriedly finished packing her bag.

She looked up at him, and after all these years, was still bowled over by his dazzling green eyes and crooked smile. And man, he managed to make a pair of jeans look so sexy. Why hadn't he gained baby weight along with her?

"It's not you, dear," she said, approaching him and planting a gentle kiss on his nose. She added in a whisper, "It's our adorable children."

"I can't believe you want to leave all this for the night." He gestured down the hall, where little Emma was using their always-stoic dog, Atticus, as a horsey while the off-key musical stylings of Tori Brandt soared from the karaoke machine that Jayne regretted ever buying.

"I love them, but I love my friends too," she said, swatting him on the butt. "And you're so chicken."

"What's that supposed to mean?"

"You can't even handle them for one night on your own."

"Sure I can."

"Then why are you taking them to your parents'?" She crossed her arms and raised her eyebrows.

"I *can* handle them on my own, but I thought it would be some great grandma and grandpa time for them." His crooked grin grew broader as he ran his fingers through his dark mop of hair. "And you've got to admit that it was pretty smart on my part to rope them into letting the kids stay a second night so I can come join you tomorrow after the girls leave the cabin." He put his arms around her and kissed her neck.

"Gray said it's a chalet."

"I don't give a shit if it's a hole in the ground, as long as you and I get to be there alone together." They both giggled.

Jayne leaned into his strong, masculine frame. "I know, how long has it been, a night away for the two of us?"

"Um…if we can't remember, it's been too long."

"It was before Emma was born." Jayne pulled away, zipped up her overnight bag and turned back around. "Which reminds me…since someone in this room hasn't gotten around to having that vasectomy, you better make sure you bring some condoms or there won't be any more action at the chalet tomorrow night than there will be tonight with the girls there."

"Yes, ma'am," he said, grinning. "That is one thing I will be sure to remember."

"Once again, I maintain your chicken status. You're afraid to watch the kids on your own and you're afraid of a little snip-snip down there." She pointed to his crotch.

"Excuse me if I'm a little protective of that region, but it happens to be one of my favorite things."

"But I thought you preferred sex without a glove."

"I do," he said as Tori came dancing into the room, once again in full ballerina regalia with her microphone. "But I also like to keep my stuff intact."

"Chicken." Jayne stuck her tongue out at him as she grabbed her bag.

"Mommy just called you a name, Daddy," Tori said, giggling. "Daddy is a chicken! Daddy is a chicken!"

Jayne burst out laughing and snuck out of the room.

"Tori, you know I'm not a chicken," he roared in a boisterous voice. "I'm a tickle monster!"

"Aah!" she screamed, running from the room. Emma followed them both down the hall, well versed in the Tickle Monster routine of Josh chasing them to the family room and tackling them with a barrage of tickles.

Jayne watched the trail of little girls, her handsome husband, and one excited Labrador run down the hall. As much fun as it looked, she was excited to get away for some grown-up time. No diapers, snotty noses, or sibling squabbles for forty-eight hours.

And she had packed her version of hard liquor: blackberry wine and Mudslide mix. Who said Jayne Brandt didn't know how to party?

****

"How long has he had this place?" Karen asked, her mouth agape.

"A couple of years now," Jayne said, closing the door behind them.

"This is fucking gorgeous."

Karen walked across the room, and decided Gray was right—the word cabin did not quite do it justice.

Innsbrook was a beautiful resort community about an hour west of St. Louis. Karen read up on it in the car ride there, and was surprised to find out that the 7,500-acre resort boasted one hundred lakes and was a certified Audubon Sanctuary. As they pulled past the guard shack, it was as if they were entering a whole new world.

On that cold, wintry December day, an inch or so of snow capped the trees like delicate white lace and blanketed the leaf-scattered grounds. It was about a ten-minute drive from the entrance to Gray's place, and in that short drive they oohed and aahed as they spotted three deer, a wild turkey and countless squirrels. It took a lot to impress Karen, but the majestic beauty of this peaceful, wild place did it.

Gray's chalet was nestled among enumerable hardwood trees and scattered with evergreens. It was completely secluded, hidden from the road and so buried in the woods that it provided total privacy. And when they walked inside—wow!

The A-frame chalet was the perfect combination of rustic and chic. Exposed wooden beams, an open loft and huge walls of windows at every turn gave the feeling of being in a high-priced tree house. Every kid's fantasy in adult size.

In sharp contrast was the modern, chic, spa-inspired interior design. Karen half expected a hunky masseuse to appear or a woman asking if she wanted a mud facial. Everything about the place said relax in nature.

Okay, Karen thought, *I will.* With that, she pulled off her ankle boots and sunk her feet into the plush carpet. "I am so glad your brother-in-law has more money than he knows what to do with."

"No kidding," Claudia said, standing in front of a massive wall of windows that overlooked the wooded grounds.

"I guess when you make good money and don't have to spend it on a wife and kids, you can splurge," Jayne said, plopping down on the couch.

Karen sat next to her. "So do we start eating first or go straight to the liquor?"

"Both," Claudia said, walking to the kitchen table. "I brought all kinds of goodies."

"Me too," Jayne said, popping up.

Soon they had each poured a beverage of choice—of course Jayne's was the sweet blackberry wine, Claudia had a glass of Merlot, and Karen went straight to rum and Coke. What the hell. If things worked out (which she was beginning to doubt), she'd be pregnant soon and wouldn't be able to drink.

In addition to the drinks, they decided to make the biggest mound of nachos they'd ever seen. Ground beef, loads of gooey cheese, black olives, black beans, sour cream and jalapenos. They put the huge pan of nachos in the center of the coffee table along with a stack of napkins and swarmed it like kids around an ice cream truck.

They were laughing and joking like they always did. Karen couldn't seem to keep the nacho goo out from underneath her perfect French manicure, but she didn't care. There were only two places in the world where she felt truly relaxed. With Rick—and with Jayne and Claudia. And by relaxed, she didn't mean a normal person's version of relaxed. Karen didn't even think she was capable of that.

But for her, this was heaven.

Eventually the topic of conversation turned to fertility. Or her apparent lack of. She knew they would bring it up at some point…and a part of her did want to talk to them about it. About how frustrated and angry and afraid she was. They would be there for her. They would let her talk through it.

But she just couldn't quite go there. Not even with them. She'd spent way too many years carefully laying the bricks to build the walls that surrounded her. Not even the most devastating time of her life was going to make them just start to fall.

"So what's next with the whole fertility thing?" Jayne asked. Karen liked how Jayne managed to make it somehow sound like it was no big deal. Even infertility could be fun with Jayne.

"Oh, jeez." Karen sighed, wiping her hands on the third napkin she'd destroyed. "I guess we're going to try IUI again next month."

"And what if that doesn't work?" Claudia asked.

"Thanks for the vote of confidence." Karen crossed her arms.

"I'm sorry, I didn't mean it that way…."

"I know you didn't, I'm sorry. But that's kind of how I feel too. I'm starting to wonder if it's ever going to happen."

"Oh, Karen," Jayne said, her puppy-dog eyes turning moist. "Don't say that. You'll be a mom—I just know it."

"No one knows that."

"Well…I just have a feeling. I just really think, one way or another, it will happen for you."

Karen chuckled and gave Jayne a grin. "I will tell my doctor to take that under advisement."

"You should!" They all laughed.

Claudia took another bite of nachos and looked at Karen with eyes full of caring. "So how are you holding up with all of this?"

Damn it, Claudia, knock it off. I don't want to talk about it. I don't want to dredge it up, I don't want to admit what a fucking mess I'm feeling like inside.

"Oh, you know me. Just getting bitchier but otherwise I'm fine."

"Do you want to talk about it?"

Karen raised her eyebrows and set her mouth in a firm line. "What do you think?"

Jayne giggled. "Seeing how you just made your face scrunch up to look like the Wicked Witch of the West, I'm going to guess the answer is no."

Karen couldn't resist a smile. "If that was a thinly veiled attempt to make fun of my long nose, then game on."

"It had nothing to do with your nose. Although now that you mention it…."

Karen grabbed the pillow off the chair next to her and pretended to hurl it at Jayne.

"Are we like thirteen years old now?" Claudia said, laughing.

"Maybe."

"Well, Karen," Claudia said in her soothing motherly tone, "you don't have to talk about it if you don't want to. But just know that we're always here if you do."

After taking a long swig of her drink, Karen said with a subdued voice, "I know. Thank you." She hopped up and headed to the kitchen. "I'm getting a refill and then I want to talk about Jayne and why although she's still cheerful, the rainbows I usually see dancing in her big, hopeful eyes seem to be dulled."

Jayne stuck her tongue out at Karen. "I am not that perky or whatever you're always accusing me of."

"The hell you aren't. Except lately."

Claudia nodded her head. "Karen's right, you know."

Jayne sighed. "Everything's good…it's just that life is so hectic. I never knew it would be so hectic. Hey can you bring my bottle of wine in with you, Karen?"

Karen grabbed her drink and Jayne's bottle before she went back in the great room and found her spot around the coffee table/feeding trough.

"And…." Jayne looked down at the floor. "We're broke all the time."

Karen had gotten a sense of that but wasn't sure how bad it was. "How bad?"

Jayne looked embarrassed and shrugged her shoulders. "I mean, I knew we'd never be rich—Josh is a teacher, after all. And I've been doing the same job in customer relations for almost nine years now, which doesn't pay the best. But with kids and daycare and diapers…wow, it just adds up. And we really need a bigger place, but there's no way we could afford it."

"That sucks," Claudia said, squeezing Jayne's shoulder. "I mean, you know I don't make much being an office manager, but I've always had Sam's lawyer income to fall back on. He pays for everything for Isabella and was more than generous about the house and everything when we split."

"Guess I should have married a lawyer," Jayne said, pouring more deep aubergine-colored blackberry wine.

"Fuck that," Karen said, shaking her head. "Sam is a sleaze and you have a prince."

"Yeah, I do." Jayne grinned. "A hot prince." She grabbed another nacho, which Karen was amazed could still be intact under the weight of all the toppings. "And in addition to not making much money at work, now my supervisor's leaving and I have to worry about whether or not I'll like my new boss. And I'll have to practically train my new boss. More stress."

"Why don't you become the boss?" Karen asked, looking directly into Jayne's eyes.

Jayne looked confused. "What do you mean?"

"Why don't you apply for the supervisor position?"

"Me?"

"Yeah." Karen took a drink. "If you have to practically train the new boss anyway, that means you could do the job yourself. And you were just talking about how money is tight, so you could use the raise."

"I don't know…" Jayne looked uncomfortable with the

suggestion.

Claudia nudged Jayne. "Karen makes some good points. Why not?"

Jayne sighed. "I don't know. I just never pictured myself heading up a department. I've always just been a worker bee."

"Maybe it's time you become the queen bee. You've been there for years, you're the best one in your department…it makes perfect sense."

"I just never thought about it. That's a lot of responsibility. And with the kids and everything…."

"Would you have to work more hours?"

Jayne took another drink as she considered it. "Not necessarily. I might have to put in a few more hours here and there with more responsibilities. But overall…no."

"Well," Claudia piped in, "if you have to be away from those adorable girls of yours every day, you might as well be making more money while you're there."

A small smile played at Jayne's lips. She shrugged her shoulders. "Do you guys really think I can do it?"

"Of course you can," Karen said. "You're Jayne Fucking Brandt. You can do anything you set your mind to."

"Absolutely," Claudia agreed. "What have you got to lose?"

"Well, I need to lose a few pounds," Jayne said with a chuckle.

"You can join a gym with the extra pay."

Jayne laughed. "True. I think I *will* go for it."

"That's the spirit!" Karen said, patting her on the back.

"I wonder how much of a raise I could get?"

"With all of your years of experience there, you need to lobby for as much as you can. Remind them you practically trained your last boss."

"This is exciting…and scary."

"Jayne," Claudia said, "you have nothing to be scared about. Worst-case scenario, they don't promote you and you keep the job you've already got. But best case—you walk away with a better title and more money."

Karen held up her glass. "I propose a toast to Jayne, moving up the ladder!" They tapped their glasses and the ping of crystal meeting crystal sounded pretty good to Karen's ears. And for a split second, she was able to get rid of the thoughts of babies and fertility that insisted on haunting her mind.

****

It was almost ten o'clock and the girls, in their tipsy state, had moved on from the loaded nachos to dessert. A St. Louis favorite: Gooey Butter Cake. It was one of Claudia's specialties and never failed to please any crowd. As she chewed on her second rich piece of gooey goodness, she was glad there were only three of them there so they could each have more.

"We should have brought milk," Jayne said, talking with her mouth full. "A glass of milk would be awesome with this."

"You're so lit up from the blackberry wine, I'm surprised you can still talk," Karen said.

"Me too." Jayne giggled.

Claudia finished her piece of cake. "I say it's time to put on our pj's and get comfy."

"Yes!" Jayne said, hopping up from her spot on the couch. She wobbled a bit.

They went their separate ways and stripped off their daytime duds for comfier slumber party attire. Claudia had brought her favorite flannel pajama pants, pink and grey with whimsical white sheep scattered about and a pink fitted sleep shirt. Claudia looked in the mirror as she carefully removed her makeup. The thought crossed her mind that it had been years since she'd worn anything sexier than flannel to bed. With no make-up on, her hair in a ponytail and sheep scattered across most of her body...she thought she looked like a thirty-five-year-old kid.

She remembered feeling sexy...vaguely. It was a long-forgotten feeling...one that hovered in the dusty recesses of her mind. Like the feeling of anticipation you could still recall from the first day of school or when you started a new job. It had been so many years since she'd experienced those things, but she kind of remembered it. The rush, the excitement.

But the thought of experiencing any emotion regarding sex or being sexy produced only anxiety now. Maybe she'd never have any of that again. And although she was terrified at the thought of ever being with another man, there was a part of her that was sad, wondering if that part of her life was over. Was watching old DVDs of Patrick Swayze in *Dirty Dancing* and the hotties in *Magic Mike* as close as she was going to get to being with a man?

As she stepped away from the mirror, she figured that buying matching pajama pants for her five-year-old didn't do much to help up the sexy quotient.

When she walked out of the bathroom, Karen and Jayne were already in the great room, giggling in their pj's. Claudia smiled, always amused at how little it took for Jayne to get tipsy. And she was such a happy drunk.

"Oh…my…God," Karen said, looking at Claudia. "You ironed your pajamas before you packed them, didn't you?"

Claudia felt her face grown warm. "What do you mean?"

"You did!" Karen shook her head, laughing. "It's like a sickness with you, isn't it? Everything has to be perfect. You even iron your pj's."

"They're one hundred percent cotton—"

Jayne giggled. "But they're *pajamas*, Claud."

"Oh, you can both just shut it," Claudia said, laughing herself. "I can't help that I'm particular. I just am."

"Well, little Miss Perfect," Karen said with a distinct twinkle in her eye, "Jayne and I had an idea."

Why do I get the feeling this is not going to be good? "Idea about what?"

"Since we've covered my shitty reproductive system and Jayne's woes, it's time we focus on you."

"Oh really? I'm good. I've got nothing to complain about."

"I beg to differ," Jayne said, plopping down on the couch, wine glass in hand.

Karen joined her. "Did you ever call that hot doc we met at Hacienda?"

Claudia's chest tightened at the very thought of calling him. She tried to sound cool when she said, "Uh, no, I never got around to it." She sat down on the floor across from them, using the coffee table as a buffer.

Jayne giggled. "Uh, no, you're avoiding him. That's what you always do."

"Listen to your drunken friend," Karen said, crossing her arms. "You never had any intention of calling him, did you? You are a beautiful young woman. You've got to get back out there. And here you get the attention of a hunky doctor, and you still weren't going to call."

"I'm going to call him. I've just been busy."

"Bullshit."

Mind your own business, Karen. I wish I had the guts to say that to you. "It's not bullshit. I will call him."

"Did you even keep his card?"

"Yes, of course I did." *Only because I haven't cleaned out my purse in weeks.*

"I don't believe you. I bet you went home that night and threw it in the trash."

"Whoa," Jayne said, grinning. "She just called you an l-i-a-r."

Claudia was getting pissed. Maybe she never did intend to call him, but it was none of their business. So what if she'd decided to live the rest of her life as a celibate old maid? That was her choice. Maybe it wasn't the healthiest choice, but this was America and she didn't need anyone telling her how to live her life.

Even if they did have a point.

Indignant, Claudia announced, "It's right over there in my purse, Karen, as if it's any of your business."

"Of course it's my business," Karen said, leaping up

and rushing over to Claudia's Coach bag. "When one of my best friends spends five years alone for no reason, I'd be a horrible friend if I didn't try to light a fire under her ass."

Again, the pressure in Claudia's chest grew as Karen started digging around in her purse. "What are you doing?"

"Wow, I'm impressed," Karen said, pulling the doctor's card out. "You really did keep it. That's progress."

"I told you I did."

"But do you have the guts to call him?"

"I told you I had the card and I told you I'll call him. So drop it."

"Call him now," Jayne said, putting down her glass and clapping her hands. "Drunk dial him!"

Claudia did not like at all where this was going.

"Great idea, Jayne," Karen said with what Claudia determined was an evil grin.

"First of all," Claudia said, trying to sound unaffected, even though her palms were growing sweaty and her heart was beating out of her chest, "I'm not drunk like the two of you. So there won't be any drunk dialing. And second of all, I am not going to call him tonight…not with the peanut gallery in attendance."

"You'll come up with any excuse, won't you?" Karen's eyes met Claudia's, full of challenge. "You tell Jayne she should put herself out there and apply for a supervisor position, but you won't put yourself out there to meet anyone new. Kind of hypocritical, don't ya think?"

"Wow, way to have my back, Karen," Claudia said, clearly hurt.

Karen's face softened a bit. "Oh, come on, Claud. You know I didn't mean that in a hurtful way. But you know I'm right."

"If I want to date, I'll date. Why can't you just leave me alone?"

"Because I give a shit about you. Just like you guys made it clear when I was considering dumping Rick all those years ago that I'd be making a mistake. What if I hadn't listened to you? What if you hadn't kept reminding me how wrong you thought I was?"

Jayne nodded her head. "We did do that to her, Claud."

Claudia couldn't deny that. But throwing herself back out there...it was just so scary. She didn't think she'd ever love a man other than Sam. And he had hurt her so deeply. How could she ever trust in another man? And what if he was *the* man for her, and she spent the rest of her life looking for someone who was never meant for her?

"So, what, you want me to just call him now, out of the blue?"

Karen said softly, "That's kind of the idea."

Claudia glanced at her watch. Nine-forty. "Don't you think it's too late?"

Jayne chuckled. "Maybe for a twelve-year-old, but not for a grown man on a Friday night."

Claudia knew this was a bad idea. Her heart was now pounding in her ears, but she heard herself saying, "Fine, bitch, hand me his card."

Jayne started clapping her hands and Karen looked absolutely thrilled as she placed the glossy card in Claudia's fingers.

Claudia felt nauseated while she pulled her phone out of her pocket. "Now you two keep your mouths shut while I call him, okay? It's bad enough that I'm caving in to peer pressure like a teenager...I don't want him to think that I act like one with my BFFs giggling like inebriated idiots in the background."

"I'm pretty sure she's talking to you, Jayne," Karen said, grinning. Jayne just shrugged her shoulders as another giggle escaped. She covered her mouth. "Put it on speaker."

Taking a deep breath, Claudia dialed the number for Dr. Kurt Klatt. *Please don't answer. Please don't answer.* She turned it to speaker and the line began to ring.

"Dr. Klatt," he answered on the second ring.

Shit. What do I say? "Umm...."

"Hello?"

"Hi, Kurt?"

"Yes, this is Kurt Klatt." He was starting to sound

annoyed.

"This is Claudia Knight. You probably don't remember me, but you gave me your card a few weeks ago at Hacienda—"

"Of course I remember you. Stunning divorcée with tipsy friends."

Jayne's laughter was barely being stifled by the hands over her mouth.

Claudia chuckled. "Well, good, you remember."

"I was beginning to think you weren't going to call. Thought I was losing my charm."

"Oh, no, you're very charming. I've just been…busy."

"I understand. So does this mean I get to take you to lunch?"

Claudia looked at Karen and Jayne. Karen was giving her a thumbs up and Jayne was vigorously nodding her head up and down. What a couple of knuckleheads.

She cleared her throat then said quietly, "That would be lovely."

"Well, since these last couple of weeks of December are so crazy with the holidays, why don't I call you after New Year's and we'll set something up?"

Relaxing a little at the temporary reprieve, she answered, "Perfect."

"Can I call you at this number?"

"Sure. I look forward to hearing from you."

"And trust me, you will hear from me. Have a great holiday season, Claudia."

"Thanks. You too."

"Bye."

She hung up and Jayne pulled her hand off her mouth and screamed.

"Oh my God, Claud, I'm so proud of you!"

"See, was that so hard?" Karen asked, looking pleased that her coercion tactics had worked.

"No, not hard at all," Claudia said, thinking to herself, *But that doesn't mean I'm ever going to answer his call.*

****

Jayne couldn't remember the last time they'd slept in. It had literally been years. The sun was shining in the master bedroom at the chalet from the skylight above and the east facing windows. This time of year, she usually never saw sunlight in bed…she was always up while it was still dark outside. She rolled over and snuggled into Josh. She looked at him as he stared into his book and tousled her hair.

"Good morning, sleepyhead," he said, his voice textured with an early-morning scratchiness. "Do you want some coffee? There's none of your flavored creamer here, so I didn't know if you'd want any or not."

"No, I'm just fine. Better than fine, actually." Her seductive tone made him tear his eyes away from the book.

He grinned at her, his eyelids still heavy with drowsiness. "Would you like to do a replay of last night?"

Jayne was aware of the old adage "absence makes the heart grow fonder," but what she found out last night was a new concept: sex-deprived parents with toddlers could get crazy in bed when there were no kids around.

Jayne smiled, a small chuckle erupting from her throat. "I don't even know that I could. And I have to pee." She grabbed the blanket and wrapped it around her naked body as she climbed out of bed.

"You know, you don't have to cover up. It's just us in the middle of the woods."

There was a time when Jayne was comfortable walking around naked in front of Josh. But that time had passed. Somewhere after baby number two and the extra pounds she'd added. The stretch marks didn't bother her that much, but the roll of fat on her midsection and extra junk in the trunk made her feel anything but sexy. Of course the fat didn't migrate toward her A-cup breasts where she would have been happy for it to settle. Nature could be cruel that way.

From the bathroom she hollered, "Unless there are some miracle fat-diminishing powers in these woods, I don't want you to see me naked." After going to the bathroom, she came back into the bedroom to see Josh with a concerned, and maybe even irritated, look on his face.

"Jayne, what are you talking about? Are you serious about you not wanting me to see you naked?"

She was surprised by the stern tone in his voice, as she was careful to ease herself under the covers. "Well, yeah."

He sighed, shaking his head. "Jayne, you're gorgeous."

She rolled on her side, away from him. "I'm fat."

"Hey," he said, tugging on her shoulder, pulling her to face him. His brows were furrowed. "That's my wife you're talking about. And you're not fat."

Looking away from his stare she whispered, "Chubby at the very least."

"You're perfect. You are sexy as hell."

"How would you know?" she said quietly, still avoiding his eyes. "I haven't let you see me naked in months."

Josh put his fingers on her chin and turned her face directly in front of his. There was no escaping his green eyes, which looked at her with sadness. "But I see you in your clothes every day...."

"Clothes can hide a multitude of sins."

"They're not sins. They're part of you. You've grown two beautiful babies inside of you...of course your body has changed. And sure, I feel the extra curves. I felt them last night when we made love. The way you look right now, the way you feel in my arms, is sexier than ever. You're a real woman, Jayne. Not some stick figure in a magazine. And I'm even more attracted to you than I was the day I married you."

She wanted to believe him, she really did. The earnest look in his eyes made hers tear up. "Then you must be crazy, Josh Brandt."

He smiled, his morning scruff making him look even more handsome than normal. "I think that goes without saying, my dear. I'm crazy for you. All of you."

"Or maybe you need glasses."

"Stop it. Get over whatever BS hang-ups you have about your body and let me see you." He threw back the blanket, and Jayne suddenly felt way more than naked. She was terrified that once he got a good look at her, he'd be crazy to think she was sexy. But as his approving eyes devoured her and he ran his hands with gentle strokes over her body, she started to feel a little less vulnerable. A little more attractive.

****

"Wow, twice in twenty-four hours. I thought those days were over until the girls are in college and I need Viagra," Josh said with a chuckle. As they cooked breakfast together in the gourmet-appointed kitchen, Jayne loved that they were surrounded by windows showing trees as far as the eye could see.

"Maybe we need to schedule more alone time like this," she said, dishing hash browns out of the pan onto chocolate brown Asian-inspired plates. "I mean, between your parents and mine, I wonder if we could get away for one night every couple of months?"

"I don't see why not. They all adore the girls. I don't think we could convince them to do two nights in a row—I mean, they are a handful—but I'm guessing both sets of grandparents would be willing to take them two or three nights a year."

The bread popped up in the toaster, and Jayne pulled the slices out and started buttering them. "Do you think Gray would be okay with us borrowing this place from time to time? Because we certainly can't afford to go anywhere else."

"He's always said we can use it whenever we want. We just never took him up on it until now."

"Okay, then, let's try to make it happen. I'll talk to my mom and dad and see if maybe we could plan for something around Valentine's Day."

"Sounds perfect to me." He put expertly fried eggs onto their plates. "Let's eat!"

They sat down at the table, and Jayne decided breakfast tasted better when you could eat it without helping two little ones with their plates. She let out a huge sigh with a contented smile on her face. "You have no idea how much I needed this."

"Yeah, I was starving too," Josh said, shoveling a huge mound of hash browns in his mouth. *How is it that he is still so thin?*

"No, I don't mean breakfast. I mean *this*. Time away from the kids. Does that make me a terrible mom?"

"Jeez, Jayne, you're an amazing mom. Don't even think that. But everyone needs a break."

"I know I sure did. I miss them this morning, but I have to say…I didn't miss them at all yesterday." She bit her lip and he laughed.

"You said yourself we haven't had any real time to ourselves since Emma was born, and she's nineteen months old."

"True." She was trying to pace herself with the food, but she just wanted to eat as fast as she could and then lick the plate. "I liked cooking together this morning. It reminded me of when we were first together, and we were always in the kitchen, making meals together."

"Yeah, that was nice. Now it's one of us cooking while the other monitors the natives."

"Except for when you're not home and I end up trying to do both."

He polished off his toast. "I'm sorry about that. I'll try to do better."

They'd been so busy with just enjoying time without toddlers that she hadn't gotten around to telling him her plans about applying for the department head position. She sat up straighter and said, "I might need a little more of your help soon."

Josh looked up from his plate. "Okay. Why?"

"Well," she said, a smile spreading across her face, "I've decided to apply for the position of Consumer Relations Department Head."

Grinning, he said, "So you want to be the boss lady, huh?"

"Well…yeah, I guess I do." Her shoulders slumped.

"Do you think I can get it?"

"You practically run that department anyway, you've got seniority and you're a great employee. Why wouldn't they hire you?"

Her smile was grateful. "Yeah, they'd be crazy not to."

"Exactly." His plate empty, he sat back in his chair. "So when did you decide this?"

"I was complaining to Karen and Claudia about having to train a new supervisor, and they made me realize that I should just apply for the position myself."

"They're absolutely right. I'm proud of you, sweetheart."

"Thank you." She looked intently at him. "It might require a few more hours of my time…I might have to bring home a little work now and then."

Josh picked up their plates and kissed her on the head. "I'll make sure I help pick up the slack. I'll do whatever it takes."

"And it would mean a raise."

"I figured that much. We could definitely handle some more money." He started rinsing off the dishes and looked at Jayne with mischief in his eyes. "Wanna go for three times in twenty-four hours?"

She grinned, shaking her head. "Puh-lease. Don't push your luck, Brandt."

"Can't blame a guy for trying."

"I miss my babies and we've got a long drive to your parents'. Let's get this place cleaned up and go get our girls."

"Are you sure…?

"Josh!"

He laughed. "Okay, okay."

Looking at him standing in the kitchen in nothing but his boxers, with his stubbly beard, messy hair and playful eyes…she felt happier than she had in a long, long time. Maybe she'd been wrong lately.

Maybe she could have it all.

Chapter Five

Karen was surrounded by a sea of boxes. Somewhere beyond the corrugated was her new kitchen, though from where she was standing, she couldn't see any of it.

"These new cabinets completely transformed the space," she heard Gabe say from behind a stack of Chiquita Banana boxes filled with dishes. "It's like a whole new room."

"Thanks," Karen said, pulling down a box to reveal Gabe and Anthony, each with a child in their arms. "Hello Miss Simone! Mister Colton!" She gave them her biggest, brightest smile. They both regarded her with suspicion and looked at her a bit like she was crazy. *Good judge of character, kids.*

"Don't mind them," Anthony said with his usual charming grin. "They take a bit to warm up to people."

"Oh, that's fine. A lot of people look at me with suspicion." She sighed. "So I guess I need to start unpacking this stuff. Yesterday I was so exhausted all we did was put sheets on the bed and fall asleep."

The day before they had movers arrive at their loft at seven o'clock and the empty truck didn't back away from their new house until almost eight that night. It was a long day and Karen was not only tired but in shock. They were officially suburbanites.

"Well, let us help you," Anthony said, putting Colton down on the kitchen floor. He handed him a big plastic spatula from the box in front of him. "He entertains himself very well. This spatula is good for at least twenty minutes."

Rick had put their dog, Kramer, outside because he was extremely fascinated with the kids, which translated into wanting to jump on them or—at the very least—bat at them with his paws. Poor pup had his wet nose pressed up against the glass for the first few minutes, but then he apparently realized he had a huge yard to run around in and he took off. Chasing leaves, sniffing bugs, the usual. Karen knew he would love having his own yard. And she would love not having to walk him at six in the morning in the middle of winter.

"Oh, guys, you don't have to help," Karen said. "It was so sweet of you to come by. I'm not going to put you to work." They had dropped by to welcome Karen and Rick to the neighborhood and brought a gift basket with a nice bottle of wine, stoneware coasters hand painted by Gabe and an assortment of crackers and cheese.

"Shush." Anthony tore open a box. "We're happy to help."

"Well, if you really want to, I'm not going to stop you," she said with a chuckle.

"Really," Anthony said in a whisper, leaning into her, "I just want to stick around to see more of that gorgeous man of yours."

Gabe crossed his long, thin arms. "Anthony, you are such a..." He covered Simone's ears. "Whore."

Anthony rolled his eyes. "Don't tell me you didn't notice how fine Rick is." Anthony turned to Karen. "I mean, don't get me wrong, you're an attractive woman and your bosom is nothing short of amazing. So I knew your hubby would have to be some sort of a hunk. But with that long, dark wavy hair and those big dark eyes...my God, he's like a real, live Bohemian Rhapsody."

Karen laughed out loud.

"Oh Jesus, Anthony," Gabe said, putting Simone down and handing her his iPhone. "Go play on the couch, sweetie." As soon as she left the room, he hissed at Anthony, "Too bad for you he isn't into queens."

Anthony sighed, then reached up and started rubbing Gabe's shoulders. "You are so sensitive, Gabey. Calm down."

"Well, you practically came just talking about him."

"And what about you calling out the exterminator three times a month, just so you can watch him bend over while he sprays the floorboards?"

Gabe looked at Karen, shaking his head. "Like I would ever do anything with him."

Anthony hugged Gabe from behind. "And like I would ever be able to tear that hetero hunk of man away from those breasts," he said, pointing at Karen.

"True." Gabe grinned, pushing up his glasses. "Just stop gushing so much about him."

Just then Rick came down the stairs. "Hey guys—is she actually putting you to work?"

"We insisted on helping," Anthony said, his face growing crimson.

"Well, she's a slave driver...don't let her work you too hard." He winked at Karen as he grabbed a water bottle out of their brand-new stainless steel armoire-style fridge.

For once, Anthony was speechless as Rick went bounding back up the stairs.

"I have to admit," Gabe said quietly, "that ass is just gorgeous."

Karen chuckled. "You're right about that."

"*Now* who's gushing," Anthony said, beginning to unpack the closest box.

****

Two hours later, they'd managed to put Karen's entire kitchen together and flatten the boxes into a big pile that they threw in the garage. One room done.

"I say we crack open this wine and cheese and crackers," Karen said, grabbing a bottle opener and the basket and heading to the family room. Rick grabbed some glasses and Anthony followed him as he sat down on the comfy old couch that Karen now realized probably needed to be replaced.

"Too bad Gabe had to take the kids home for a nap," she said, holding out her wine glass to Rick to be filled.

"Yeah, as you saw, they were getting a little cranky,"

Anthony said, grabbing a hunk of cheese. "Sorry about that."

Karen took a grateful drink from her glass. Yum. This moving business was stressful and the wine was exactly what she needed. "Oh, they were fine. Such cute kids."

Anthony smiled. "Yeah, we got lucky, that's for sure." He looked at Rick, and then back to Karen. "Well, I saw you with that longing for motherhood look on your face while you were watching them. So are you guys planning on a family?"

Rick put his arm around Karen, and she didn't mind. She wasn't sure she was ready to discuss her failures with a virtual stranger. But Anthony and Gabe seemed like good friends already. What the hell. "Actually, we've been trying for a year and a half now. Fertility has not been our friend."

"Oh, sweetie," Anthony said, patting her leg. "I'm so sorry. I didn't mean to bring up a painful topic."

She smiled, feeling okay with saying it out loud. It wasn't as bad as she'd imagined. "That's okay. We're going to do another round of IUI and see how that works. Maybe third time's the charm."

"Well, you know," he said with a grin, "Gabe and I had a little trouble in the fertility department ourselves. Neither one of us could get pregnant. That's why we went the adoption route." He winked at her.

"What a shame," Rick said, throwing back his head with laughter.

"I know, right?" Anthony seemed thrilled to have gotten a laugh out of Rick. "So I certainly hope IUI or whatever it is works for you. But if it doesn't, we can hook you up with all the necessary people to explore adoption."

"You know, Karen," Rick said, "that's something we haven't really discussed."

"Yeah, we'll definitely keep that in mind. Thanks, Anthony."

"No problem. And of course when I say that we can give you the info, I mean Gabe. He's amazing. He did everything…I have no idea who we went through or any of that. I'm just the pretty face—he's the brains in the relationship."

Karen chuckled. "Although he's a good-looking man, too."

"Are you kidding me? He's adorable. And such a good dad. Amazing, really." He turned to Rick. "I bet you'll be a good dad. I can see that about you."

"Thanks." Rick smiled. "I sure hope so."

"Anthony, I can't thank you enough for coming over to help," Karen said. "And this wine is delicious."

"It's one of my favorites," Anthony said, looking pleased. "I had a feeling you'd like it." He stood up. "I should get out of your hair, and I'm sure Gabe would like some help at home. Those little rug rats may be cute, but they're a lot of work."

Anthony put his glass in the kitchen sink, and Karen followed behind him. He gave her a quick kiss on the cheek. "I'm so glad you guys moved in here—we needed some fun new neighbors."

"And you give me hope that suburbia isn't the soccer mom wasteland I was worried about."

Anthony patted her back. "Trust me, there are plenty of those around here, but you'd be surprised at how wicked fun some of them can be when you get them away from the carpool."

Karen laughed. "That's what I'm hoping for." They headed to the front door. "As soon as I get these boxes all unpacked and things in order, we'll have you guys over for dinner."

"Oo, sounds like fun. Maybe we could even get a sitter and make it a grown-ups night."

"Works for me."

Rick waved from the couch. "So nice to meet you, Anthony."

"Likewise." Anthony winked at Karen.

Karen still had a smile on her face as she closed the door behind him. She headed to the couch and sat down next to Rick. Kramer promptly jumped up and curled in next to her. He had a serious habit of invading one's personal space, but Karen let it go because he was so damn cute.

"So how's it going upstairs, Mr. Gordon?" she asked, putting her feet up on the distressed wood coffee table.

"Pretty good. I've got all my art supplies unpacked in the studio and your office is set up and ready to go."

"I knew I married you for some reason."

Rick took a drink of wine then put his arm around Karen. "So what do you think about what Anthony brought up…adoption?"

Karen sighed. It's not like the thought had never occurred to her. She looked at Rick. "Would it make me a bitch if I said I really want my own biological child?"

"No, you're already a bitch for a lot of other reasons." He laughed as she elbowed him, hard. "Ow!" Kramer jumped up, tail wagging, hoping this meant playtime.

"Very funny. I'm serious."

Rick kissed her. "I know. I'm sorry. It's just that you set yourself up perfectly for that one."

"I did."

"But no, I don't think you're a bitch for wanting your own child. But just so you know, I'm okay with adoption."

"And I am too…if that's our only option. But I really want a shot to make a baby from the two of us, if we can. A little baby with your dark eyes, my smile…."

"What's wrong with my smile?"

"Oh, jeez, nothing. I was just babbling. But I would like to see what kind of little person we could make together. Don't you?"

"Well sure. But if it's not in the cards for us, and you really want a child, I'm open to adoption."

"I am too. I just want to feel a baby growing inside me." The further they went through the process unsuccessfully, the more she seemed to want it. She was beginning to wonder if all the effort was worth it. Or would all the time and money and agony be for nothing? "Are you saying you want to give up on fertility?"

"No, not at all. I just want you to know that if things don't work out, I'm on board with adoption if you are. Families come in all forms, like we just saw today."

Karen closed her eyes. "One more round of IUI and if that doesn't work, IVF."

She felt Rick's gentle hands on her cheeks. "I'm here for you. Whatever you want to do, I'm game. Okay?"

She opened her eyes and saw his searching hers. He was so strong, while she only pretended to be. He was the calm, sure presence she needed to keep herself from completely losing her mind with the whole fertility debacle. How had she ever made him fall in love with her?

"Okay. Now get off of me so I can make some dinner in my new kitchen."

"Yes, ma'am."

****

Claudia was relieved to get a break. After caring for a sick child for three straight days, she was exhausted. Between the puke, snotty Kleenex, giving regular doses of ibuprofen and comforting a justifiably whiny five-year-old...the usually together Claudia Knight was anything but. Sam had actually laughed at her when he walked in the door.

"What is so funny?" she asked with obvious irritation.

"Sorry, Claud, but have you looked in a mirror today?" He was grinning, and she wanted nothing more than to smack the cocky smirk off his face. But the truth was she hadn't looked in the mirror.

"No, I was too busy taking care of your daughter."

"Our daughter," he said, the smile evaporating from his face. "It's just that you always look so beautiful, even when you're not wearing makeup and you've only got on a pair of sweats and a T-shirt." She blushed at the compliment. "But today your hair is kinda crazy and you look a little...flustered."

"Well, taking care of someone else's bodily fluids for days can do that to you."

"I wasn't criticizing..." Sam took off his coat and

tossed it over the arm of the high-back chair they'd bought together nearly a decade ago. A peace-offering smile spread across his face, and Claudia smiled back.

Looking in the mirror above the dining room serving table, she shook her head. She looked like a crazy person. No wonder he'd laughed. "Okay, Sam, you have a point. Jeez. Looking at me probably made poor Isabella throw up."

Sam laughed. "You don't look that bad."

"Almost. But anyway, thanks so much for coming over."

"Well, it's not fair for you to be the only one on flu duty. So why don't you go take a break and I'll take over?"

"That's exactly what I'm going to do."

So there she was, soaking in the tub, trying not to doze off. She could hear the low murmur from the TV in Isabella's room…sounded like *Good Luck Charlie* from the Disney channel. The fact that she recognized the characters' voices from down the hall told her she really needed to get a life.

"Hey, Claudia?" Sam asked, tapping on her bedroom door as he pushed it open. Claudia could see him clearly through the open bathroom door, and the look of shock on his face said he could see her in the bathtub, too.

"Shit, Sam!" she hollered, crossing her arms to cover as much of her strategic parts as she could. He quickly shut the bedroom door.

"I'm sorry…I thought you were just lying in bed."

"You should have waited to see!"

"Well, it's not like I haven't seen you naked before…."

"Not since we got divorced six years ago."

"Well, from what I just saw, you still have all the same parts." Even through the closed door, she could almost see the smug little grin on his face. *Jerk.*

"Grow up, Sam. I can't believe you did that."

"I said I'm sorry. It wasn't intentional." He cleared his throat. "But I can't say I minded the view."

Claudia rolled her eyes as she sighed. Once upon a time

she would have found him charming. But not anymore

Well, maybe a little.

Ignoring his comment, she asked, "So what do you want?"

"Oh, yeah, I almost forgot. I wanted to know if it was okay to give Isabella some ice chips."

"Yes, that's fine. Put them in one of her *My Little Pony* cups—those are her favorites."

"Will do. While I'm heading to the kitchen, do you want anything?"

"No. Thanks, though."

"Okay." She heard his footsteps clambering down the stairs and she sighed.

So much for a relaxing bath. She decided to give up and unplugged the drain. Climbing out of the old claw foot tub, she quickly wrapped a large bath sheet around herself and then shut the bathroom door.

****

It was a couple of hours later as she lay in bed that Claudia began to wonder if Isabella had shared her flu. Her stomach was a little unsettled and achiness was starting to spread across her body.

The TV in her room was tuned to a *Sex and the City* marathon, and she tried to focus on the show and convince herself she wasn't getting sick. She didn't have time to be sick; she had a daughter to take care of. Maybe she'd feel better if she took a nap....

The sound of her cell phone ringing from her nightstand woke her up. It was her generic ringtone so she didn't know who it was.

"Hello?" she answered, trying to sound alert but not sure she achieved it.

"Claudia?"

"Yes."

"This is Kurt Klatt." *Who? The name sounded familiar...* "From Hacienda, the doctor—"

"Kurt. Yes. Hello!"

"For a minute there you were bruising my ego. I

thought you'd forgotten all about me."

"No, not at all." *Say something, Claudia. Anything.* "So did you have a nice holiday season?"

"I did, but I'm glad it's over." He chuckled, and she thought he had a nice laugh. "You?"

"Yeah, it was good. I just love Christmas."

"Well, now that the season has passed, are you ready for that date?"

She didn't like that he called it a date. That made it sound scarier. She'd never really planned on going out with him. How was she going to get out of this? She had to come up with something. Then she heard herself saying, "Sure. When did you have in mind?"

"I know we talked about lunch, but let's make it dinner instead. What part of town are you in?"

"I'm near Forest Park."

"That's not too far from what I had in mind...I was thinking something kind of fun and casual...I don't want to scare you off, after all. Have you ever been to the Fountain on Locust?"

"Sure, I love the Fountain." She relaxed a bit; it *was* a more casual, laid-back environment known for good food, great desserts and a unique setting.

"Are you free later this week?"

Feeling the unsettled rumbling in her stomach and the aches in her bones that had gotten even worse...she didn't know if she would be well enough. "This week is kind of crazy."

"Well, I've got a conference next weekend, so I'll be out of town. I hate to put you off any longer. What about next Tuesday night?"

Tuesday...in her flu haze she was trying to focus. She would have Isabella, although she could find someone to watch her. But she really didn't want to go out with the hot, blond doctor. Did she?

Just then, there was a knock on her door and Sam said loudly, "Can I come in? Or should I just open the door and hope for another strip tease?"

"Um, Claudia?" Kurt said. "Who is that?"

"It's just my ex...."

Sam's voice raised even louder, "Claud?"

She covered the mouthpiece of her phone, "Sam, just a minute!"

Kurt sounded irritated when he said, "If you're still involved with your ex, I don't know that I want that kind of hassle."

"No, I'm not...involved with him. It's just...."

More knocking on the door and Sam asked, "Are you talking to me?"

"Kurt, I'm sorry, I need to go," she said, flustered. "But Tuesday night sounds good. I can meet you there."

"Okay," Kurt said, sounding less than enthused. "Seven o'clock?"

"Sure. Bye."

She hung up just in time for Sam to ask loudly, "What's going on?"

"Come in," she said with a sigh, sitting up too quickly and realizing that she shouldn't have as her stomach responded with a wave of nausea.

Sam's head popped in, and she thought about wringing his neck. "What took so long?"

"I was on the phone." Irritation was thick in her tone as she closed her eyes.

"Oh, that's why I heard talking. Did I hear you say Kurt?"

Claudia covered her eyes. Maybe she shouldn't have asked him to come over and help with Isabella. So far he'd seen her naked and interrupted a phone call with her date. Not that she really wanted to go out on a date, but still. "Yes."

"Who's Kurt?" Sam sat on the edge of the bed and even that slight movement of the mattress made her stomach churn.

Opening her eyes, she glared at him. "As if you have the right to ask me that question."

"Oh," Sam said, looking surprised. "Okay, I

understand, you're right. But remember that we agreed not to bring partners around Isabella...."

"Christ, Sam, I haven't even been on a date with him yet. Of course I won't bring him around Isabella. *I* have always had our family's best interests in mind."

He stood up, and his usual congenial expression turned to one of anger. "Don't rewrite history. There was no family when I decided to leave. We didn't find out about Izzy until after I left."

"But becoming a parent didn't change your mind." She couldn't disguise the hurt in her voice.

Sam sighed. "I thought we were past all this. I thought we were in a good place."

"We are, Sam, I'm sorry." Claudia rubbed her eyes, which were starting to burn from what she was pretty sure was a fever setting in. "I just got a little defensive when you asked about Kurt."

"Okay, and I'm sorry for being nosey. You're right—it's none of my business. It's just that from what I gather, there haven't been a lot of dates in the last few years."

Claudia managed a grin. "Some of us have decided to be celibate."

"Some of us could never do that." He smiled back.

"That was pretty obvious the last time I saw you in a bed. With company." Seeing him in bed with his assistant was enough to make Claudia buy new bedroom furniture and, of course, a new mattress.

"Ancient history, Claud." He shook his head. "So anyway, the reason I was interrupting your important phone call...."

"It wasn't that important."

Sam seemed to like that response. "I want to know if I can give Isabella anything to eat. She said she hasn't gotten sick since this morning, and her fever is gone. I thought I'd start with a couple of crackers but wanted to check with you first."

"What time is it?" Claudia glanced at her phone. Six-eighteen. She must have been asleep for over an hour.

"Yeah, I think that's safe. Or if she wants some Jell-O, I've got some in the fridge."

"You know, you look really pale." He moved closer and put his hand on her forehead. "You're burning up."

His cool hand felt good on her skin. She still remembered what his hands felt like, after all these years. "Yeah, I think our daughter shared her flu bug with me. My stomach's upset, too."

"Let me get you some ibuprofen for your fever and a cool rag to help until the meds kick in. What else can I get you?"

"That's all, thanks. But I didn't call you to take care of me."

"I don't mind. I'll be right back."

She watched him leave the room as the uneasiness in her stomach kicked into high gear. Although she was used to controlling everything in her life, praying for the nausea to subside didn't seem to be working.

The Supermom a.k.a. Claudia apparently had met her match in this virus.

Surprised she made it to the toilet in time, she hugged the cool porcelain as she watched the contents of that morning's breakfast come back up. Yum.

When the retching stopped, she heard Sam say from behind her, "Personally, I liked the vision of you in the tub this morning better than this one."

"Me too," she said, as she felt him press a damp washcloth into her hand. "Thanks."

He left the room and she cleaned herself up, realizing this was going to be a long night. Claudia really just wanted her mom. Even at thirty-five years old, she still wanted her mom when she was sick. But her parents had been spending the winters in Florida for years now so she was on her own.

Climbing back into bed, she found Sam waiting at her bedside. He handed her a glass of water and three pills. "I can stay and take care of you, if you want."

"No," she said, shaking her head and wondering how

long of a reprieve she'd have before her stomach started churning again. The last thing she wanted was for her ex-husband to nurse her. They'd been getting along well for a few years now, but that didn't mean they were buddy buddy. It was obvious from their earlier conversation that there was still a lot of hurt there, just under the surface. On her side, anyway.

"Well then, if Izzy holds down those crackers and Jell-O okay, why don't I take her home with me so you can do the flu thing on your own, without us bugging you?"

She nodded her head. "That would be great, thanks."

"No problem." Looking at her, he seemed like he wanted to say something else. After a moment he said, "I'll leave you alone. Holler if you need anything, and I'll give it another half hour or so before I decide to put a formerly puking kid in my BMW."

Claudia managed a small smile. "Thanks, Sam."

He looked at her with kindness in his eyes as he whispered, "No problem."

Chapter Six

Jayne's phone rang and she glanced at the display. An internal call whose extension she didn't recognize.

"This is Jayne," she answered in her usual friendly tone.

"Mr. Brandt would like to see you in his office," was the response she heard from the woman at the other end of the line.

She frowned. If Gray wanted to see her, why didn't he just call or text her himself? "Right now?"

"If you're available, yes." The woman sounded older; she must be a new assistant because his last one couldn't have been a day over twenty-five.

"Uh…" Jayne glanced around her department. "Sure. I'll be right up."

"I'll let Mr. Brandt know."

Jayne rolled her eyes. Mr. Brandt? She didn't think she could ever call him that without giggling. After all, he'd been her brother-in-law for five years now and, as much as she tried to put it out of her mind, he'd been her boyfriend six years ago. She'd be more apt to call him knucklehead than *Mister* anything.

But at Nixon Pharmaceutical, the large drug manufacturer they worked for, she had to show him the respect he deserved—at least when his office door was open. Jayne headed to the elevator, and when she reached the third floor that housed the "bigwigs," she was impressed as usual. The grey no-man's-land of partitions where she spent her days was in stark contrast to the luxurious furnishings and large offices of the third floor. When she and Gray had been dating years ago, she thought his office then was great. When he was promoted last year to president of marketing and customer relations, he stepped up to one of the best offices in the whole building.

Jayne wondered if Gray's office was as large as her house as she approached his administrative assistant's desk, which sat outside his door. The woman sitting there was at least fifty-five years old and looked every day of it. Her frumpy suit and grey hair said Grandma. Even though Jayne didn't like the way her own body looked at the moment, she decided it was all relative because she felt pretty damn attractive standing next to this woman. And Jayne always wore stylish high heels and eye-catching accessories...she had decided it didn't matter how much weight she gained, her jewelry and shoes would always fit.

"Hi," Jayne said, smiling. "I'm Jayne, here to see Gr— Mr. Brandt." She suppressed the giggle that the formal title desperately called for.

Without smiling, the woman pressed a button on her phone. "Mr. Brandt, Jayne Brandt is here to see you."

"Send her right in please, Nancy," Gray's voice boomed from the speakerphone.

Jayne opened his heavy dark cherry wood door and saw him sitting at his desk across the room, staring at his computer as he typed rapidly.

"Hey, Jaynie," he said, barely looking up as he motioned her in. "Close the door behind you."

She did, relieved she wouldn't be expected to call him Mr. Brandt. "Good. Now I can call you Gray."

"Yeah, I'll allow that," he said, his dimples popping up.

"Why did your admin call me up here? Your fingers broken?" She settled into the enviably comfortable leather chair across from his massive desk.

"Oh, that was just me being a smart ass. I thought it would irritate you." He winked as she stuck her tongue out at him.

"Well, it worked," she chuckled, crossing her legs and bouncing her foot up and down, admiring her favorite black high-heeled Mary Janes. "And who's that new admin, anyway?"

"Nancy. She started a few weeks ago."

"What happened to that young girl…was it Tiffany?"

"Yeah…let's just say Tiffany was a little too distracting for me. So I sent her to another department so I could get some work done instead of staring at her legs and chest all day through my door."

"That explains the dowdy older woman out there."

Gray nodded, looking like a kid that got caught with his hand in the cookie jar. "You betcha."

"Well, for the record, she's not very friendly."

"Not everyone is as chipper as Jaynie."

She laughed. "True. So…what did you need to see me about?"

His jovial expression turned more serious. "It's about you applying for the department head position. You really should have given me a head's up about this."

"What do you mean?" Jayne stopped bouncing her foot.

"This puts me in a very difficult spot."

"How does this have anything to do with you?"

"Because I'm president of marketing and customer relations. If you're applying for customer relations department head, I'll be your direct boss. And I have final say about who gets hired in that position."

Jayne slumped down in her seat a bit. She'd never thought about that. "So you don't think I should get the promotion?"

"That's not what I'm saying at all. But you're my sister-in-law."

"How is that a problem?"

Gray shook his head and stood up, walking around to her side of the desk and sitting on the corner. "I swear sometimes you're so naïve."

Jayne crossed her arms. "I am not naïve, Gray. I just don't know where you're going with this."

"It's a conflict of interest, hiring my family for a supervisory position. It looks like nepotism."

"But I'm sure I'm the most qualified applicant…."

"There's no disputing that."

"So the fact that we're in-laws has nothing to do with it."

Gray rolled his eyes. "I know that and you know that...but what do you think everyone else will think when they look on the company's organizational chart and see one Brandt listed directly above another?"

Jayne was starting to get nervous. Was he saying he wouldn't hire her? They really needed more money, and ever since Karen gave her the idea to apply for the promotion, her heart was set on it. "They'll think that the Brandt family has hard workers."

"Jesus, Jaynie, they'll think I just handed you the job...that I abused my power."

"So are you saying I can't have the job? That because of you, I'm stuck in the same position forever?"

He sighed and stood up, walking to the window that overlooked the lake on Nixon Pharmaceutical's grounds. "I'm not saying that. But we have to be very careful."

"Is there a company policy against it?"

"Well, I checked with HR and it's kind of a gray area." Turning back to face her, he added with a smile, "No pun intended."

"So what do we do?"

"Since Nixon Pharmaceutical was founded by two brothers several decades ago, there's a strong precedent of families working together. And we have several other instances now where there are spouses both working here, or in-laws."

"Then this shouldn't be an issue."

Gray headed back to his desk and sat down. "But it becomes an issue because I would technically be your boss. And I'm third in command of the entire company."

"But how often do you really get involved with the customer relations operations?"

"Not much. But if you got the job, I'd be responsible for your performance reviews and for handling any issues anyone has with you."

"But you're forgetting that I'm an unbelievably good

employee." Jayne smiled, bouncing her foot again. "There won't be any issues."

Gray rolled his eyes. "Well, Miss Perfect, that solves everything."

"I'm going to take that as a sarcastic remark. So spit it out, Gray. What do you think we have to do here to make this work?"

"First of all, don't tell your boss to spit it out."

"You're not my boss yet."

"No, right now I'm your boss' boss. Even more intimidating." He glanced at his computer and started typing again.

"Well then, your highness, what are we going to do?"

He laughed, turning his attention back to her. "I think if we have a committee choose the new supervisor, that will help show an effort at fairness. Also, I think we'll have to use a committee for your performance reviews as well."

"That only happens once a year. Shouldn't be a big deal. So that's it?"

"And you have to be aware that you will be under a great deal of scrutiny. You'll have to literally be Miss Perfect. I don't want you making me look bad."

Jayne sighed, shaking her head. With Gray, it always comes down to Gray. "You know what a good worker I am."

"Of course I do. I wouldn't even be considering any of these hassles if I didn't think you'd be perfect for the job."

"Then what are you getting at?"

"Well, I pulled your employment records and there are a couple of things you'll need to work on."

She wasn't surprised he'd pulled her files. Gray might have been arrogant, but he was thorough and excellent at his job. But she was surprised he acted like there were areas for improvement. Jayne prided herself on being the best. She leaned toward him. "Like what?"

"Don't get all worked up."

"I'm not."

"Jaynie, I know you. So just chill and hear me out." He

opened her file, which she strained to see. "Of course your performance appraisals reflect what an excellent job you do, team player, shows initiative, etc. But the last couple of years it also shows that you've had a lot of instances where you've come in late…."

"Well, you know what the traffic's like coming across the bridge. And you should try to get two little kids out the door in the morning…."

"Hey," he said in a calm tone, holding his hand up. "I'm on your side here. Just listen, okay?"

She sat back in the leather chair and crossed her arms again. She felt like she was in the principal's office.

"Your boss noted that it was never really an issue, because you always indicated the tardies on your time sheet, so you were docked for coming in late."

"Well, of course I've never fudged my time sheet."

"I know that. But the supervisor position is salaried, not hourly. So it's important that you get here on time…nothing irritates employees more than their boss not following the rules. Do you think you can make that happen?"

She nodded her head, starting to feel stressed already and she didn't even have the job yet.

"Also it says you've had to leave early on several occasions to get sick kids."

"I can't change that, Gray. Kids get sick and daycares don't want them there when they're spreading germs."

"Then Josh might have to pick them up sometimes."

"You know how hard that is for a teacher. They have to get a substitute…."

"As your brother-in-law, I say that sucks. As your boss, I would say it's not my problem. An occasional absence or having to leave early is understood. But you need to make other arrangements if it happens often."

Jayne chuckled. "Wow, sounds like my new boss is an inflexible jerk."

Gray put his face in his hands. "I am not a jerk. But I expect excellence. You know that." He sat up. "And since we're family, you have to go the extra mile to avoid scrutiny. That's just how it will have to be."

She swallowed. "I get that."

"Do you?" He raised his eyebrows, and Jayne realized that his expression was just like Josh's when he questioned her. Damn Brandt brothers were too good looking. "See, that's why I wish you would have come to me first so we could talk about it."

"I'm sorry...I never even thought about it. But I do completely understand what you're saying. I won't let you down."

"I know you won't. I just want you to know upfront what you're getting yourself into. Are you sure you want this?"

She looked down and said quietly, "We really need the money."

Gray leaned across the desk and grabbed her hand. "Then as your brother-in-law, I'll tell you that I'm going to recommend you for the position and try to get you even more money than the current supervisor, based on your twelve years of service and exemplary performance."

She looked up and their eyes locked. She knew he would take care of his family if it were in his power. "Thank you, Gray."

"That's Mr. Brandt to you in this office," he said, shoving her hand away and offering a smirk. "Now get out of here. I've gotten eighteen new emails since you came in. What is it about you that always causes me problems and makes me work late?"

"Good things are never easy."

"Yeah, I bet my brother could attest to that," he said, a deep laugh escaping.

"Screw you," she said, getting up. "*Mister* Brandt."

"That's much better." As she headed to the door, he said, "Kiss those beautiful nieces for me, okay? And make sure they know it's from Uncle Gray."

She smiled as she opened the door. "You bet."

When Jayne returned to her desk, her mind was still

reeling. Along with the stress of a new job and added responsibilities, she'd have the extra pressure of being beyond reproach. She couldn't give anyone an excuse to point fingers and say she'd moved up the ladder because of her connection to Gray. That meant she'd always be under a microscope.

Great. As if being a frazzled working mom wasn't enough. Let's just add another layer of anxiety to the crazy layered baklava of her life.

Actually, baklava sounded pretty good.

With no baklava in sight, she settled for grabbing a couple of chocolates out of her desk drawer that she kept for emergencies. Which, lately, meant every few hours. She was savoring the last sweet creamy bite of chocolate when her phone rang. An outside line she didn't recognize. Time to use her chipper voice. "Nixon Pharmaceutical, Jayne speaking. How may I help you?"

"Uh, Jayne, it's Sam. Sam Knight."

Claudia's Sam. Well, he used to be, anyway. Why on earth was he calling her? Was something wrong with Claudia? *Oh God, please let her be all right.* In a panic she answered, "Hi, Sam. Is everything okay?"

"Oh, yeah, I'm sorry. I guess hearing from me would make you think there was an emergency or something."

Jayne relaxed in her chair, slipping her shoes off. "Yeah, my brain went into panic mode. So what's up?"

"Well, Claudia's got the flu really bad, so I've had Isabella stay with me for the last two days. Which has been fine, it's just that I've got an important business dinner tonight and I don't think Claud's well enough for me to take Isabella back home." He sounded stressed.

"The dinner is tonight? And you need someone to watch Isabella?"

"Yeah, I was hoping you might be able to since she loves you and your girls so much."

Jayne smiled. "Oh, the girls would love to see her, I'm sure, but tonight Tori has dance lessons and Josh is working late running concessions at the school basketball game. It's pretty hectic…I don't think there's any way we could watch her."

"Oh, okay," Sam said, sounding completely deflated.

"I'm so sorry, Sam. I wish I could help."

"I know it's really last minute, I just figured Claudia would be better by now. But when I talked to her a bit ago, I can tell she's still miserable. So I can't leave her with a kid when she's so sick, but my boss is gonna kill me. This is a huge client."

"Why don't you call Karen? She might be free."

He chuckled. "I'm *not* calling Karen. No way."

"Oh, that's right. She can be a little tough on you."

"That's an understatement. She hates me. I'm her archenemy."

Jayne laughed. "You might be right. Why don't I call her for you?"

"I really appreciate that, Jayne, but there's no way she'll do me a favor."

"Well…I can convince her that it would be more of a favor for Claudia."

Sam didn't speak for a minute, and Jayne heard him sigh. "I don't know…."

"Let me call her and see what I can do." After her stressful conversation with Gray, Jayne was anxious to get her mind off Nixon Pharmaceuticals.

"You've sold me, Jayne," Sam said with a chuckle. "You sound pretty sure that you can make this happen."

"If Karen's available tonight, I'll make sure she watches Isabella, okay?"

"And you promise Karen won't meet me at the door with weaponry?"

Jayne giggled. "I promise. She's not a violent person. She prefers verbal abuse."

"So I've noticed."

"But if Isabella's there, Karen will be on good behavior. Trust me."

"I do trust you. I really, really appreciate you trying to help me out."

"No problem. I'll call her now and call you right back." They hung up, and Jayne was happy to immerse herself in a problem that for once lately, wasn't her own.

****

When Karen heard the doorbell ring, she had to remind herself: *Sam has a child with him. Be civil.* It was crazy…she felt like she was the scorned woman and he was her ex. But she couldn't help it if she felt so protective of her friends. Maybe that was proof she had some mothering instincts in her somewhere.

She opened the door and there stood the man she once liked but had quickly learned to despise. Holding his hand was one of her favorite little girls in the whole wide world. Karen had held her when she was just a few minutes old. Karen may not have been her biological aunt, but there was no doubt that they were family; they were connected.

"Aunt Karen!" Isabella shouted, running in and throwing her arms around Karen.

Karen couldn't help but eat it up. "How is my favorite five-year-old girl?"

"Good. Mom's sick. I gave her the throw-up kind of flu."

"So I hear," Karen said with a chuckle. She looked up at Sam. "Come on in. I won't bite when children are present."

"Yeah, I was kind of hoping she was my insurance policy," he said, giving up a tentative smile. He stepped inside. "Nice house. But I never thought I'd see you in the 'burbs."

"Yeah, well, I never thought I'd see you on my doorstep."

"Touché." He watched Isabella running around, checking out the new house, stopping every few seconds to pet Kramer, who was more than excited to have a little one in the house. "Well, here's her bag. Jammies, her favorite stuffed animal, toothbrush, some books. You don't need to put her to bed, but if my dinner runs late, is it okay if she crashes on the couch until I get here?"

"We'll just have a slumber party on the couch. Maybe watch some TV, huh?"

"Do you have satellite?" Isabella asked.

Karen laughed. "Yes ma'am. We even have HBO."

"Where's Uncle Rick?"

"He's upstairs in his art studio. I think he might even have a little surprise for you up there. Wanna go check it out with me?"

"Yeah! Let's go."

"Hey, Izzy," Sam said, catching her attention. "Behave, okay? And use your manners."

"I will, Daddy." She ran up to him and gave him a big hug and a kiss. As much as Karen hated to admit it, she knew he was a good dad and they were close. But that didn't make up for what he did to Claudia.

"Well, Karen," Sam said, looking a little like the picked-on kid at school suddenly being cornered by the bully. "I can't thank you enough for doing this for me."

"I'm doing it for Claudia and Isabella."

"I know. But thanks anyway."

She met his stare. "You're welcome, Sam. Stay out as late as you need to. I know how business dinners can go."

"Okay. Bye, Isabella."

"Bye, Daddy! Come on, Aunt Karen—let's go see Uncle Rick!"

With that, Sam was gone and Karen's night of playing the cool aunt had begun.

****

Sure enough, while Karen cooked what she hoped was a kid-friendly dinner, Isabella was in heaven upstairs with Rick. He'd put some thick paper on his easel and let her use some of his less expensive paints while they created art together. She wanted them both to paint My Little Ponies, and he begrudgingly obliged. When it was time to eat, they had both completed their pastel-colored equestrian masterpieces. Karen loved the big grin on Isabella's face when they came downstairs. She noticed Rick shared an equally pleased smile.

As Karen dished up the homemade macaroni and cheese, green beans with bacon, and candied apples, Isabella talked non-stop. Karen and Rick exchanged amused expressions as they listened to the little girl babble on about an array of topics ranging from Barbies to her love for noodles to the hope she would someday get a dog.

She finally seemed to take a breath when she started eating. "Oh, Aunt Karen, this is yummy. You should give my mom the recipe. These noodles are really good."

"Thank you," Karen said, relieved that she had hit the jackpot.

"Don't give it to my dad, though, he doesn't cook much." She swallowed another big bite of macaroni. "Why don't you like my dad?"

Oh, shit. What do I say to that? Because he's a selfish prick that broke your mom's heart? Think, Karen, think. "Um…what makes you think I don't like your dad?"

Rick looked at Karen with terror in his eyes. He knew her well enough to know she had trouble holding back her opinions.

"I heard him thanking Aunt Jayne on the phone for calling you, and he said he couldn't believe she convinced you to do a favor for him since you hate him so much. Plus I've noticed that you guys are always giving each other dirty looks. Just like Justin at daycare gives Samantha dirty looks all the time."

"Oh, Isabella, I don't hate your daddy."

"Why does he think you do?"

Karen took a bite of green beans as she tried to come up with something that this inquisitive girl would buy. "He was probably just kidding around with Aunt Jayne. I mean, your dad and I aren't great friends or anything—"

"Why not? He's a really funny guy. And he's handsome, you know. Mommy thinks he's handsome."

"I'll give him that," she said, stuffing her face some more, trying to stall.

"Sometimes," Rick piped in, "when a mom and dad get divorced, their friends get upset watching those two people hurt."

"You mean when my mom and dad got divorced?"

"Well, yeah," he continued, sounding as panicked as Karen felt. "So Aunt Karen had to watch your mommy be upset and so it made it hard for all of us to be as good of friends with your daddy as we used to be."

"So you all used to be good friends?"

"Oh, sure. But when people get divorced, there are a lot of hurt feelings and sometimes it's hard to stay friends."

"But my mom and dad are friends."

Karen took over. "That's because they love you so much and worked really hard at getting along and being friends so they could raise you together. I think they're doing a great job."

"Well, I *am* pretty smart," Isabella said, bobbing her head up and down. "These apples are good. I've never had these kind of apples before. Give my mom this recipe, too."

"I'll be sure and do that," Karen said with a sigh, glad to have an official subject change.

****

Karen was nodding off on the couch with Isabella curled next to her. She knew this was a favor to Sam and Claudia, but it really was more of a reminder to Karen of why she was going to so much effort to have a child of her own. Spending the evening with Isabella solidified the fact that even though kids could be a lot of work…there was nothing else like them.

Isabella was giving, smart, inquisitive and just plain fun to be around. And somehow with children, Karen's thick, sturdy walls that she'd built to keep people out just seemed to crumble down. With kids, Karen could be vulnerable. She didn't feel judged or frightened. She just felt content.

Kramer the dog had decided Isabella was his new favorite person, so he'd abandoned his usual spot next to Karen so he could snuggle up with the girl. Isabella had been delighted, and even after she stopped petting him and fell asleep, Kramer didn't leave her side. It made Karen feel good to know he would probably be as welcoming of a baby.

If they were ever lucky enough to have one.

There was a quiet knock at the door, which woke Karen out of her semi-asleep state.

"I'll get it," Rick said, since he was the only one that hadn't yet crashed. "Hey, Sam."

"Hey, Rick," Sam said warmly, stepping inside. "I really like your new place. Looks like a great neighborhood."

"Yeah, we've only been in for a couple of weeks, but so far we're enjoying it."

"So how was she?" He pointed to Isabella, who Karen decided looked like an angel when she was sleeping.

"Oh, she was a blast," Rick said with a grin. "That's quite the kid you've got there."

Sam, looking every bit the proud papa, said, "I'm a lucky guy."

"You are," Karen said, giving Isabella a gentle shake. "Your daddy's here, sweetie." The little one stirred and then finally opened her eyes.

"Daddy," she said, reaching her arms out toward him. Sam gently picked her up, cradling her pajama-clad body in his arms.

"Here's her bag," Karen said, putting it over his arm.

"Thanks again, you guys," he said quietly, heading toward the door. "If I can repay the favor, please let me know. Everybody needs a nasty letter from a lawyer now and then, right?"

Rick chuckled. "I'll definitely keep that in mind."

"Hey, Sam," Karen said as he was starting to go out the door.

"Yeah?"

"We'd love to watch her, anytime, okay?"

Sam smiled. "Okay."

Karen closed the door behind him and felt Rick's arm around her. She buried her face in his chest and for some reason, felt tears well in her eyes.

Chapter Seven

Helen Taggart was a lot like her daughter Karen, except she managed to make even Karen look like a positive person.

There was no doubt for Karen where she'd acquired her less-than-hopeful demeanor: her mother. And although she loved her mother immensely, there were times even she just couldn't deal with her pessimism and judgment.

Today was one of those days.

As Karen watched her mom steal packets of Splenda and Sweet-n-Low from the container on the restaurant table and slide them in her purse, she wondered which came first: the pessimism or her divorce from Karen's dad? Did the divorce make her a downer, or did being the human equivalent to a tranquilizer ultimately cause the demise of her marriage? Hard to say.

"Mom," Karen said, shaking her head. "Why are you stealing packets of sugar substitute?"

"I'm not stealing them," Helen said with indignation. "They put these on the table for a reason. They're ours for the taking."

"Yeah, for a cup of coffee or two. Not to sweeten the drinks for everyone at your next Bunko party."

"It's not stealing." The insistence in her voice wasn't worth Karen arguing with.

Karen was always relieved to see that although her mom clearly had some wrinkles, she looked pretty damn good for being fifty-nine. Karen hoped she had inherited those age-defying genes from her mom. There was no doubt she had gotten her looks.

"So what's new with you, Mom?"

The older version of Karen shrugged her shoulders,

making her big silver hoop earrings sway. "Nothing new, really. Do you remember Mrs. Nestor at church?"

Karen hadn't been inside her childhood church since a high school friend got married there about fifteen years earlier. "Can't say that I do."

"Of course you do. She used to babysit the next-door neighbor kids."

"Don't know."

"Well," Helen said with irritation, "she's got cancer real bad. It doesn't look promising."

"That's a shame."

"And then you know your Great-Aunt Edna?"

Karen searched the recesses of her memory. Her mother had a habit of bringing up obscure relatives she'd never met, as if they'd been close and spent every holiday together. "Do I know her?"

"Well, of course you do. She's your grandma's sister."

"I mean, have I ever met her?"

"Maybe not."

"Then I obviously don't know her, Mom."

"Anyway, she fell a couple of weeks ago and broke her hip. And you know, once you break a hip—"

"It's all downhill from there." Helen's favorite expression and her life's mantra. She lived for gloom and doom...there was never a time Karen talked to her when she didn't hear about some person she probably didn't even know but was forced to hear their tale of medical woe. Although Karen was worried her mom had a strange fascination with the macabre, maybe it was really that she was just glad it was these other people, and not her. "So, Mom, any uplifting or less depressing news? What have you been up to, other than cataloging people's illnesses?"

Ignoring her daughter's snide remark, Helen said, "By the way, I don't like that dark nail polish on you. It's not attractive."

Looking at her greyish-taupe nails, Karen thought they looked pretty. "I think it is."

"Oh, I took the kids to the Magic House this

weekend."

The "kids" were Karen's niece and nephew, her brother's kids. They were adorable; Dawson and Ashley reminded Karen of when she and her brother Jonathan were young. Two irresistible blonde-headed little cherubs that probably got whatever they wanted.

"Oh, that's cool," Karen said, remembering going there herself as a kid. It was a massive old house that was renovated and expanded to create an incredibly imaginative place for kids to explore and learn without feeling like they were getting a science or history lesson. It just felt like playing in the ultimate indoor playground. Karen's favorite thing was the giant electrically charged ball that you put your hand on, making your hair stick straight out, all around your head. "Do they still have the static ball?"

"They sure do." Helen held up her phone, proud to display a picture of her beloved grandchildren, their light blonde tresses standing on end.

Karen grinned. "Wow, they are getting big so fast."

"I know. You should see them more often."

"It's only been a few weeks since I saw them at Christmas. And I've been a little busy moving and unpacking."

"Well, from what I saw this morning, you're not done unpacking."

Leave it to you, Mom, to negate all that I've done and only point out what I haven't. "I'm almost done."

"Well, anyway, it's a very lovely home. So much more homey than that loft you lived in."

Karen rolled her eyes. "Our loft was homey. Maybe not by a fifty-nine-year-old's definition, but I made it warm and inviting by any modern definition."

"And this neighborhood is so much nicer."

"The Central West End is actually a very desirable part of town."

It was Helen's turn to throw back the eye roll to her daughter. "Maybe if you're a hippie."

"What is this, 1967? Last time I checked there wasn't

anyone walking the streets of the Central West End with flowers in their hair, promoting free love."

"You know what I mean. Those people are different down there."

"Mom," Karen said with a sigh, "we lived there for eight years. So are we 'those people'?"

"Not since you moved."

"You know, whatever, Mom." The waitress showed up with their food. They'd decided to go to Miss Aimee B's Tea Room. It was a quaint, elegant restaurant, housed in an historical building from the 1860s and gave the feeling of dining in a woman's parlor one hundred years ago. But Karen doubted the lace-trimmed, dress-clad ladies from a century ago would have been stealing sugar packets in their white gloves. And although Karen tended to gravitate toward more modern things, even she couldn't resist the charm of Miss Aimee B's. Not to mention they had a killer baked chicken salad pie, which Karen had paired with a side of their decadent mac 'n' cheese. Comfort food. Boy, could she use some comfort.

"So, Karen, you look tired. I'm sure it's stress about the whole fertility thing. What's going on?"

Karen took a bite of the warm, delicious pie. She hadn't mentioned the fertility debacle because she didn't want to talk about it. Didn't want to think about it. But she couldn't stop thinking about it, pretty much non-stop, so she might as well talk about it with her mom. "Well, so, we've decided to try IUI one more time."

"Then what?"

"Well, hopefully it will work, Mom."

"I know you think I'm being pessimistic, but you need to be realistic and have a Plan B."

IUI *was* Plan B. Plan A was have sex like the majority of the population and have a baby. So, Plan C. "If it doesn't work, then we have enough money for one round of IVF."

"Is that in vitro?"

"Yeah. Where they take some of my eggs, his sperm, and create an embryo in a petri dish."

"Shhh," Helen said, looking around. "Don't say that so loudly."

"What, sperm?" Karen couldn't resist a grin spreading across her face.

Helen frowned at her daughter. "What is it with your generation, just blurting out whatever, whenever?"

"Oh, we just do it to irritate our parents."

"It's working." Helen chewed a bite of her quiche before saying quietly, "I wish I had some money to give you toward IVF in case one round doesn't work."

Karen was touched...her mom lived like she'd been a child of the Depression (although she wasn't), so for Helen Taggart to even consider the thought of offering Karen money for IVF...that was huge. "Mom, wow, thanks. But we can afford one round. And IVF is like the rock star of fertility. It's a big deal. It should work."

"If your selfish father had left me or you more money...."

"I know. That would have helped, for sure." That was a sore subject for her entire family. When her parents divorced, Helen was more than gracious to her ex-husband. She took less than she was entitled to have, less than her lawyer advised, in an effort to maintain a good relationship between them for the family. She didn't want to tear the family apart with bitterness. So she only took a very small amount of his retirement, despite all the years they'd socked it away together.

Karen's father, Hal, apparently didn't feel the same sense of loyalty to his first family. When he passed away, Karen found out her stepmother, who he'd only been married to for eight years—got a life insurance settlement of hundreds of thousands of dollars. Karen and her brother Jonathan had each only been given a very small amount.

Of course Karen knew money didn't equate to love. But she had been his daughter for nearly thirty years, and that's all he thought to leave her? That, and a fucked up heart that struggled to trust after the father she adored left them. Quite the legacy.

And then her stepmother spends a few years as his wife and got to retire after he died, or so she heard. She hadn't really kept in touch. Too many hurt feelings. Too much pain.

She sure could have used an extra ten grand or so now for fertility. She'd socked away most of her inheritance into her retirement fund and used a few thousand to put into renovations at the new house.

But in the back of her mind, she wondered if she had uprooted them and moved to the suburbs for nothing. If she didn't have a baby, the house was useless. Just an homage to a dream that died.

Gobbling down her mac 'n' cheese, Karen paused long enough to ask, "If all this fertility BS doesn't work...what do you think about adoption?"

"I think adoption is wonderful."

"You do?"

"Of course. Being a mother isn't about giving birth. It's about all the moments after that."

Karen was surprised by her mom's perspective. But pleased. She trusted her mom, believed in her mom. And she was right—as much as she longed to carry a child inside of her, what she really wanted was a baby to call her own. *Who cares where it comes from?*

Helen whispered, "Just don't get an Oriental or a black baby."

Karen shook her head. "Why not? And no one uses the term Oriental anymore. How about Asian?"

"Asian, whatever." Her voice still low, she added, "They are beautiful, but I just think it would be so hard to be adopted and everyone could tell at one glance. It's no one's business if you're adopted, and I think it would just be harder for a child to walk around with everyone knowing right away."

"I don't know if that's true."

"Look it up. I mean, *The Blind Side* makes you think everything is hunky-dory, but it's got to be hard on everyone, I'm telling you."

Karen had a sudden urge to adopt a mixed race African-Asian baby just to prove her mother wrong. "Well, I'll take that under advisement."

"I'm not being close-minded, Karen. I'm just trying to avoid a lot of pain for everyone." She patted Karen's hand. "But whether it's adoption or IVF or whatever…I just think you'll make an unbelievable mother. I can't wait to see you with your own child."

The smile on Helen's face made Karen feel like somehow, someway it would all work out. And that was exactly what it was to be a mother.

****

Claudia couldn't believe she'd agreed to this date. That morning she'd put on one of her favorite sweaters with a short skirt, extra-dangly earrings and sky-high sexy heels, trying to make an effort. Why, she didn't know. As she sat, nervous, in a booth at the Fountain on Locust restaurant, she desperately wished she were anywhere else. She'd been there about ten minutes, grateful the décor gave her plenty to look at while she waited.

The Fountain on Locust was in a building that in the early twentieth century served as the showroom for the Stutz Blackhawk and Stutz Bearcat, considered high-end vehicles in the day. Today it was a restaurant whose walls had been turned into a massive art deco gallery. Old-fashioned chrome and black soda bar style stools perched at the bar made of decorative wood, polished to perfection. Black and white tiles on the floor were laid to create interesting patterns. Everywhere Claudia looked there was something fascinating to see. But so far, no Kurt.

Maybe he'll stand me up, she thought with optimism. That would be a stroke of good luck. She could get points from Jayne and Karen for trying but then if he called again, she could feign outrage and tell him he'd blown his chance. Yes, that would be perfect.

"What are you thinking about to put that pretty smile on your face?" Kurt asked, standing beside the booth, bringing her back from her well thought-out fantasy.

"Oh, hello," she said, standing up to greet him as he gave her a quick kiss on the cheek. He smelled good. As they both sat back down, she said, "I thought you were going to stand me up."

"Never," he said with a smile. "Traffic was a bear. And then I had to be careful about where I park my Jaguar."

"Jaguar, huh?" she asked, thinking he was trying to impress the wrong woman by talking about his expensive car. Cars didn't matter a lot to Claudia.

"Yeah. She's my baby."

Claudia thought she actually saw him checking out his own reflection in the gleaming wood of the tabletop. *Really?* Maybe she was just imagining it. He was attractive, though, no doubt about it. Sort of like a Ken doll. Blond hair, swept off his forehead. Bright white teeth set in a mouth with full, pouty lips. Large blue eyes with long lashes.

She certainly could have done a lot worse for trying to break back into dating.

The waitress was quick to take their orders; Claudia ordered the Royal Grille sandwich that she always loved there. It sounded like an odd way to make grilled cheese, with the unusual ingredient of Fuji apple slices. But the combination was somehow delicious.

The Fountain was known for serving retro-style drinks, and Kurt ordered a high ball. Claudia turned down his repeated offers for alcohol, since she knew she had to drive home. But she sure would have liked to reach across the table and suck down his high ball in one gulp. Liquid courage sounded like a good idea.

"So, Kurt, what kind of doctor are you?"

"I'm a plastic surgeon." He winked at her. "I've done the work on some of the most famous and prestigious women in town."

"Well, that's fascinating." She sipped her coffee, with a sudden feeling of being under a microscope. Here was a man who made a living by fixing people's physical flaws. She felt frantic, wishing her nose was straighter and the crow's feet that were appearing beside her eyes weren't evident under the lights.

"So if you ever need something done, I could give you a discount."

"Duly noted, Doctor." She smiled at him. "I've never given plastic surgery much of a thought."

"Oh, come on. Isn't there anything you've ever wanted done? Every woman has something they'd like to improve upon."

A man telling her on a first date that she needed plastic surgery. Great. Worse than she had imagined. "Well, you tell me. What should I have done?"

He shook his head. "Oh, I'm not saying you need work done. I'm saying most women think they do."

"So you do it even if they don't really need it done?"

"It's all about perspective, isn't it? Like I might think you're gorgeous, but maybe when you look in the mirror, you notice a slight bend in the bridge of your nose. If you want to correct that, who am I to tell you no?"

He just said my nose is crooked. I don't believe it. "So you think I need a nose job?"

"On the contrary. I just said you were gorgeous, remember?" His smile pissed her off more than charmed her. "I just said that if it would make you feel better about yourself, I'm happy to make people more comfortable with how they see themselves."

She still wasn't sure if he was complimenting her or pointing out her flaws. Maybe both. "So what types of procedures do you do the most of?"

"Lots of rhinoplasties and breast augmentations. I'm kind of known as the best breast guy in town." He sat back in his seat. "Yours are real, right?"

She felt her cheeks grow warm. "Definitely."

"I thought so. They're spectacular." His smile grew larger. "And that's a professional opinion."

The waitress brought their meals, and Claudia was relieved as she hoped it would result in a change of topic. Because this was more bizarre than anything she had imagined for their date.

Digging into the grilled cheese sandwich gave her a moment of bliss before she remembered Kurt was still sitting across the table. She was quickly reminded as he began a barrage of new topics—all of which she assumed were designed to impress while they came across to Claudia as materialistic and an attempt to merely show-off.

Kurt droned on about his home on Cape Cod and his condo in Deer Valley, Utah, near Park City. From the right guy, she figured she would be wondering if maybe someday she'd be lucky enough to join him, but Claudia didn't think she would ever want to join him again, anywhere. After all, all his chatter between broad white-toothed grins was about himself. His only question to her so far was clarifying if her breasts were real.

But maybe he's just nervous too, she thought, although she doubted it. But she should give him the benefit of the doubt. After all, it's not like she went into this "date" with an open mind. She had set him up to fail. And he did have pretty pale blue eyes, those full lips, and although she didn't usually go for blondes, he had a nice, thick head of hair. Of course being in his business, maybe none of it was real.

As she neared the finish of her gooey, yummy sandwich, he touched on a subject that she thought maybe they could find some common ground on. Maybe the night could be salvaged.

"So usually my kids and I spend Christmas up there in the mountains. It's beautiful, the shopping is great and then of course we go skiing."

"How many kids do you have?" she asked, perking up.

"Two. Boy and girl."

"That's nice—one of each. How old?"

"He's fifteen now and she's thirteen. Getting to be a bit of a handful these days, so we sent them off to private boarding school."

"Oh, really?" Boarding school? Really? She knew people did that, but she only saw that on TV or in movies. Isabella was in private school, but locally, of course. She came home every night. The thought of sending her away...wow. She could barely comprehend it. "Where do they go?"

"In Massachusetts. That's why I bought the place in Cape Cod. We usually spend spring break out there and a few weeks in the summer after school lets out."

"I can't imagine my daughter going away to school...I would miss her so much."

"How old is she?"

"Five."

"Yeah, well," he chuckled, "wait a few years. You won't feel the need to see her all the time anymore and they won't want to see you much, either."

Claudia couldn't disagree more. She'd been very close to her parents and her siblings. But now was not a time to have a debate. "Doesn't your ex miss them?"

He shrugged his shoulders. "It was her idea to send them to boarding school."

"Does she have a busy career?"

That question produced his biggest smile of the night. "Only if you consider spending my money a career. She does a really good job of it, so you could probably consider it a career path." Claudia realized she must have a smirk on her face because he was quick to say, "I'm sorry, I didn't mean to imply that all ex-wives do that."

"I don't get maintenance or alimony. I support myself. My ex only helps with our daughter."

"Oh, so you work?" It sounded like it was a foreign concept to him.

"Sure. I'm an office manager for a small company." It wasn't a glamorous job, but she liked it. She'd been there since just a couple of years after college, and they were like a big family. Over the years, she'd made herself so valuable to the owners that she really knew more about running their company than they did. But it freed them up to handle the sales aspects and bring in more business while she ran the show. She wasn't getting rich from working there, but they paid her well for her position, treated her like gold and gave her four weeks of vacation each year plus sick days.

"You sound surprised that I have a job."

"Well, no offense, but you're beautiful and divorced...in my world that usually means ex-trophy wife that rides off the lifestyle of her ex."

"I'm beginning to think we live in very different worlds."

"Maybe. It's kind of nice to have a date with a woman that supports herself. What does your ex do?"

"He's a partner at a law firm."

"So that explains how he screwed you out of maintenance."

Claudia shook her head. "No, I never asked for it. I'm a big girl. I can take care of myself. He was very generous in dividing our assets and pays more than required for our daughter. But he's not paying for my mortgage or car or anything like that. Just expenses for our daughter."

"Wow, wish you were my ex-wife." He winked at her. "If things go well after tonight, maybe we could be on our way toward that."

Uh, no. Claudia smiled. "So if your ex doesn't have a job and your kids are away at boarding school...what does she do?"

"Hell, I don't know. Shops, lunches with friends...I think she does some charity work here and there. Usually just at functions where she can dress up."

"Like those women on *Real Housewives*?"

"Exactly! I'm sure if they ever made a St. Louis edition there's no doubt she would make the cut, along with half of her friends and my clients, too."

"Then you could be breast guy to the stars."

"I like the way you think. I should get an agent. Maybe I could get my own reality show." The sad thing was Claudia didn't think he was kidding.

They moved on to dessert...after all, why pass on a free dessert at a restaurant known for great ones? Unfortunately, the conversation didn't get much better. Very few questions or inquiries directed at her, mainly just more bragging about his lifestyle or expertise as a surgeon, etc. He was good looking, successful for sure (and he definitely wouldn't let her forget that), and not without his charms. But he just wasn't her type.

What is my type? She wondered as he rattled on about his speedboat docked at his condo in Lake of the Ozarks, the Midwest's closest thing to experiencing the beach life. Even if he wasn't her type, she really did give it an effort. Didn't she?

The thing was she'd fallen in love with a man in college whom she thought she'd be with forever. And although Sam was very successful, too, he didn't feel the need to brag about it or make that the emphasis of his life. Sure, they had bought an expensive home and drove nice cars and enjoyed the finer things in life. She had been pampered, sure. But their lives had been centered on their love, their families, their friends. Sharing real moments together and enjoying each other's company. He cared what she thought, asked her opinion, appreciated her. They were best friends. They laughed a lot, enjoyed doing the same things, and he made her feel special and important.

Well, until that day. When she found out there was a side to Sam that no longer valued monogamy or his wedding vows. The Sam who wanted to be free to explore other things…or, more specifically, other women.

With Kurt, though, even if he was the most monogamous man on the planet (which she found hard to believe), there wasn't much else there to share. He made it clear he didn't value family. He didn't care what she had to say or want to learn more about her. And he spent the day looking at other women's breasts.

No, not her type at all.

As Claudia finished her Black Cadillac sundae with black cherry ice cream and creamy hot fudge, Kurt asked, "So…do you like to party?"

"Party?"

"Yeah, you know…a little somethin' somethin' to take off the edge or hype things up a bit? I've got some excellent bud if you're into that or some pills that will really light up the night."

Drugs? Was he serious? She knew more people, even successful people, did drugs than she cared to think about. But Claudia Knight was not one of them, never really had been. Besides a few joints at parties back in her college days—the occasional drink here and there was the only thing she used to alter her mood. That, and end a date that was clearly going downhill fast.

"Uh, no, that's not really my scene." She wiped her lips with a napkin and grabbed her purse. "It's getting late for a work night. I really should be going."

"It's not even nine."

"Well, my daughter's not away at boarding school, so my mornings start pretty early to get us both out the door." She edged herself closer to the end of the booth, trying to make a quick getaway. "Thank you so much for inviting me out tonight."

"Okay," he said, looking irritated. "I'd like to do it again sometime. Someplace nicer, on a weekend."

"Maybe," she said with a small smile, not wanting to encourage him. She knew she would never answer any of his calls ever again.

"Just let me pay the bill and I'll walk you to your car."

"Oh, that's sweet, but I'm fine—I've got a spot right out front." She stood up and he did as well, reaching in for a kiss. She turned her cheek so he settled his full lips there. "Thanks again."

"I'll call you," he said as she escaped the booth that had imprisoned her for the last couple of hours. *I won't answer.* Thankfully the wonderful meal and great atmosphere had helped take the edge off a night that had otherwise been a waste of time. She'd have to come back with the girls soon…now *that* would be a good time.

She felt like she was making the getaway from an ill-fated heist as she drove away. So there. She'd gone on a date; she'd tried. Now she could tell the girls to back off and leave her alone. One date every couple of years was enough. She didn't need a man. Claudia was fine with her life the way it was.

At a stoplight she sent a quick text to Karen and Jayne: *So I went on a date. It was a disaster. Will fill you in when we do lunch on Sat. Luv u both!*

When she pulled into her driveway, seeing Sam's car there surprised her. She'd forgotten he was there, watching Isabella. Normally he would have watched her at his place, but he had an early morning meeting and didn't want to risk trying to get a kindergartner out the door on time. So he was nice enough to agree to watch her but asked if he could do it at Claudia's, so she'd be on kid duty in the morning. That was fine with her...she'd missed her little girl tonight.

Walking through the front door and slipping her pea coat onto the coat rack, she could hear the TV on in the family room. The flat screen TV above the fireplace was playing an episode of one of the *Law & Order* shows. Sam never could get enough of crime and law shows.

"How'd it go?" she asked and then saw Sam was asleep on the couch. He was still wearing his dress shirt and pants but had thrown his suit coat, tie and shoes onto the overstuffed chair in the corner. Sometimes it surprised her, even after six years, that he wasn't still hers. Although it no longer seemed normal to see him asleep on the couch they'd picked out together years ago...it didn't seem altogether wrong, either.

Claudia went into the kitchen, pulled off her high heels and grabbed a glass of water. She sighed. What a night. The kitchen was clean, which didn't surprise her, since Sam had always been a neat and tidy person. The black-and-white paper hat sitting at Isabella's spot at the table was the only hint that they'd picked up Steak-n-Shake for supper on their way home.

Feeling a sudden exhaustion, she headed back into the family room to wake up Sam and send him on his way so she could crawl up the stairs and into bed. She shook him, not very gently, since she knew he was an incredibly sound sleeper. "Sam...wake up, Sam."

He stirred and then his eyes popped open. "Oh...hey. Guess I fell asleep."

She chuckled, still leaning over him. "You guessed right."

Sam's eyes focused on hers. "Wow, Claud, you look beautiful tonight."

She looked away, focusing on the floral pattern of the rug. "Oh, whatever, thanks."

"So how did your big date go?"

"It wasn't a big date. And it was even worse than I'd imagined."

"So he was a flake?"

"An arrogant plastic surgeon who likes nothing more than talking about himself."

Sam chuckled. "That good, huh?"

"Yeah," she said, giggling, looking back at him. "Well, you need to get home, and I'm ready to go to sleep and forget tonight ever happened."

"I meant what I said," he whispered, making no attempt to get up. He touched her arm. "You really are stunning tonight. That guy was an idiot to blow it by talking about himself."

She was uncomfortable, being that close to him, but she didn't look away. "I know another idiot that blew it."

"Touché." He didn't smile. Instead, he looked into her eyes with even more intensity. "But maybe this idiot is smart enough to have regrets." Before she knew what was happening, he'd put his arm around her and pulled her against him as his lips found hers. Those lips she knew so well, so warm, so soft—

"Sam, what are you doing?" Claudia attempted to push away, but even she was surprised at how weak her protest sounded. His strong arms pulled her tighter and she was now on top of him. Lying against his body, the heat was undeniable. Their lips fell into a familiar yet exhilarating rhythm as her body experienced a rush she'd forgotten it was capable of. "Sam..." Even Claudia didn't know any more if she was objecting or consenting.

He tore his lips from hers, both of them breathless as their eyes searched each other. "Do you want me to stop?"

Did she? This was so wrong. No good could come of this. She knew that...right?

He didn't let go. His arms felt so good, so comfortable. He'd awakened something in her...something that longed for him. Ached for him. Or maybe just any man.

But this wasn't any man. This was Sam. She'd loved him for fifteen years. And he broke her heart.

"Sam, I don't think this is a good idea—"

"I know we weren't expecting this, but it feels so right. Doesn't it?"

It did.

"Claudia, I never stopped loving you. Not for a second." He kissed her again; this time his kisses were more forceful, full of intention. She didn't pull away. She moved in.

When they'd both reached a fever pitch, she finally let go and sat up. "I don't think I can do this...."

"Don't think about it," he said, never looking away. "Let's explore this moment, whatever it is. Let's not analyze it now. I want this... I can tell you do, too." He grabbed her hand.

Claudia didn't know if it was the bad date, her overactive hormones surging from lack of use, or the look in the eyes of the man she'd never totally been able to let go. But she squeezed his hand, stood up and led him upstairs.

Chapter Eight

Sometimes there was just no substitute for pasta.

Karen was the first to arrive at Cunetto's House of Pasta on The Hill. The Hill was an Italian-American neighborhood in St. Louis settled largely by Italian immigrants in the late nineteenth century. Today it was known to St. Louis residents as by far the best place to get delicious, authentic Italian fare. Restaurants, bakeries or delis to delight just about anyone's palate were on almost every street. It was hard to choose a favorite restaurant…they were all so good.

While she waited for Jayne and Claudia to arrive, Karen really wanted a drink. But just the day before, she'd had her final IUI procedure and certainly didn't want to turn her potential little embryo into an alcoholic. She was filled with an uncharacteristic hopefulness this go-round. Maybe that meant something, maybe it meant nothing. Maybe it was her attempt to trick her reproductive system into making a baby. Plus she'd read somewhere recently about self-fulfilling prophecies or some BS. Well, whatever it was, she wondered if there were cells dividing inside her at that very moment, creating a human life. The possibility was enough to put a smile on her face.

"Hey, lady!" Jayne said, approaching the table with Claudia in tow.

Karen waved them over and gave them both hugs before they sat down. "I'm starving. Figure out what you want so we can order."

"Yes, ma'am," Jayne said, smiling. "You're bossy as usual, but you seem like you're in a good mood."

"I am in a good mood. I'm here with my two favorite women on the planet, and I'm about to overeat on delicious pasta and hate myself for it later. What could be better?"

They all laughed, then quickly studied their menus and placed their orders with a handsome waiter within a few minutes. Karen ordered her usual fettuccine—a simple, classic dish without a lot of fuss. Full of flavor and to the point.

After the waiter left their table, Karen could see that old spark in Jayne that she had grown to love over the years. Tonight she could tell the girl was bursting with some good news.

"So, Jayne, what's the big news?"

"Am I that transparent?"

"Yes," Claudia said with a chuckle, exchanging a knowing glance with Karen.

Jayne's face lit up with a huge smile. "I got the job!"

"The promotion?" Karen asked.

"Yep. You are dining with the new director of consumer relations for Nixon Pharmaceutical."

"Way to go!" Claudia said, beaming at Jayne.

Karen was so proud of her. "I knew you could do it, Jayne Brandt."

"Thank you both so much for pushing me to go for it. It comes with a hefty raise—thanks in part to Gray—and a nice boost in the self-confidence department."

"That's fantastic," Claudia said. "Was it hard to get?"

"Not really. I think I was the most qualified and I'm a proven performer. The hardest part was actually the conflict with Gray."

Karen frowned. "He didn't want you to get it?"

"Oh, no, that's not what I meant."

"Well, I hope not because I was just learning to tolerate him."

Jayne chuckled. "No, it was just kind of tricky since he'll be my direct supervisor now and he's also my brother-in-law. He was really worried that it would look like nepotism. So he set it up so that a committee made the decision and will oversee my performance appraisals and things like that. He also warned me that I will have to be on my best game so no one thinks I'm riding on his coattails."

Karen smirked. "Technically, you rode much more than his coattails, back in the day."

Jayne smacked Karen's arm. "Don't remind me, you smart-aleck."

"Only until the day you die, my friend." Karen turned to Claudia. "And what's the story on the disastrous date?"

Claudia rolled her eyes. "He was a buffoon."

"Do tell."

"Well…for starters, he's incredibly arrogant. I think I caught him checking himself out in the reflection of the table."

"No!" Jayne said, her mouth dropping open.

"Pretty sure. And then really the only thing he wanted to know about me is whether or not my breasts are real."

"Jesus," Karen said, shaking her head.

"Well, he is a plastic surgeon, so I suppose it was a valid question."

Jayne piped in. "Still has a major creep factor, though."

"I thought so too. And then he just went on about himself…he owns a home in Cape Cod, a condo at the lake, a place in the mountains near Park City…."

"Holy shit," Karen said, devouring a roll the waiter just dropped off. "Must be one hell of a good plastic surgeon."

"According to him, he's the best." Claudia buttered her roll. "Then he mentioned his kids, and I thought we might find some common ground there, but he said he sends them away to boarding school. Can you believe that?"

"No, I can't," Jayne said, shaking her head. "I mean, I'm not saying that I wouldn't *occasionally* want to send my kids away, but just for a day or two."

Karen nodded in agreement. "No kidding. I'm not going through all this fertility crap just to ship the kid away."

"Speaking of that…?" Claudia asked quietly.

"Last round of IUI yesterday. I'm really hoping it worked this time."

"Let's think positive," Jayne said, offering her most

supportive smile.

"I'm trying my best to take a page from your playbook and do just that, Jayne."

"Good. When will you know?"

"A couple of weeks." Long, agonizing, excruciating weeks.

"Well, let us know as soon as you find out," Claudia said, her big eyes looking right at Karen. "Whether it's good or bad. We're here either way."

"I'll let you know."

After the waiter brought their food, Karen kept her eye on Claudia while they chatted. There was something different about her tonight, Karen was sure of it. She seemed a little more...something. After polishing off a fair amount of her huge mound of pasta, Karen said, "So Claudia, anything else new with you? You seem like you're holding out on us."

"Me? No." But Karen was sure she saw Claudia's face grow pink. Something was up.

"I know you said the date bombed, but did you maybe...mess around a little bit anyway?"

"Karen!"

"Well, it has been a long time for you."

Jayne agreed. "It's true, Claudia."

"Not that it's anyone's business, but no, the most he got from me was my cheek to kiss."

Karen pressed on. "You seem a little more...relaxed tonight."

"Oh, I don't know," Claudia said with nonchalance and a shrug. "Probably just glad it's over with. And glad the flu bug has left our house. By the way, I hear you watched Isabella one night, Karen. Thanks so much."

"She was great." Karen smiled. "Such a little talker, so smart. I just wanted to gobble her up."

"She apparently had fun with you, too. She came home with the paintings she and Rick made and talking about Kramer and your great mac 'n' cheese. She said I need to use your recipe."

"Look at me, ousting the resident Martha Stewart."

"Pretty impressive," Jayne said with a giggle.

"One meal does not a chef make," Claudia said, grinning. "But you always have been a good cook."

"Thank you. Whereas you are a great cook, a master at plating and renowned for your table settings. I just cook."

"I just eat," Jayne said, polishing off her dish of linguini with asparagus. "Which reminds me, I have to start dressing up a little more for my new position. The bad news is that most of my suits and dressier outfits are too small for me now."

"Well then, you've got a great excuse to go shopping," Claudia said with enthusiasm. "Want some help?"

"Sure, that would be great. I was kind of hoping to go tomorrow."

"Sam's got Isabella this weekend, so that would be perfect."

Jayne turned to look at Karen. "Do you want to go, too?"

"I would, but I still have a lot of stuff to do around the new house. I swear it's taking forever to get everything done. So I'm gonna pass."

"Are you going to have a house-warming party?"

"You know, I was thinking I might have a little something in a few weeks. Maybe just you guys and my favorite new neighbors, this great gay couple."

"That would be fun!" Jayne sat back in her seat. "We'll get a sitter and have a real grown-up night. Just don't do it on Valentine's Day weekend…Josh and I are going out to Innsbrook again for a little one-on-one time."

"Oh, that sounds romantic," Claudia said, and Karen saw a faraway look in her eye that, again, didn't seem quite right. There was something up; that was for sure.

****

"If I tell you something, you have to promise not to tell Karen," Claudia said nervously as she and Jayne browsed through the racks at Ann Taylor Loft at the outlet mall.

Jayne looked at Claudia like she had two heads. "I don't

want to keep a secret from Karen."

"What about when you started dating Josh, but you didn't tell me, you only told Karen?"

Jayne looked hurt. "That was years ago, and it was only because Sam had just left and your heart was broken. Plus, she guessed something was up. She's hard to trick."

Claudia wanted to tell someone—had to tell someone—what had happened between her and Sam. But she couldn't deal with Karen's reaction. She would absolutely flip out. She would never understand; she would just berate Claudia and probably tell her everything she needed to hear.

She just wasn't ready to hear it yet.

But she knew it wasn't right to ask Jayne to keep a secret. "I'm sorry, Jayne, you're right. It wasn't fair of me to ask you that. Never mind." She pulled a cute blazer out and held it up. "What do you think of this?"

Jayne looked at the tag. "It's cute, but unfortunately, not big enough for me."

"Sure it is."

"No, it's not," Jayne said, looking embarrassed. "Okay, fine, tell me what you were going to tell me. I can't stand it anymore. I'm fat and I need something to distract me from my woes."

"No, I really shouldn't—"

"Just tell me why you don't want her to know."

Claudia sighed. "Because she'll judge me. And I just can't handle that right now. I just need someone to listen."

Jayne gave her a warm smile. "I'll listen."

Claudia swallowed. "I slept with Sam."

Jayne didn't say anything, but her expression was a mixture of shock and terror.

"I know, I know it was dumb and reckless and you've probably lost all respect for me—"

"I have the utmost respect for you. But how did it happen?" She pulled two skirts off the rack.

"I'm not sure. It was the night of my date and he was

watching Isabella at my house. So I came home, he was there, he said some sweet things—"

"Like what?" Jayne moved onto another rack, and Claudia was pretty sure she was avoiding eye contact.

"Like…I don't know. That he had regrets, that he never stopped loving me."

"Do you believe him?"

"I have no idea. I mean, we're not *together* if that's what you think. It was just one night together."

"So…." Jayne looked at Claudia, her eyes full of questions. "So how was it?"

Claudia sighed. "Like it always was, only better."

Jayne went back to searching through the racks, finding a blazer and a pair of slacks. "So…what does this mean? Was it a one-time thing?"

"Yeah, I guess so. I don't know." Claudia knew it needed to be, but there was a part of her that wanted him again.

Jayne stared right at Claudia. "You know what he said when he left. He told you then that he loved you. But he also said he wasn't made to be with just one woman."

"Of course I remember that." Like it was yesterday. She could still remember the physical pain she'd felt when he left. But now she also had memories from the other night…and how good it felt to be back in his arms, after all these years. Despite all they'd been through, he still had the power to make her feel amazing. In all the right places.

"I don't feel like trying these on. I'm just going to buy them and see how they fit at home. I'd rather be humiliated in my own room."

"Oh, Jayne, don't be so hard on yourself. You are beautiful."

Jayne attempted a smile. "I wish I thought so."

As they walked up to the checkout and stood in line, Claudia asked quietly, "So do you hate me?"

"What? Of course not. Why would you even ask that?"

"Well, because I'm so weak and stupid—"

"You are not. I'm not going to stand here and say that I

think it was a good thing to sleep with Sam. But what do I know? Maybe it's exactly what you need to move on. You've never gotten over him, I know that."

Claudia looked down, noticing that her pewter-colored ballerina flats had a large scuff on the toe. How did she miss that? They looked unkempt. "You're right."

"So maybe this will...I don't know, help." Jayne giggled. "Or just do what I do. Sneak cookies from the pantry when no one's looking."

Claudia joined in the laughter, relieved to have told Jayne. It didn't change anything, but she felt a little lighter. Someone else knew, and her world didn't come to a screeching halt. So she slept with Sam. Probably a lot of people slept with their exes. It didn't mean anything had to change. But, at least for one night, it had felt pretty amazing to have sex again.

****

When Claudia got home, Sam's car was parked in the driveway. She glanced at her watch: five-forty. He wasn't due home with Isabella until six.

She walked inside and Isabella came running up to her. "Mommy!"

Smothering her daughter with kisses, she pulled away and asked, "Did you have a good weekend?"

"Yeah, Daddy took me to the Science Center and then we played Barbies today. He was all the boys and I was all the girl dolls."

Claudia grinned, trying to picture Sam voicing various prince dolls and Malibu Ken. "That sounds like fun." They headed toward the kitchen and Sam poked his head around the corner. Claudia said, "You're here early."

He smiled. "Yeah, I hope you don't mind—"

"Daddy said we could all eat together tonight!" Isabella said with the kind of enthusiasm only a child can conjure. "He said you would like that."

"He did, huh?" Claudia asked, her heart beating faster as she approached a sheepish looking Sam.

"Well, I thought you'd be okay with it. We picked up

122

some pizza from Pi and I was hoping their Bada Bing salad was still your favorite, 'cause I grabbed one of those, too."

"Yep, still love it." Sam kissed her on the cheek and she felt her face grow warm.

She looked at the table, and he'd really made an effort. He'd put the salad in her decorative glass bowl. The salad plates had been chilled and he'd pulled out some of her linen napkins and even lit candles.

"Let's eat," Isabella said, climbing into her chair.

Sam pulled out Claudia's seat and whispered in her ear, "It's good to see you."

She smiled back at him, wondering what on earth they'd started.

****

Valentine's Day. Never a big deal in Karen's book. She didn't need a day for Rick to profess his love; he did that every day. In words, in actions. Having said that, she didn't mind getting a huge bouquet of her favorite flowers—calla lilies—to make her dining room table look divine.

Rick brought them home with him the night before, and hid them in the garage. When she woke up that Saturday morning on Valentine's Day, they were waiting for her on the kitchen table.

"Very nice, Mr. Gordon," she said, giving him a kiss as they both hovered around the coffee maker, waiting for it to finish brewing.

His sleepy grin and overnight beard made him look even more attractive to Karen. "I thought you might like them."

"You thought right."

He knew her well enough to know she didn't want a sappy, sentimental card. She, in turn, knew exactly what he always wanted. She handed him a small box with a huge grosgrain bow she'd made herself.

Grinning, he opened it to find a gift card to his favorite art supply store. "I was hoping you'd get me another one of these."

"My baby can never get enough art supplies."

"So true." He put his arms around her waist. "Well, what do you want to do today?"

"I don't know…wanna just chill this morning?" She didn't waste any time with the coffee; the minute it was done, she poured two cups. She left hers black, and put one scoop of sugar and a dash of creamer in Rick's. Soon they were both sipping the steaming hot beverages, desperate for their first kick of caffeine for the day.

Rick smiled. "Ah, that hits the spot. And yes, I can chill. I'm very good at chillin'."

He grabbed the newspaper off the kitchen table; she loved that he still read the paper. She wondered how many people still did that. She grabbed her e-reader and followed him into the family room where he turned on a laid-back Pandora station that played softly in the background while they both read, sipped their coffee and chilled. Kramer climbed on the couch, blissful to be snuggled between them.

Karen figured Rick would get bored after an hour or so, he'd take off to go somewhere, and she'd get his second gift of the day prepared. She snuck a peek at him as she looked up from what she was reading, her excitement building. He was so handsome and perfect for her. Just the right amount of tenderness and the right amount of manliness.

She was thinking this just might turn out to be the best gift ever.

****

Sure enough, Rick bolted about an hour and a half later. Instead of a full breakfast, they had just nibbled on some toast, so the plan was for him to go spend his gift card on some new brushes he'd been eyeing, and then he would grab lunch for them on the way home from the yummy Chinese place they'd discovered just down the road.

Right after he left, Karen looked at Kramer and announced, "I think today is the day, my handsome pooch!"

He, of course, didn't understand what she was saying, but easily picked up on her excitement and the tone in her voice. He jumped up, putting his paws on her chest and licking her face with desperately happy slurps. Karen scratched behind his downy soft ears and then pushed him down.

She just knew that this time the IUI had worked. All the signs were there. Her breasts were tender, she felt bloated, tired and she maybe even thought she'd been having the urge to pee more often. All good signs. All pointing towards a baby.

The previous day had been the two-week mark, and she could have tested then, but she felt like waiting that extra day would be a good idea. She'd hate to get a false negative and stress herself out.

So her plan was to take the pregnancy test and then put the stick with the plus sign in the gift box she'd already wrapped. She'd taken special care to wrap it to perfection…she felt like Claudia, as she'd made sure the bow was perfect and every corner was precise. But this was no ordinary gift.

She was going to give Rick a baby.

Instead of the usual dread she'd felt the past year and a half when taking a pregnancy test, this time her stomach fluttered with excitement. This time was different, she was sure. From now on, Valentine's Day would take on a whole new meaning: the day they found out they were going to be parents.

Kramer followed her into the bathroom, his tail wagging.

"You can tell, too, can'tcha Kramer?" Karen went through the ritual she knew all too well. No need to read the instructions; she'd done this so many times she could post an instructional video on YouTube.

After following all proper procedures, she placed the cap back on the test stick and set it on the sink. Now the wait. Two minutes had never seemed longer. Karen's usual tactic was to stare at it obsessively, but this time, she decided to wait the two minutes before she looked.

Kramer sat next to her, expectant, his eyes on her. He

knew they were waiting for something, but what, he didn't know. She rubbed his chest as his tail wagged tentatively, not entirely sure what was going on.

"Okay, two minutes are up!" she said, hopping up, looking forward to finally seeing a plus sign on the stick.

She picked it up, her body surging with adrenaline and there it was....

The same straight line of failure she'd seen on every other pregnancy test.

"No," she whispered, shaking her head. *I must have done something wrong. I was in such a hurry, I must have screwed something up.*

She grabbed another test from the bathroom cabinet and this time, read the directions carefully as if she'd never taken one before. She had to drink more coffee and waited about thirty minutes before taking the test.

Another straight line. Not pregnant.

****

Rick walked into the house, surprised Kramer didn't greet him at the door as he usually did. Karen wasn't in the family room, so he headed into the kitchen, expecting to find her there. Nope. He put the bag of warm Chinese food on the counter, along with his new paintbrushes.

"Karen?" he hollered. No response. Something wasn't right. He headed down the hall and walked into their bedroom.

There she was, lying on the bed with her back to him. Kramer was snuggled up next to her, his head draped over her side and he looked at Rick with sad, mournful eyes. Rick could hear Karen's quiet whimper. Alarmed, he was about to ask what was wrong when he saw two familiar white plastic sticks sitting on the nightstand.

Fuck. Why was this so hard? Why did she have to keep getting her heart broken, over and over again? It was so hard for him to see her struggle with this. And he'd never seen her cry about it before...Karen was tough. She almost never cried.

Rick wanted to say something to her, something to ease

her pain. Something to give her hope or at least comfort. But he didn't have any words, and was pretty sure she wouldn't want to hear them anyway.

So he slipped off his shoes and climbed onto the bed next to her. He put his arms around her and held her close as her whimpers turned into full-out sobs. They lay together like that for a long time, until her crying stopped and he could tell she had fallen asleep. But he didn't let her go, even when his own eyes filled with tears.

****

"I can't believe we're getting here so late," Josh said, his irritation obvious as he pulled their overnight bag out of the trunk. It was already getting dark outside at the Innsbrook chalet. "We wasted the whole day."

"Well, I'm sorry," Jayne said, following him inside. "I just didn't want to come home to a dirty house."

"So you'd rather waste our day together cleaning than spending it together out here?"

"It would have gone faster if you'd helped clean." Jayne was irritated, too.

Josh put the suitcase down, rolling his eyes. "I was watching the girls."

"And reading."

"But still watching the kids. Besides," he said, looking at her with accusations in his eyes, "maybe the house would have been in better shape if you hadn't worked late every night this week and brought work home, too."

He was right. But what was she supposed to do about it? Although she figured her new position would take a little more time, so far she had underestimated the additional hours. She kept trying to tell herself it was just while she was getting things under control, but she was worried that was just being optimistic.

Sure, the new position came with more money, which was nice. But after taxes it didn't seem to add up to much…but the stress sure was adding up. She'd been working late and missing out on time with the girls. The house was more out of control than ever.

Jayne sighed. "So are we going to spend our Valentine's arguing or do we want to enjoy our time here together?"

"I'm sorry," Josh said with a sigh. He put his arms around her and kissed her forehead. "You're right. We're here to enjoy the peace and quiet of the woods and a house without kids."

"Absolutely." And she knew he was looking forward to a hot night of passionate lovemaking, but if she was honest, all she wanted was a nap.

She hoped that the chocolate-covered strawberries they'd brought along with the takeout dinner they'd picked up would get her in the mood. Because all she was feeling was stressed.

****

Claudia had no idea what she was doing. She just knew that in the moment, it felt good.

Sam was over again, and they'd shared a heart-shaped pepperoni pizza from Papa Murphy's with Isabella. Then they gave her a little Valentine's basket with a box of chocolates, a stuffed animal and a gold heart necklace. When they all sat down to watch a movie together, Isabella sat in between her parents, proudly wearing her new necklace and clutching the fluffy panda bear.

By the time the movie was over, Isabella had fallen asleep.

"I'll take her upstairs," Sam whispered. Claudia nodded, glad she'd been proactive and put Isabella in her pajamas before they watched the movie.

She watched Sam carry their daughter up the wooden staircase, realizing having him around was becoming more comfortable than she should have ever dared to allow. Claudia knew she was playing with fire. Her mind told her she was being foolish, she was making a huge mistake. Sam had left her, making it abundantly clear he had no desire to be monogamous.

But every instinct in her body told her to go for it. It felt good; it felt right. Long forgotten emotions were taking over…emotions that made her feel wanted, and sexy, and

128

desirable. Simply put: she wanted him.

As she sat on the couch, these thoughts tumbling through her mind, she heard a creak on the stairs. She looked up to see Sam standing there in nothing but his boxers. He smiled at her, and she admired the way his abs were still flat and his chest was ripped with muscles. It was obvious he made time to work out.

Sam motioned for her to follow him, and she did. He led her to the bathroom where he started filling the tub. She looked over to her vanity to see a bottle of champagne chilling in an ice bucket, and two glasses already poured with raspberries coloring the bottom of the glasses like red rose petals.

"When did you do that?" she asked, surprised.

"While you were getting Izzy in her pajamas and having her brush her teeth."

"Sneaky, Mr. Knight." She didn't resist as he started to unbutton her shirt. Her mind was screaming *don't give in to him, don't be so foolish.* But as his fingers touched her skin with fiery seduction, she told her brain to shut up and became a woman ruled by desire.

Chapter Nine

Injections. Pills. Timers. Calendars.

This was what Karen's life had been reduced to. For most people, having a baby meant making love to your husband on a Saturday night after a glass or two of wine and a nice meal. For some, it was a quick romp in the back seat of their parents' car after staying out past curfew and figuring they didn't really need a condom—it was only one time, right?

But not for Karen and Rick and the other couples like them. *Unexplained infertility.* Fuck unexplained infertility. *Our reproductive systems are so dysfunctional and/or lazy they don't even get a name for what's wrong with them.* Karen would have preferred a disease or syndrome or something that had an exact reason, a cause and a fix.

Gray areas were a bitch.

So after the day that Karen vowed she would despise more than ever (which the rest of the world called Valentine's Day), she called her fertility specialist's office that Monday to get the ball rolling for IVF.

Gone were any normal, romantic, sentimental moments to create their baby. The IVF process was clinical, calculated. It made Karen feel like a walking scientific experiment...like she was no longer a woman. She was more like a bloated petri dish.

And bloated she was. Along with emotional. As if the whole process itself wasn't enough of an emotional roller coaster, the hormones they were giving her had reduced her to a weeping pile of feelings she wasn't accustomed to giving in to. But now, thanks to the wonders of modern fertility treatments—she didn't have a choice.

She had been turned into a character she loathed and

liked to call Crying Karen.

Crying Karen would show up while watching TV shows, touching movie trailers, and even while reading. The *Today Show* in the morning was known to make Crying Karen appear. Just about any feel-good news story would turn on the waterworks. And crying uncontrollably made Crying Karen cry even more.

And she was crabbier than normal. Yes, even she could see that. Poor Rick walked around with a dazed and fearful look on his face most of the time. He never knew if Karen was going to snap and start yelling at him or if Crying Karen was going to suddenly make an appearance. Hell, Karen didn't even know from moment to moment.

Along with the tears and anger management issues came a whole new medical vocabulary. Ovarian hyperstimulation. Follicle stimulating hormones. Injectable gonadotropins. Egg retrieval. She felt like she was taking a crash course in clinical baby making in med school.

Feeling crabby and bloated and just in no mood to socialize on a Saturday when she was getting ready to meet Claudia and Jayne for lunch—Karen was considering canceling. Then she saw the look of joy on Rick's face. He knew she was getting ready to leave the house. It was the happiest she'd seen him all week. *Might as well give the poor guy a break.*

So off she went, to meet the girls at their favorite little Mexican place. El Maguey had a few locations in town and was known for tasty, economical and fast Mexican food. Service was good, the food was served in minutes and the chips and salsa flowed. What Karen really wanted was a margarita, but it was obvious that was out of the question.

They'd decided to meet up at the location in University City, otherwise known as The Delmar Loop. The Loop was a few blocks of town that bordered the western St. Louis city limits. It was a busy, vibrant cultural district full of restaurants, eclectic shops, live music venues, a restored movie theater and St. Louis' own Walk of Fame.

Karen loved the St. Louis Walk of Fame, comprised of

stars imbedded in the sidewalk commemorating famous St. Louisans. She always enjoyed reading the names on the plaques as she walked along Delmar, and today was no exception. The weather was pretty mild for early March in St. Louis…the sun was shining and it was sixty degrees. After a cold, snowy winter they'd planned do some browsing around the eclectic neighborhood after lunch.

But as Karen made her way from the parking garage to El Maguey, she was trying desperately to get rid of Crying Karen, who'd decided to show up after listening to a song on the radio as she parked her car. As she stepped onto the star for Charles Lindbergh, she took a deep breath and tried to compose herself. Her high heel boots stomped on Vincent Price and she wiped her eyes with a frantic motion, trying to erase the evidence that Crying Karen had paid a visit. By the time she reached Maya Angelou, Karen felt it was appropriate that she finally had things under control on the star of the great female-empowering writer.

Walking into the restaurant, she saw Jayne and Claudia in a booth, and the looks on their faces told her that they could tell she'd been crying.

"What's wrong?" Jayne asked as Karen threw her purse onto the wooden bench across from them and sat down.

"Fucking John Mayer," Karen said, wiping her eyes again. "These hormones are making me crazy and then that damn song *Daughters* came on."

"And that made you cry?"

"Yes, Jayne," Karen practically hissed. "All I could think about was how my dad screwed me up—like Mr. Mayer warns fathers not to do—and then I started crying thinking that if I ever do get pregnant, I'll probably screw the kid up anyway. Maybe the Big Guy Upstairs knows what he's doing and won't let me get pregnant."

Claudia handed Karen a tissue. "Here. And don't think like that. We're all screwed up."

"I can't believe I'm crying."

"Neither can I," Jayne said, and she let the smallest of giggles slip through her lips. "I mean, it's so unlike you."

"If I wasn't so hungry, I'd stab you with this chip," Karen said, grinning as she shoved the warm tortilla chip in her mouth.

Jayne laughed. "Food fight!"

Claudia shook her head. "I can't take you guys anywhere, can I?"

The waiter took their orders and Karen continued to gorge on chips like there was no tomorrow. "So what's new with you two?"

"Not much," Claudia said, and Karen noticed that her eyes darted away. *There is something up with her. I just know it. It's been going on for a while now.*

"Nothing?" Karen asked pointedly, catching Claudia's eye. "You act like you're hiding something. Is there some new guy you're not telling us about?"

Claudia took a drink, a little too slowly, Karen thought. "There's no new guy."

"A woman? Because you know we're all accepting here. Nobody would care. I mean, I might wonder why you never made a pass at me, but other than that, I'm totally cool with it."

Jayne laughed. "What makes you think she wouldn't go for me?"

"Oh, you are *way* too straight."

"What is that supposed to mean?"

"You are like the epitome of the girl-next-door. I'm sure casting directors have your picture in mind when they're looking for that."

"Who says the girl-next-door isn't a lesbian?"

"Oh, you guys," Claudia said, shaking her head. "I'm not a lesbian. Not that there's anything wrong with that."

"So what are you up to, Claudia?" Karen asked, pointing directly at her.

"I didn't know I was having lunch with the Gestapo," Claudia said, challenging Karen with a stare.

Karen wondered if maybe the hormones were making her more than just crabby and weepy. Maybe they were making her paranoid, too. She'd have to look that up when she got home to see if paranoia was a side effect. "Fine, Knight. So everything's status quo with you. What about you, Mrs. Brandt?"

"Oh, I don't know." Jayne shrugged. "This new job is taking up more time than I thought and it's stressing me out."

"That sucks," Claudia said.

Jayne sighed. "Yeah, it does. Because lately when I get stressed, I eat. I've put on another ten pounds in the past few weeks."

"Well, yeah, I can tell you've gained some," Karen said, dunking another chip in the bright red salsa. "But you're still beautiful."

"Karen!" Claudia said, her eyes bugging out.

"What? I'm not going to lie and say I can't tell she's put on some weight. I mean, if your friends aren't honest with you, who will be?"

"She's right," Jayne said, nodding her head.

"And I said you look beautiful," Karen said, touching Jayne's hand. "I meant it. So you're a little thicker...you're still a knockout. There's absolutely nothing wrong with the way you look. Any guy would love a shot with you."

"Thanks, Karen." Jayne smiled. "Josh doesn't seem to mind, but it bothers me."

"Well, maybe we could start working out together or something," Claudia suggested.

The waiter brought their steaming plates of food.

"Sure," Jayne said with a chuckle. "As soon as I finish this deep-fried chicken chimichanga drowning in cheese sauce."

They all laughed, and Claudia nudged her. "Well, there's always tomorrow, right?"

"Right. And maybe we could do something soon...spring's just around the corner. Maybe we could get together and bike ride or walk or something."

Karen shoveled some refried beans onto her fork. "If I don't get pregnant, I'm considering drowning my sorrows with crystal meth. Or maybe I'll just start scrapbooking and will make my dog the subject of every scrapbook."

Jayne laughed. "I will pee myself if you ever make a scrapbook of your dog."

"Trust me, sister, you won't be the only one."

After they finished lunch, they took to the streets of The Loop. Everyone seemed to be so relieved to get a glimpse of the spring that was imminent. They shared laughs together and it felt like old times. Before husbands and mortgages and babies (or lack of babies).

When they slipped into Vintage Vinyl, it was like a time warp. Flipping through the record albums took Karen back to when she was a little girl and her dad used to play records. And her first album had been a classic, Michael Jackson's *Thriller*. She realized her child would never know the unique experience of putting a needle down on a spinning disc.

The three of them cracked up over horrible albums that should have probably been burned years ago and oohed and aahed over classics. Karen kept her eye out for some with great cover art—Rick liked vintage items and of course loved interesting artwork.

"I probably need to get going," Jayne said, looking at her phone. "I worked late a lot this week and I miss my girls."

Karen hated to leave; this was the most relaxed she'd felt since all the shots and pills of the IVF cycle had started. But she had one furry little guy and one handsome man waiting for her at home—if she hadn't scared them away yet. Chances are, she'd go home and find out they'd packed up and moved to safer ground.

"Well, it's been fun," she said as they stepped out of the store. "I parked in the garage. Did you guys?"

"I did," Claudia said.

"No, I'm this way." Jayne pointed in the opposite direction. She hugged Claudia, then Karen. "No crying on the way home, okay?"

"Go to hell," Karen said with a smirk. As Jayne started to walk away, Karen hollered, "And don't forget about my housewarming party. Two weeks from today!"

"I can't wait!"

Karen and Claudia headed toward the parking garage. Claudia cleared her throat. "You know, I'm glad we have a few minutes together. There's something I've been wanting to talk to you about."

I knew it! Something is going on. "What about?"

"Well…" Claudia was uncharacteristically unpoised. She looked down at the sidewalk as they stepped on the star for Bob Costas. "I want you to know that if it would help, I mean, if this round of IVF doesn't work and the doctor thinks you could benefit from a surrogate…I would be happy to be a surrogate for you."

Karen stopped walking. She looked right at Claudia, whose face wore a nervous smile. "You would carry a baby for me?"

"In a heartbeat."

Oh God, don't let Crying Karen show up. Stay away, you blubbery wench! "Claud…that's like the nicest thing anyone has ever said to me."

Claudia hugged Karen. "Well, I know how much you want this. And I'll do anything in my power to help."

Karen's heart swelled with emotion, and it took all of her energy to keep Crying Karen at bay. "I'll keep that in mind."

They started walking again and Claudia said, "And I know it costs a fortune…so I want to offer some funds if you need them."

"Claudia—"

"Karen, just listen for a minute. You know Sam gave me more money than I needed when he left. I invested it for a rainy day. Well, it's raining on my friend. I'd love to give you some of it if that would help."

Karen knew there was absolutely no way she would ever take money from Claudia. But there was a part of her that would love to take Sam's hard-earned money and put it in her uterus. That would probably really piss him off. "Claud, that is so sweet and so generous of you. I don't know that a surrogate would make a difference or not, and no, I'm not going to take money from you. But just the fact that you offered...."

They stopped at Karen's car and hugged again. Claudia said quietly, "Just keep it in mind, okay?"

"Okay."

"Well, I'll talk to you soon."

"Yeah. And give Princess Isabella a kiss and hug from Aunt Karen, okay?"

"I will."

Karen started to climb into her car and then popped back up. "And Claudia, if you ever tell anyone I cried from a John Mayer song, I will kill you." She could hear Claudia's laughter echo through the garage.

****

It had been a long week. Jayne was exhausted and so glad it was Friday. She'd worked late every night, and Josh had picked up the girls every day from daycare and made dinner. She felt like she hadn't seen them at all.

To make matters worse, she and Josh had gotten into a fight the night before. Her sweet, easygoing, lovable Josh had reached his breaking point. He'd been doing double-duty for three months now and finally had it. Jayne made the mistake of pointing out he'd forgotten to take the trash out.

Not a good idea.

When all was said and done, she was crying and apologizing as he stomped out the front door. She knew everything he said was right...home was more important than work, she'd left him holding the bag, the girls were acting out because they missed their mom. And the house was in utter disarray.

Even though she couldn't blame him and she felt lucky to be married to a man who had put up with so much for so long—he was home in ten minutes and apologizing. It was unlike them to argue. But it was bound to happen. They were both tired and sick of trying to juggle twenty-eight hours of work in a twenty-four hour day.

But now on Friday, Jayne thought she might actually see a light at the end of the tunnel at work. It had taken extra time to get things in the department organized the way she thought would be best. After putting in the extra work, it seemed like maybe things were settling down a little bit.

So Jayne glanced at the clock on her computer after cleaning up the last of the lingering emails from the week: it was two-thirty. *That's it, I'm going home. I'm the boss in this department and I've been putting in extra hours for weeks.*

She sent a text to Josh: *I'm leaving work early & getting the girls. I'll make a big pot of chili so u can relax when you get home. I luv u.* She felt better as soon as she sent it.

After turning off her computer, she grabbed her purse and slinked out of the department, feeling like she was playing hooky. Once she hit the parking lot, she was home free. Then her phone rang, and she glanced at it—"Gray Brandt."

"What do you want?" she answered with a smile in her voice.

He chuckled. "Is that any way to speak to your superior?"

"It is when you call my personal cell phone."

"Well, what are you doing leaving at two-thirty in the afternoon?"

Jayne scrunched up her face. "Do you have a GPS tracker in my purse or something?"

"Naw, but those sure are pretty red high heels you're wearing today."

"What?" She stopped at her car and turned around. There, up on the third floor corner office, she could see him waving through the big glass windows. She would have flipped him off for fun but decided that might not be a good idea in case anyone else saw. So she waved. "Is that how you spend your days, staring at the parking lot?"

"I'm very good at staring. They pay me a lot to do it." He moved away from the window. "Actually, I was just stretching my legs and saw you heading to your car. I thought it was a good chance to give my favorite sis-in-law some shit."

"Well," she said, climbing into the car, "I'm your only sister-in-law."

"That's just a technicality. Anyway, so why are you leaving so early? You know what I said about that—"

"Gray, chill out. I've worked late nearly every day for the past few weeks. Even leaving early today, I've probably put in five hours of overtime this week. Not to mention eating lunch at my desk every day."

"Okay, just checking. I've heard good things about how you're doing. I just wanted to make sure you're not sneaking out early on a regular basis."

Jayne sighed. So much for leaving undetected. "Well, I'm not, okay? And if I don't stop working late all the time, Josh is going to kill me."

"My brother? Mister laid-back? Mister easygoing?"

"Yes. Mister my-wife-is-shirking-her-family-responsibilities-for-Nixon-Pharmaceutical."

"Wow, it takes a lot to piss him off."

"Yes, it does. So that tells you how much I've been working lately."

"I guess so." He sounded surprised.

As she pulled her Honda Civic out of the parking lot, she said, "So, you've been hearing good things about me?"

"Yes. Of course you knew I'd be checking up on you."

She rolled her eyes. He expected a lot from his employees, no doubt. She was certain she was no exception. "Of course, Mr. Brandt. And of course you knew you'd hear nothing but positive remarks."

"That's why we hired you." She could hear him typing and knew from experience that he was done talking and onto the next thing. "Well, enjoy the afternoon, slacker."

"I will. Bye." As she hung up, she was still slightly annoyed that he'd questioned her, especially after she'd been working so damn hard. But she had more pressing things to worry about.

****

Josh sat in the school auditorium, waiting for a staff meeting to begin when he remembered he'd heard his phone beep with a text message about an hour earlier as the last period class was letting out. He read the message from Jayne and smiled. It would be nice to enjoy the evening with her at home instead of him scrambling to take care of the kids and dinner on his own. Plus, he wanted a chance to spend some time with her after their argument the night before. He hated fighting with her...he adored her and was angry with himself for losing it like that.

Glancing at the entrance to the auditorium, he saw Jason Scharp, a social studies teacher, walk in. Jason was hard to miss because of the long white cane he was always swinging in front of him. What he lacked for in vision he more than made up for with his great personality and self-deprecating sense of humor. He and Josh were around the same age and often hung out together. Josh saw Jason pause inside the doorway, taking in his surroundings.

"Hey, Scharp," Josh hollered, getting out of his seat and heading toward his friend.

Jason smiled as he approached. "Did you save me a seat so we can talk about girls and video games?"

"You betcha," Josh said with a chuckle. "Wanna hand?"

"Yeah, thanks." Jason held out his hand and Josh put it on his arm, guiding Jason to their seats.

"So where's Shawn?" Josh asked. Shawn was Jason's usual cohort, a math teacher who coached wrestling with Jason.

"He somehow wheedled his way out of the meeting and left early." They sat down.

Josh looked at Jason. "How'd he do that? The meeting is mandatory. I'd like to leave early on a Friday, too."

Jason shrugged, smiling. "You know Shawn. He somehow gets away with doing whatever he wants."

"I need to find out his secrets."

"Let me know when you do." The seats were filling up fast as the meeting was about to start. "Hey, Josh—you live in St. Charles, don't you?"

"Yeah, near the historic district."

"I thought so. Where's a good place to eat down there? I'm meeting my wife at Picasso's Café later tonight to hear one of her musician friends play. But I've got some time to kill before then so I thought I'd take a cab to Main Street and grab a bite."

"Well, there's a lot of good places, but you don't need to take a cab. I'll give you a ride."

"No, that's okay," Jason said, shaking his head.

"No, really, Jason—I live just a few blocks off Main Street."

"I don't know…I mean, normally I would drive myself, but my car's in the shop."

Josh laughed. "If you drove a car, I think it would need to be in the body shop after every quarter mile or so you drove."

Grinning, Jason shrugged and said, "You've got a point there."

"So let me give you a ride, and instead of dropping you off at a restaurant or pub, why don't you come home with me? Jayne's making a big pot of chili and we can have a beer or two before you go to Picasso's."

"Are you sure Jayne won't mind?"

"I'm sure."

Jason smiled. "Does she make good chili?"

"Delicious." Josh chuckled.

"Okay, count me in. If you're sure it's okay."

"It'll be fine. I'll text her right now." *Look forward to having u home early. Put an extra bowl out—I'm bringing Jason home w/me. Luv u.*

****

Jayne had been home with the kids for an hour when she finally felt like she could take a few minutes to do what she needed to do. She'd oohed and aahed over the artwork and crafts they'd made at pre-school. She gave them a snack and got them set up with Play-Doh. Then she made the chili and could smell it filling up the house with its inviting aroma as it simmered on the stove. Sure, the kitchen and the family room were a wreck, but at least she was home. After dinner she'd start cleaning up.

Finally, she went to her bedroom and changed out of her work suit that was a little too tight and a little too uncomfortable on her waist. On went the sweat pants and T-shirt. And on with what she didn't want to do but had to.

Jayne checked on the girls before grabbing the small bag from Walgreens out of her purse—they were content as they created something with the Play-Doh. So she went to the bathroom, closed the door, and locked it. As a mother, she almost never locked the bathroom door because it seemed like someone always needed her for something. She probably hadn't had an uninterrupted bathroom break in at least two years. But this required the lock.

Tearing open the pregnancy test, she just wanted to get it over with so she could put her worries to rest. Sure, her period was late and yes, she was bloated and tired and her breasts hurt. But her period was likely just late from all the stress she'd been under. And being bloated and having sore breasts were also symptoms of PMS. So she knew she wasn't pregnant, but also knew that until she saw the negative test, she'd be worried about it.

As always, she was careful to read the instructions—she always read instructions, whether she was assembling a high chair or putting on a new mascara. She wanted to do it right.

After successfully peeing on the stick, all she had to do was wait two minutes and she could relax. While she sat on the toilet seat, waiting, she heard the girls moving around the house. Tori's feet padded down the hallway into Josh's office.

"Tori, what are you doing?" Jayne yelled, looking at her watch. One minute and ten seconds down.

"Just looking in Daddy's office." It was really a tiny butler's pantry they'd converted into an office, just barely squeezing in his desk.

"Leave his stuff alone."

"Okay, Mommy."

"What's Emma doing?"

"Um…I think she's still playin' with Play-Doh."

One minute and thirty-five seconds. "Okay. Emma?" No response. "Emma?"

"Momma," came Emma's little voice from maybe the kitchen.

"Emma, what are you doing?" One minute and fifty seconds.

"Lotion."

Lotion? What lotion? Two minutes. *Thank God.* Jayne grabbed the stick off the counter and—

What? Why is there a plus sign?

Frantically, she snatched the instructions from the box again. Yep, a plus sign means the test was positive. And yes, the test window showed the results were accurate.

"No," she whispered, feeling like she was suddenly, slowly drowning. She was sure the room must be filling up with water and somewhere in the distance she could hear Emma saying slowly, "Lootioon."

Tears sprang to her eyes as she buried her face in her hands. Drowning, still drowning. She felt like she couldn't breathe. *This can't be happening. This just simply cannot be happening. We haven't even had sex….*

Valentine's Day. Damn it. She hadn't even wanted to, she was so tired. Josh seemed to enjoy himself, but she just couldn't wait to be able to go to sleep.

What was she going to do? She couldn't handle life now… How on earth was she going to manage a third child? With this baby, she'd end up with three kids aged four and under. How would they ever afford daycare? And their house was already cramped. *And I can't go back to sleepless nights and endless feedings….*

"Mommy?" Tori said, trying to open the door. "I want to show you the pretty art I made."

Trying not to hyperventilate, Jayne wiped her eyes and took a deep breath. "I'll be right there, sweetie."

Pull it together, Jayne. You have to pull it together.

Despite the waves rolling around her like she was a buoy tumbling in a thunderstorm, she somehow managed to stand up and open the door. Tori stood there in the hallway, jumping up and down in excitement.

"Mommy, why does your face look funny?"

"No reason, sweetie."

"Your face is all red."

"Never mind. Where's this neat art work?"

"It's in the office."

Beaming with pride, Tori grabbed Jayne's hand and pulled her into the office to show off her masterpiece.

Instead of using paper or canvas, Tori had apparently found Josh's antique desk to be a good medium to use. And wood carving was her new art form.

"Isn't it pretty? There's a flower and a butterfly and my name, 'cause I can write my name. So now Daddy will always have my drawing on his desk."

"Tori…" Jayne said but hardly any sound came out. She saw a screwdriver that Josh had left out, which was obviously what Tori had used to make her work permanent. On Great-Grandpa Brandt's desk, which dated back to Germany in the early 1800s. More waves came tumbling in.

Just then, Jayne heard Emma talking in the kitchen again and she took off down the hall.

"Mommy, do you like my art?" Tori asked, following her.

"No, because you ruined Daddy's desk…." Her voice trailed off when she saw Emma in the kitchen. The toddler had managed to pull a kitchen chair up to the refrigerator and grab out the giant tub of I Can't Believe It's Not Butter!

Emma stood on the chair with the refrigerator door open, her arms and legs covered in the gooey, greasy pale yellow butter substitute. She smiled at Jayne as she rubbed it on her cheeks, in a slow chant of, "Loootiooon."

The waves came crashing down with such force that Jayne dropped to her knees and started crying. Full-out, snot running down her face sobbing. Tori's own cries

144

blended in as she wailed, "You don't like my art!" and ran from the room.

As Jayne cried uncontrollably, Emma—probably frightened at her mother's apparent meltdown—started to whimper, too. Jayne opened her eyes when she heard the sound of the front door and then footsteps approach. She looked up to see Josh and his friend, Jason, standing above her.

"What's wrong?" Josh asked, his voice frantic. He glanced over at Emma. "Oh, Emma…."

"That's not even the half of it," Jayne said in-between sobs. "And Jason's here and the house is a wreck, I'm a wreck, Emma's…well, Emma's covered from head to toe…."

Jason, holding onto Josh's elbow, looked scared to be in the middle of the chaos. Apparently it sounded as crazy as it looked. He chuckled, a nervous sound. "Jayne, everything looks fine to me. I swear."

For some reason, that made her cry harder.

"Really, it's okay," Jason assured her as Tori came running down the hall, whining.

"Daddy, Mommy's being mean. She doesn't like my art I made you!"

Josh looked from Tori to Emma and then to Jayne—who was still crying. "Jayne, sweetheart, calm down. I'm not sure what's going on, but it can't be all that bad."

"It's worse, trust me," she managed to say through her tears.

"Daddy!" Tori yelled.

"Tori, wait," Josh said, clearly not knowing where to start.

"Hey, Tori," Jason said, facing the little girl. "Do you have any swings in your backyard?"

"Yeah."

"Why don't you show me your swing and I'll push you?"

"I 'member you. You're Jason and you can't see."

"Guilty as charged."

"Tori!" Josh reprimanded, shaking his head.

"She's fine," Jason said. "Tori, grab your jacket and then let me hold your hand so you can lead me outside. Then let's see how high I can push you, okay?"

"Okay!" she said with enthusiasm, running off to get her coat.

"I don't know if I can handle the little one," Jason said, motioning to Emma who'd obviously made herself known to him with her whimpering.

Josh sighed. "She's going straight in the tub."

Jason grinned. "Okay then. Should I even ask…?"

"No, please don't."

"Here I am!" Tori yelled, wearing her coat and grabbing Jason's hand. "The backyard is this way." She started pulling him through the kitchen, to the back door.

"Okay," Jason said, his white cane picking up where the three year old's guidance ended.

"My sister has butter *all* over herself."

He chuckled as they walked out the door. "Oh, really?"

Jayne had managed to stop the crying but now her breathing was uneven as she tried to recover. "We just let a blind man babysit our daughter outside."

"He's fine, don't worry about it." Josh rushed to grab a towel out of the linen closet in the hallway and wrapped it around Emma. "You, my dear, are going in the bathtub." Careful to hold her away from his body, he carried her down the hall to the bathroom.

Jayne followed behind them, watching through swollen eyelids as Josh sat Emma in the tub and turned the water on. After he poured in bubble bath and the tub started to fill, he turned to look at Jayne.

"So what could be so bad to cause the hysterical scene I just walked into?"

Jayne started crying again. "I'm pregnant."

It was Josh's turn to look like he'd been hit by a tidal wave. "What?"

"And don't even look at your desk."

Chapter Ten

Tense didn't begin to describe the interaction between Jayne and Josh. It was as if they were both dazed and in shock, lone survivors of some baby-apocalypse suffering from post-traumatic stress disorder.

It had only been twenty-four hours since that little blue plus sign had appeared on the stick. But their lives were forever changed.

They had dropped the kids off at Jayne's mom's house and were back at home, getting themselves ready to go to Karen and Rick's housewarming party. This should have been a fun night—it wasn't often they got to have a night with their friends, away from the kids.

Instead, as Jayne tried on the third outfit she hoped didn't make her look as fat as she felt, she wanted to do nothing more than crawl into bed and cry. Like she had last night. She looked in the mirror and sighed. No, she didn't like the way she looked, but it would do. These days she wasn't going for looking good, she was settling for not being totally disgusted with the image in the mirror.

Of course with another pregnancy, she would just gain more weight all over again.

In the reflection of the mirror, she saw Josh behind her, pulling on a casual blazer over his T-shirt. She wasn't sure she'd ever seen that exact expression on his face before. It wasn't anger, or sadness. It looked more like fear, really. Terror.

He'd looked like that ever since he'd heard the news.

Under normal circumstances, they would be joking and laughing while they got ready for a night out. But tonight there was a sense they were both hanging on by a thread. Any quick movement or loud sound might make the thread snap.

Jayne cleared her throat.

Josh looked her way. "Huh?"

"What?"

"I thought you said something."

She grabbed her favorite scarf and wrapped it around her neck. "No, I didn't say anything."

"Oh. Okay." Josh stepped away from the mirror.

"Um…" Jayne swallowed. "We can't let anyone know tonight that I'm…pregnant." It didn't matter how many times she said it out loud or thought about it, it seemed like an impossible reality.

Josh seemed surprised. "Really? Why?"

"Well, for one, I honestly don't think I'm ready to talk about it yet. I'm still in shock."

He chuckled, though it came out more like a painful moan. "No shit."

"And then there's Karen."

"What do you mean?"

Jayne grabbed the first earrings she found in her jewelry box and slipped them on. Her voice was quiet. "How on earth am I going to tell one of my best friends that I accidentally got pregnant, when I certainly never wanted to…while she's spent the last couple of years trying to have a baby?"

Josh sat on the bed, putting his head in his hands. "Oh Jesus…I didn't even think about that."

And Jayne hadn't at first, either. It was enough just thinking about the implications for their family. But after the first hour or so, it dawned on her and then the overpowering guilt was almost as bad as the shock of the situation.

Of course none of this had been intentional, but the fact of the matter was Jayne had a fetus growing inside of her. That was something she'd never intended to do again in her lifetime. That was Karen's dream now.

She felt like she'd stolen her friend's dream.

Like Karen had been training and practicing for years to

be in the Olympics. Maybe as a downhill skier. And, at the last minute, Jayne was standing by her at the top of the slope at the Olympic trials and accidentally slipped. Jayne's fall down the slopes beat Karen's time. All of Karen's practice and efforts meant nothing. Jayne was going to the Olympics instead.

And she'd already gone to the Olympics twice and didn't even want to be there again.

"So…yeah," she said, turning to face Josh. "We have to keep this between us. Until I figure out how to tell her. I don't want to break her heart."

Josh stood up, grabbed Jayne in his arms, and held her close. She loved that he knew her so well. Knew when she needed him.

Jayne finally pulled away. "We better get going."

"Okay," he said, his arm still around her, still holding on.

Jayne took one last look in the mirror. The couple staring back didn't look at all like them. They were always both so full of smiles; they were everyone's favorite happy couple. Tonight they looked like a couple of zombies from *The Walking Dead.* Or maybe that was too generous a description.

"I don't know how I'm going to get through tonight," Josh said, grabbing her hand as they headed out of the bedroom.

"I'm sure there will be plenty of alcohol there."

He nodded his head. "That just might help."

****

Karen was excited to be having her friends over to see her new home. She and Rick had worked hard to get everything ready for their housewarming party. New blinds were installed, curtains hung, great examples of Rick's artwork filled the walls, knickknacks and books and candles brought out their personalities in the décor. Everything looked great.

If it had been a little warmer, she'd have suggested Rick grill something outside. But it was still only late March…at

149

night it was a little too cold for her to ask Rick to stand on the patio while they all were toasty and warm inside. So she decided to make chicken Acapulco, one of her favorite meals. Who wouldn't like chicken, sour cream, and gooey melted Monterey Jack cheese served over rice? She was starting the meal with a salad and serving asparagus as a side dish. Claudia had offered to bring dessert, so the meal was complete. And Karen had whipped up some homemade guacamole and salsa to serve with chips when everyone arrived.

This was the first time the girls would be meeting Gabe and Anthony, her neighbors. But she just knew they would all get along and it would be a great night. She really needed this. She'd been so cranky lately and just overwhelmed by the whole IVF process that she needed a night with her friends. Next week the actual IVF procedure would be performed.

But tonight was all about fun.

Claudia was the first to arrive, looking beautiful yet casual in her featherweight chocolate colored turtleneck, long cream-colored cardigan and skinny jeans tucked into deep brown riding boots. Karen wished she had thought to have Rick invite a friend to set her up with.

"Wow, Karen, your place looks great!" Claudia gushed as she stepped through the front door. "I love this big, open great room and the warm colors you've chosen." She petted Kramer, who begged for attention with his wagging tail and sad puppy dog eyes.

"Thanks." A part of Karen was relieved…she really valued Claudia's opinion when it came to decorating. They had completely different styles—Karen was more earthy and eclectic while Claudia's place was more Cape Cod chic. But they both shared a good eye for interior design. "Here, hand me that dessert so I can take it in the kitchen. What is this?"

Claudia followed Karen into the kitchen. "I made two different cheesecakes—a raspberry drizzle cheesecake with a chocolate crumb crust and a pumpkin cheesecake with graham cracker crust."

"Screw dinner," Karen said, winking. "Let's just eat these now."

After Karen finished giving Claudia the grand tour, Jayne and Josh arrived. By then, Karen was in the kitchen, cooking the asparagus. So Rick started showing them through the house when the doorbell rang again; it was Gabe and Anthony.

Soon enough, they were all sitting down at the dining room table, which was set with new woven bamboo placemats, thick dark brown square chargers, and her assorted Fiestaware plates she'd had for years and still loved. They'd all dished up from the serving table and were starting to dig in.

Karen looked around the table, so thrilled to have most of her favorite people in the world right there. The table looked great, the food smelled delicious, and her heart was soaring.

"Is something wrong?" Rick asked, staring at her with a look of concern on his face.

"No, not at all." She smiled, hoping to God that Crying Karen didn't all of a sudden make an entrance. "Just so happy to have all of you here."

"I'm just happy to have a night away from the kids," Gabe quipped, taking a drink of wine.

"Amen to that," Josh said, grinning. Karen thought he looked a little *off*. He normally exuded a laid-back aura and calm that made her think of a surfer. But tonight he seemed to have a bit of an edge to him.

The two men clinked glasses and Karen noticed Josh took a pretty big gulp of his drink. She glanced over at Jayne, who was busy shoveling food in her mouth. A lot. *Must have been a tough week with the kids.*

"So, Claudia," Anthony said, turning to her in the seat beside him. "Is it true you're single?"

Claudia blushed. "Yes, it's true. Divorced."

"Honey, you're absolutely gorgeous. What kind of a moron would lose you?"

"A giant fucking asshole moron," Karen said with no hesitation whatsoever.

"Karen," Claudia said with a sigh, shaking her head. "Thanks, Anthony."

He chuckled. "God, I love you, Karen. You have absolutely no filter."

Gabe nudged Anthony. "You love that about her because you're exactly the same way. It's like the two of you have some disorder."

"So *that's* what's wrong with you," Rick said, looking at Karen with raised eyebrows. "I was never quite sure." Karen thought he looked even more handsome than usual in a deep purple sweater with a grey T-shirt peeking out underneath. She flipped him off but with a smile on her face.

"It's not a disorder, my dear," Anthony said. "It's an inability to bullshit."

"Exactly." Karen nodded her head in agreement.

"Well, whatever it is," Jayne said, taking a break from her all-you-can-eat buffet, "it's fun."

"Unless it's directed at you," Claudia said, shooting a look at Karen.

Karen sat back in her seat. "I didn't direct anything at you, just your selfish prick ex-husband."

"Who is also the father of my child."

"Yeah, Karen, you should lay off of Sam," Jayne said quietly.

"Whatever," Karen mumbled, wondering what the big deal was. After all, he deserved every rude remark she ever made about him.

"So enough about this Sam character," Anthony continued. "Why are you not with someone?"

"I don't know," Claudia said with a shrug. "It's just kind of hard getting back out in the dating world. I was with Sam since college."

"Well, we know the perfect guy for you, don't we, Gabe?"

"Who?" Gabe asked, his long fingers pushing up his

glasses. Their eyes met in a silent but mutual understanding. "Oh, yes! We do."

"And he's straight?" Rick asked.

"No, I want to set her up with a gay man, Rick," Anthony said, shaking his blond-tipped head. "Of course he's straight. Straight and *handsome*." Karen thought he made handsome sound like the most delectable, exquisite delicacy on the planet.

"Well, he can't be better looking than either of us, can he?" Josh asked with a laugh, pointing to himself and Rick. Karen noticed his wine glass was already empty. She got up to refill it.

"I'm not rating you," Anthony said, crossing his arms. "Your partners are at the table with you and so is mine."

"No, Anthony, go ahead and rate them," Gabe said with a sigh, leaning back in his seat and crossing his long arms.

Anthony rolled his eyes. "Gabe, just stop. Focus on Claudia."

"You would love this guy," Gabe said, giving Claudia a broad smile. "He works for Edward Jones—"

"Does something with money and makes a lot of it," Anthony piped in.

Karen finished refilling Josh's glass and he whispered, "Thank you." There seemed to be a desperation in his voice. He quickly took a drink and Karen patted him on the shoulder.

"Can I just say this is delicious?" Gabe said, looking at Karen as she sat back down. "I want the recipe."

"Gabe," Anthony whined. "You're interrupting our matchmaking."

"Sorry," he said, looking sheepish. "Did you mention he's built like a Greek Adonis?"

Anthony took another drink. "I was getting there. So, yes, he's built like a Greek god or something. His brother is a good friend of ours. They come from a great family, really good, fun people."

"So why isn't he snatched up?" Karen asked.

"He was," Gabe said.

"But he caught his wife cheating on him." Anthony sat back in his seat, looking satisfied with himself.

"Gee, don't know anyone that's happened to," Karen said with a smirk. "That's me, using my filter."

Jayne giggled.

"So he's been divorced about a year now," Anthony continued. "We *have* to get you two together. Oh my God, wouldn't they make gorgeous babies together, Gabe?"

"They would. No doubt about it."

Claudia smiled graciously. "He sounds amazing. I'll keep him in mind."

"This one will not last long out there on the open market," Anthony cautioned. "We ought to set it up very soon."

"It can't go any worse than your last date," Jayne said, grinning at Claudia.

"No kidding," Claudia said with a chuckle.

The banter and the wine flowed all through dinner, with plenty of laughs and empty plates when they were done. They all helped clear the table and then found seats in the family room. Rick got a small fire going along with some great folksy music playing in the background. Some of their favorites—Ryan Adams, Ray LaMontagne, The Civil Wars, Landon Pigg, Glen Phillips, The Avett Brothers, among others. Kramer cozied up to the fireplace and seemed pleased to be amidst all the excitement. It was a great blend of people and they were all really enjoying themselves. The night was a success.

After an hour or so, Karen stood up. "Who wants dessert?" Hands raised in the air. "Okay, Claudia has made two fabulous looking cheesecakes, so I think I'll just cut them and bring them in here with some plates. Then everyone can just grab a slice or two of whatever they want."

"I'll help you," Claudia said.

Jayne chimed in. "Me too."

The three women went in the kitchen and started

pulling out plates, forks and napkins while Karen cut the thick cakes into small pieces. She couldn't wait to try them. She was almost done when Claudia said, "I have to use the restroom. I'll be right back."

"Okay," Karen said, smiling at her as she walked out of the room.

"I'll carry the plates and napkins in," Jayne said, leaving the kitchen.

Karen had just finished cutting the pumpkin cheesecake when she heard her phone beep from the counter with a new text message. She glanced at it, and it showed it was from Sam Knight. *Why is Sam texting me?* She read the message: *When are you getting home? Izzy's asleep & I'm in bed, waiting for u. xoxo*

She was confused and then realized she was looking at Claudia's phone, not her own. Which only made her heart leap in her throat and her stomach suddenly feel like someone had punched her in the gut. Just then, Claudia came back in the room.

"Do you want me to take one of those in the family room?" she asked, pointing to the cakes. Then her brows wrinkled, apparently noticing a look of shock or maybe utter disdain on Karen's face.

"What the fuck, Claudia?" Karen asked, feeling like she was starting to lose control.

"What's wrong?" Claudia asked, looking completely confused.

Karen held up the phone. "You're sleeping with that asshole Sam!"

The color immediately drained from Claudia's face. "Karen, let me explain—"

"There's nothing to explain. If that's what you want, go for it." Her words dripped with accusation and disappointment.

Jayne walked in the room. "What's going on?"

"I didn't want it to happen," Claudia said, her eyes starting to well with tears. "It just...it just happened."

"Oh," Jayne said quietly. "Karen found out."

Karen turned to look at Jayne, and saw fear in her eyes. "Do you mean you knew about this bullshit? You knew and I didn't?"

"Well, I…" Jayne whispered.

Claudia interrupted. "Maybe if you weren't so judgmental and unforgiving, I would have told you."

"Unforgiving?" Karen's voice was almost at a yell now, and the men had migrated to the kitchen. "Is that what you call it? I call it being loyal, Claud. Having your back. I thought that was a good thing."

"Hey, hey," Rick said, touching Karen's arm. "Let's calm down, okay?"

Claudia was dabbing her eyes and for once in her life, Karen shut her mouth. It was probably one of the most difficult things she'd ever done. She didn't know if she wanted to punch Claudia for being so stupid or hug her and talk some sense into her.

But she just grabbed a cheesecake and marched into the family room. Anthony was suddenly right beside her.

"What was that about it?" he asked in a conspiratorial whisper.

"That asshole Sam. Maybe he's not her ex in every way."

"Oh…" he said, nodding his head in understanding.

The others joined them and everyone took a piece of cake in silence. The tension was undeniable.

"I've got a funny story," Josh said, his crooked grin attempting to break the somber mood. "Yesterday I come home from work with a friend of mine—"

"Josh, no," Jayne said quietly.

"Well, it was funny, in hindsight," he said, looking at Jayne. Karen could tell he was drunk. She wasn't sure if she'd ever seen him drunk before.

"Another time." The look Jayne gave Josh made him shut up.

"Oh, I almost forgot," Gabe said, standing up. "I brought a great dessert wine that Anthony and I discovered when we were vacationing in Napa a few years ago.

Moscato Bianco from Mondavi Winery. Let me go get it."
He headed off to the kitchen.

"It's delish if you like sweet wines," Anthony said.

"That should be perfect for you, Jayne," Claudia said.
Karen couldn't even look at her.

"No, she can't drink anymore," Josh said, then a look
of alarm came over his face like he'd said something he
shouldn't have. Karen saw Jayne nudge him.

"Because…" Jayne smiled at all of them with a terrified
look in her eyes. "I'm…uh…the designated driver tonight."

Why is she acting so weird? What is going on?

As it began to dawn on Karen why Jayne really couldn't
drink, she felt like she was going to throw up. She felt like
she was in a dream as she heard herself quietly ask, "You're
pregnant, aren't you?"

Claudia gasped, as Karen looked straight into Jayne's
big doe eyes brimming with tears. Jayne nodded her head.

"Congratulations!" Anthony said, clapping. Claudia
quickly covered his hands. "No?"

"Well, this is just the best night ever!" Karen exploded,
standing up. "I just found out that my two best friends in
the world have been keeping secrets from me. You—" she
said, full of venom, pointing at Claudia—"decided it was
okay to start sleeping with the one man in the world that
betrayed you so badly that it's taken years for you to
recover. And who was there for you when you were falling
apart and on your own with a newborn? I was. I was there
for you. But not only do you decide to go back to that self-
serving prick, you decide to purposely deceive me about it."

Claudia tried to reason with her. "I just don't know
where it's all going and I didn't want you to be angry…."

"Oh, angry doesn't begin to describe how I'm feeling
right now." She was trembling all over, and felt completely,
utterly out of control.

"Karen," Rick said in a quiet voice, touching her arm.
"Let's stop before you say things you might regret."

She jerked away. "No, Rick, there are things that need
to be said." Karen turned to Jayne. "And you, Jayne…I

know you didn't do this on purpose. I know you don't want any more kids. But that's what makes this hurt even worse. I've spent almost two years now trying to do something that happened to you on accident." Now Crying Karen decided to join the party. "Not only is it so frustrating, it breaks my heart that you didn't even tell me."

Jayne had tears in her eyes, too. "Karen, I'm so sorry...I just found out yesterday and I wasn't sure how to tell you...."

"So you just didn't! Neither of you think enough of me to share the truth. Because I'm apparently such a bitch, huh? Well, you won't have to worry about me anymore, okay? I'm done with both of you!" With that, Crying Karen ran down the hall and threw herself on the bed, sobbing into her pillow. Kramer jumped on the bed next to her, licking her face. She threw her arms around the furry bundle of acceptance and felt lucky someone still loved her.

Because she was pretty sure she'd just lost the two best friends she'd ever had.

She heard her guests leaving, Rick trying to clean up the social disaster she'd just created. It sounded like the girls left right away, and when Anthony and Gabe were heading out, she heard Rick say, "Guys, I'm sorry about how things went down tonight. But we really appreciate you coming over."

"What—are you kidding me?" Anthony said, laughing. "This was the best dinner party we've been to in ages!"

"Legendary," she heard Gabe say. "And be sure and tell Karen we had a great time and I want that recipe, okay?"

"I'll let her know."

A minute later she heard Rick coming down the hallway, his pace slow, weary. When he reached their bedroom, he leaned against the doorframe and let out a big sigh. The room was dark, but she didn't need the lights on to tell that he was disappointed in her.

Her voice quiet, she said, "I screwed up, didn't I?"

Rick approached the bed and sat down next to her. He placed a gentle kiss on her neck. "What am I going to do with you, Karen?"

She closed her eyes, feeling a loss deeper than she could have imagined. "I don't know, Rick. I just don't know."

****

Who knew that IVF would feel like going through a medical McDonald's drive-thru? As Karen lay on the table in the sterile procedure room, she felt like the bed was a car and she had just ordered one human—to go, please. Would you like twins with that? *No, thanks, hold the multiples.*

She understood the procedures they used were to prevent her from winding up on *Dateline* explaining how she ended up with a baby of Mexican heritage when they accidentally put Mrs. Rodriguez's embryo inside of her. But it was still a bit startling.

There was a cutout in the wall with a small sliding glass door. A faceless person—the embryologist—called out, "Name and date of birth?"

Karen rattled it off, feeling like she was having an out-of-body experience. Yes, she was wearing the standard-issue scratchy cotton ass-bearing gown, and yes, it was her feet in the stirrups. But it just all seemed so surreal, she felt so disconnected.

"Karen Gordon, one embryo," he confirmed. Then the embryo—her possible unborn child—was passed through the window to the nurse standing beside her. *Don't forget I need napkins and ketchup with that.*

The procedure itself went quickly. There wasn't much to it. After all the shots and pills and gearing up, it felt anticlimactic. Shouldn't there be balloons or music or high-fives?

Instead, Rick took her home and she wondered if she dared to be hopeful. She wanted to be, but after last month's round of IUI and the hopefulness she had felt...she didn't know if she could handle setting herself up for that kind of disappointment again.

And she wondered if she should have had them put in two embryos, as the doctor suggested. It would increase her chances of getting pregnant. But then the chance of twins would increase exponentially and she was certain she couldn't handle that. She considered the thought of selling one on Craigslist if that happened, but how do you choose which one? Besides, there were probably laws against that.

So she was in a weird sort of twilight zone of hoping but not hoping too much. Dreaming but just a little bit. This was it. If this didn't work, she would never have a biological child of her own.

It probably didn't help matters that her heart was heavy with the horrible state of her friendships with Claudia and Jayne. A part of her was still so angry with both of them, and another part just wanted to call them and apologize and hope to God they accepted.

They'd never really fought before. This was new territory. And they'd been friends for fifteen years…they were like an extension of her. She didn't know how to live her life without them.

But she was also stubborn and prideful and didn't know how to make things right without admitting she was wrong. Because she wasn't sure she was entirely wrong. They had betrayed her; they deceived her. Shouldn't they be the ones to apologize? If they apologized, then she would, too.

Great. She'd reduced herself to thinking like a five-year-old. But that's all she could muster at the moment.

****

Rick and Kramer stood at the front door, waving goodbye as Karen drove her car down the driveway. *Thank God she needed a pedicure.* He felt a pang of guilt for being glad she had left the house. It wasn't that he didn't want to be with her…it's just that he didn't know what to do with or how to handle this new version of his wife. The only thing giving him hope was that this was all temporary. Because loving and living with his wife right now was not easy.

Not that being married to Karen was ever easy.

It took a certain amount of intuition and patience to handle a damaged heart like hers. But Rick knew how to do it…it had taken eight years for him to perfect it, but he had. And the rewards were more than ample—she was an amazing woman.

But under the stress of trying to get pregnant and the drugs she was taking to make it happen, well, it was like some aliens had come down to earth and stolen his wife. In her place, they'd left an exact replica, but one with a brain that was emotional, irrational, and cried at the drop of a hat. This creature was nothing like the woman he had married.

"C'mon, Kramer," Rick said to the dog as he closed the door. "Let's go chill."

Rick grabbed a beer out of the fridge. It was a new pomegranate-flavored beer they'd started making at the brewery where he worked. The beer was tasty, but as the company's graphic artist, he was most proud of the label he'd created. He thought it was classic, yet *popped*, encouraging you to try the succulent pomegranate-flavored concoction.

He headed upstairs to his studio with Kramer eagerly running right behind. Not sure if he felt like painting or not, Rick grabbed his old acoustic guitar out of the corner. He smiled as he cherished the familiar feeling of the wood in his hands and the old strings underneath his fingers. It had been twenty-five years since he'd learned to play guitar. It was during his I-want-to-be-a-rock-star phase. He chuckled at the memory. But he figured most teenage boys went through that phase, if for nothing else other than the fact that girls seemed to be infatuated with any guy that could sing and play guitar.

And it never failed to impress a woman when he played it; Karen used to love it when he'd pull out the guitar and sing to her. That felt like eons ago.

As he strummed the guitar, losing himself in its simple chords, Kramer cocked his head to the side—his ears alert, his eyes open wide.

"What is that, buddy?" Rick grinned at the dark brown dog, who managed to always look a little goofy. "What should we play today? I'm thinking some blues are in order, don't you think?"

As he started playing *The Sky is Crying*, he decided to change the lyrics to fit his current dilemma. "The sky is cryin'....'cause my baby's on IVF meds...the sky is cryin'...and I don't know what it is I did...I been lookin' for my baby, even though she's right in front of me." He ended with a flourish and Kramer's tail started to wag. "Thank you, thank you very much," he said in his best Elvis impersonation.

With a sigh, he put his guitar back in the corner. He grabbed a paintbrush...his form of therapy. He'd been working on this painting for a while, but couldn't seem to get it quite right. As his brushes slowly fleshed out the canvas, his mind was swirling with thoughts of Karen.

He knew she was hurting, which killed him because he had no idea what to do about it. Normally he would just try to be supportive while she sorted out whatever her troubles were with her friends. But after the disastrous dinner party and the huge blowup with Claudia and Jayne, he knew she wasn't able to talk to them now. Besides, their estrangement was likely what was troubling her most.

He'd almost called Claudia and Jayne a couple of times, asking them to please understand the pressure Karen was under and the effects of the hormones she was on. To beg them to call her, to tell her it was okay. Maybe this new Karen would be okay with that. But the Karen he knew so well, the one he fell in love with, would have been angry and mortified if he got involved with her personal business.

As he switched from a paintbrush with a dark gray hue to a new brush he'd dabbed in a soft yellow, it dawned on him it had been a long time since he'd seen Karen truly happy. This whole fertility debacle had completely changed their lives. It consumed her and had left her more fragile than he ever imagined she could be. As thrilled as he was at the thought of becoming a father, a part of him wished they'd never gone down this path.

He missed his wife and the marriage they'd shared. And he had no idea what was going to happen if IVF didn't work. He was worried it would shatter Karen.

They would know soon enough, though. They'd either be prospective parents or he'd be left trying to somehow, someway comfort the woman he barely recognized anymore. But he loved her, so he'd figure it out. He'd have to figure it out.

With a heavy sigh, he stepped back from the painting and felt like it was finally done. It showed a deep, dark spiraled tunnel and at the very end, there was a light. A soft, warm welcoming light, drawing you in.

"What do you think, Kramer?" He rubbed the dog's silky ears, took a drink from his beer, and headed downstairs.

When Rick lay on the bed, Kramer jumped up and curled in next to him. Rick closed his eyes and decided until Karen returned from her pedicure, he was going to do his best not to have another thought.

****

Claudia didn't know what she was doing with Sam. It was becoming so easy to fall back into rhythm with him…they had been together for so long, they just…fit. She was trying not to let Isabella notice the change, since she didn't know where this was all headed. But she could tell their little girl was enjoying the joint mommy-and-daddy time.

It was time to address the situation with Sam. Claudia had to know what exactly they were doing and where this was all leading, if anywhere.

The three of them were at Isabella's favorite playground in Forest Park. Forest Park was a huge park in the city of St. Louis and one of the largest urban parks in the nation— five hundred acres larger than Central Park in New York. It boasted the world-class St. Louis Zoo, Art Museum, History Museum, Science Center, and the Muny Opera. Then of course there were ball fields, trails, lakes, tennis courts, and a golf course—among other things. Sam and Claudia sat on a circular bench enjoying the sunny, warm early April day while they watched Isabella play.

"So…" Claudia said, not knowing how to begin this

conversation. The whole situation was bizarre.

Sam smiled at her. "So what?"

Claudia looked across the playground and waved at Isabella, who was busy climbing on a large metal play set. "What are we doing?"

"Well, I thought after Isabella plays for a while we were going to grab lunch—"

"No, Sam, I mean this," she said, motioning to him and back to herself. "Is this just messing around in bed or is this something more?"

"Well, I told you I had regrets." He put his arm around her and sighed. "Maybe when I said I didn't want to be married and I didn't want to be monogamous…maybe I was all wrong."

"You're saying maybe. That sounds pretty vague." She turned and looked into his eyes. His eyes were starting to show the signs of wrinkles around the edges. He was no longer the young man she had married. She saw sadness in them, too.

"I was wrong, Claudia. I never stopped loving you, and I realize now that I ruined everything."

"Yeah, you did." It was so easy for her heart to go back to that raw, dark, painful place that she'd plunged into when he left. "You took a great marriage, a great love…and you walked away."

"I was so selfish, so stupid, Claud," he said, rubbing her arm. "Is there any chance at all that we can have a second shot at this?"

She sighed, not sure if she wanted to hear what he was saying or not. So much of the past few years had been spent wishing they were still together. But now that he was saying he wanted another chance…was that still what she really wanted? Was it too late for them? Had his actions destroyed any chance for her to truly feel secure with him ever again?

Claudia stood up, crossing her arms. Her voice soft, she said, "I don't know."

Sam stood up next to her and touched her cheek. She

turned to look at him. "Just think about it, okay? I don't need an answer right away. Just know that I'll be doing what I can to win you back, to make things right."

"But I don't know if that's possible." She felt tears catching in her throat.

"Is it okay with you if I try?"

"Is that what you've been doing?"

"Yeah," he said, a small chuckle erupting. "I think I thought things were going so well, maybe I could just move back in and it would be like it used to."

And a part of Claudia really wanted that. They had been so good together. That is, until he decided he wanted out. She tucked her hair behind her ears. "What made you finally think leaving was a mistake?"

"Because for the past few years, I've been living the life I said I wanted. No attachments. No monogamy."

"And?"

"And I realized the happiest time in my life was when I was married to you."

She leaned into him and he put his arm around her. As Isabella ran toward them, Claudia didn't know if his words were what she needed to hear or not.

Or if they were even true.

Chapter Eleven

Ever since Jayne found out she was pregnant, she felt like she'd been in a fog. She'd never planned on three kids, and her stress level was at the breaking point with the two kids they already had. She simply didn't know how she was going to do this.

She wasn't entirely upset at the thought of a baby. She loved babies, loved her children more than she ever imagined she could. So while she was terrified at the reality of raising three kids in one small house with two working parents living paycheck to paycheck...there was a part of her that was anxious to meet this new human growing in her belly.

Would it be a boy this time? Would it look like either Emma or Tori? Or would it have its own unique look? She loved being pregnant and was looking forward to feeling the first fluttery movements inside her uterus.

But realistically, she didn't know how they were going to actually make this all work. Throw in a nice dose of morning sickness here and there, add that to the stress that existed before the new baby was a factor—and Jayne was feeling more overwhelmed than she ever had before in her life. Josh was being so sweet and trying to make things easier for her around the house. He was cleaning more, getting both of the girls ready in the morning, and had apparently learned to tell other people "no" instead of always being the go-to helper for his friends.

He'd put the girls to bed and joined Jayne on the couch, where she lay, filled with utter exhaustion after working all day and making dinner. Her eyes were closed, and she was surprised she was still awake.

"Hey you," he whispered, placing a gentle kiss on her

cheek. "How are you feeling?"

Jayne sighed. "Tired. But not bad." She opened her eyes to see Josh's normally relaxed face showing extra signs of stress. It was obvious he was as worried about the situation as she was. "Thanks for putting the girls to bed."

"You're welcome." He smiled, but Jayne was able to see his smile today showed a strain that didn't used to be there.

She closed her eyes again. "So, Josh...what are we going to do?"

"About what?"

"You know, the baby situation."

"Well...what specifically? I mean, we're having the baby—"

"But where are we going to put it? Are we going to have the girls share a room? I mean, that's not a big deal, except that this is an old house and the bedrooms are so small...."

"I know. I think the only way it would work is with bunk beds."

"And we really need a bigger table to eat at. Ours only fits four."

"Where the heck would we put a bigger table?" Josh took his turn to sigh.

Jayne sat up, leaning into his warm, strong frame. He always smelled so good. "I checked out some bigger homes online."

"Me too."

She looked down at her feet, realizing she was in desperate need of a pedicure. "I don't think we can afford anything bigger, though."

"I'm sorry, Jayne, I don't think we can, either." She looked up at him and saw shame and frustration all over his face. She knew there were times that he felt bad that a teacher's salary wasn't always enough to support them. She wished she made more money so that he didn't have to feel bad about working at a job he loved that was so worthwhile.

Josh put his arm around her. "I've been tossing around

some ideas that might help. I need to check into something. Would you mind if I run over to Gray's for a bit? He's good with money...I want to talk to him about it."

"That's fine," she said, feeling ashamed Gray would know how much they were struggling. He was Mr. Moneybags, and they were his pauper relatives. Well, she'd had a taste of his lifestyle and all it meant was fancy stuff with no real happiness. Maybe they'd be stacked up with babies to the ceiling in their precious little house, but at least they had true love. A family that mattered more than anything in the world. Even Gray couldn't put a price tag on that. "I'm going to fall asleep here on the couch within five minutes of turning on the DVR, anyway."

He squeezed her and then leaned over to give her a kiss. "I won't be out late."

"Okay."

Josh stood up, grabbed his jacket off the hook by the door and pulled his keys out of his pocket. He stopped, and his vivid green eyes seemed dull, sad. "Jayne?"

"Yeah?"

"I'm sorry about...all of this." He ran his fingers through the dark, messy mop of his hair.

"This isn't your fault—"

"No, I mean...I'm sorry I don't make more money—"

"Josh, stop. You are more than I ever dreamed of. Money comes and goes. You are my forever."

The crooked grin she loved on his face made a timid appearance, and in his eyes she saw the slightest hint of a sparkle. "I'll take care of this, Jayne." He waved good-bye as he walked out the door.

Jayne sat on the couch for a minute, with their happy mutt Atticus curled up by her feet. She didn't even bother to turn on the TV; she just headed down the hall and climbed into bed.

****

"So what do you need to talk about?" Gray asked Josh, pouring himself a Scotch on the rocks.

"Money," Josh said, not believing what he was about to

do.

Gray chuckled. "And you're sure you don't want a drink?"

Josh grinned. "Maybe just a beer. I have to teach our nation's youth in the morning."

"Come pick one out," Gray said, motioning toward the fridge. He opened it, and Josh saw a few different kinds of bottled beer in the fridge—Foster's, Newcastle Ale, Corona, Bud Light—but virtually no food. The built-in Sub Zero fridge looked even emptier inside because it was so massive. Josh grabbed a Newcastle and closed the door.

The brothers headed into the two-story-tall great room that served as the main living area in Gray's house. Josh couldn't decide if it was comical or merely ironic that his brother lived alone in a posh 6,000 square foot home that was basically a mansion, while Josh and Jayne were trying to figure out how to fit their soon-to-be family of five into twelve-hundred square feet. Maybe he should have gone the corporate route like his brother.

This house looked a lot less like a bachelor pad than Gray's previous home in a high-rise condo in Clayton. He'd traded in the sterile, colorless abode for this professionally decorated estate in the posh suburb of Ladue. Ladue's 63124 zip code was the St. Louis equivalent to LA.'s 90210. Josh never understood why Gray needed such an enormous place for just himself. Sure, he threw parties (most of which were business affairs Josh was never invited to) and the home no doubt suited Gray's status in the business world. It just seemed crazy for one thirty-six-year-old guy to live by himself in a place with six bathrooms.

Not that Josh and his family didn't enjoy the perks of Gray's home. They all spent a great deal of time in the zero-depth entry in-ground pool in the backyard, complete with a slide, diving board, underwater lighting and full music system that played from the Rockustic speakers that looked like rocks and surrounded the pool. And it was nice to be able to watch the sixty-inch flat-screen TV mounted outside while wading in the water with a drink in your hand, prepared at the bar just a few steps away.

The girls loved it at Uncle Gray's. He let them run around, down the endless massive hallways and grand foyer that was the closest thing to a ballroom that Josh had ever seen inside a home. The impressive spiral staircase was perfect when Tori wanted to make a grand entrance or put on a show. And Uncle Gray had spared no expense when he had the decorator design a room for his two little nieces. It looked like a princess palace—resplendent in pink, ruffles and a mural of their kingdom painted on the wall. Two matching canopy beds had miniature versions next to them for their baby dolls. Nah, Uncle Gray didn't spoil them at all.

Despite all that, Josh's favorite spot was probably the home theater room. He felt with fair certainty his entire home would fit in Gray's theater. Complete with its own concession stand with marble countertops, a popcorn maker, soda fountain and beer on tap—the massive screen was revealed when the heavy red and gold curtain opened on the small stage. The buttery soft high-back leather stadium seats felt like you were sitting on a cloud while you watched a movie with better surround sound than Josh had ever experienced at a commercial theatre.

Come to think of it, maybe Josh could move his entire family into Gray's home without being noticed…Gray probably only used about a fourth of the house, anyway.

"So, big brother," Gray said, making himself comfortable on his overstuffed couch and propping his feet on the quilted leather ottoman. "Money, huh? What's up?"

Josh sunk into what he imagined could only be a down-filled sofa as Gray picked up a touch-screen remote control and starting playing with it. Josh was filled with major man-toy envy as he watched Gray close the blinds in the room, turn up the lights and start playing the satellite—all from the one touchscreen remote. He swallowed his pride and knew he had to get this thing started. "Well…don't say anything to Mom or Dad yet, but…Jayne's pregnant again."

A smile curled on Gray's lips as he took a sip of his

drink. "I thought you guys were done."

"We were." Josh took a swig of his beer, wishing he had gone with something stronger.

"Well, aren't you a credit to mankind? Good to know that if I ever wanted kids—which I won't—that the Brandt boys have strong swimmers."

"Apparently."

"So then you'll have, what? Three kids aged four and under?"

It somehow sounded worse when Gray said it out loud. "That's how the math came out for me."

Gray laughed, and as usual, he had a way of making Josh want to smack the dimples right off of his face. "Josh, you are so screwed. You might as well just forget about having a life. Well, not that you have much of one anyway."

"Yeah, I know." Josh shook his head while Gray seemed to revel in his brother's misery.

"So are you gonna buy a bigger place or what? You all barely fit in that little cottage as it is."

"It's not a little cottage," Josh said, beginning to think he wouldn't be able to do this after all. He knew Gray was pompous and condescending. He had just forgotten how good he was at it. "It's a meticulously restored turn-of-the-century home."

"That's the size of my pool house out back." Their eyes locked as Gray's smile turned to a smirk.

Josh didn't look away. "Well, maybe I don't feel the need to compensate for anything."

Gray shrugged. "The only guys that say things like that are the ones that can't afford the finer things. No need for me to compensate for anything...just ask Jayne."

Josh exploded out of his seat and prayed to God he could keep his fists out of his brother's face. "You're a fucking asshole, Gray!" Josh sat down his beer and grabbed his keys off the ottoman. "I'm out of here. I came to you for help, and you bring up this bullshit about my wife that we agreed years ago was off limits. Just remember that all of your money still couldn't win her over. She wanted *me*.

Not my status or sports car or ridiculous fucking house. She chose just *me*. And I think that drives you nuts."

Josh took off down the hall, hoping he could find his way to the front door. He heard Gray's footsteps pick up behind him.

"Josh—wait!" Gray grabbed his shoulder and Josh spun around to face his brother.

Gray, for his part, did look apologetic. "I'm sorry...I know I crossed the line."

"You fucking dug a huge ditch through the line."

"Listen, you started in on the whole compensating thing and that really pisses me off."

"Well, you were insulting my home."

"I didn't mean it as an insult, I was just joking." Gray nudged Josh.

"Comparing my home to your pool house was a pretty targeted bash." Josh wasn't ready to forgive his little brother. Again. He always said and did what he wanted—and had his entire life. And now, when Josh really needed his help... God, Josh just didn't know how far he was willing to stoop for his family.

"I said I was sorry. I really am." Gray put his arm around Josh. "Come back in here. You know I'm just an asshole...I didn't mean anything by all of that. I love you guys."

Just like when they were kids, Gray somehow had a way of tugging at Josh's heart when he wanted to. *How does he do that?* Maybe that's why he had done so well for himself in the business world...he was a master at manipulation. "Gray, do not *ever* make a comment about Jayne like that again."

"I won't. Scout's honor."

"You were never a Scout, you jackass."

"Well, Mom's still alive, I can't promise on our mother's grave or anything. Will an old-school pinky swear work?"

Josh sighed, shaking his head. He held out his pinky and Gray linked his up.

"Now come back here," Gray said, waving Josh onto the couch. "So how can I help? And no, I will not take one of the kids."

"Well, I've been trying to figure out how to make this whole situation a little more manageable. And what we really need is to build an addition onto the house. Extend the family room, add on a breakfast room with a small main floor laundry room and, most importantly, add another bedroom."

"That would certainly help."

"Yeah, big time," Josh said, pulling out the folded up piece of paper he'd worked on all afternoon while his last two classes took a test. He laid it on the couch between himself and Gray. "It would equate to about six hundred square feet. I should be able to get permits, since it's going to extend back into my yard. And the yard is big so we'll still have plenty of room for the girls to play back there."

Gray looked at Josh's sketch. "This looks nice. Would you make that the master bedroom?"

"Yeah, I figured that would put all the kids at the other side of the house with the family room between us and them. Can't hurt to have a little distance." They both laughed. "Oh, and a walk-in closet for Jayne. She's always talking about a walk-in closet." Josh stared at the piece of notebook paper, but he saw so much more. He saw a chance to turn this little surprise person into the blessing he knew it was, instead of the stress-inducing event it had started out as. Sure, there would still be diapers to be changed and an extra mouth to feed and body to clothe...but they would have room. Room for the new baby, to spread out, to organize—to have a better life for their family.

"So how can I help?" Gray asked, bringing Josh out of his daydream and back to the paper with lines and dimensions scribbled in pencil.

"I could apply for a home improvement loan," Josh said, his voice dropping. "But honestly, there's not much equity in our house with the market the way it is and all the money I put into the rehab a few years ago." Josh looked at his brother, feeling his heart pounding. "I want to ask you for a loan. We can have papers drawn up, and I can start making payments right away. I just...I just probably can't afford more than a couple of hundred dollars a month for now. But I'll pay back every dime, and I can teach summer school to earn extra cash—"

"How much do you think you'll need?"

Josh looked back at his sketch. "I mean, this is just a huge ballpark guess...but, I don't know...maybe forty thousand?"

"No problem." Gray sat back, took a drink and turned up the basketball game on the TV.

"I know two hundred dollars a month isn't much to start—"

"It's not a loan, Josh." Gray stared at the TV, his fist pumping the air when some team scored. "It's a gift for my nieces and—who knows?—maybe my first nephew."

"No, Gray, I want to pay you back—"

"Well, I won't let you." Gray looked at Josh, his expression serious. "Let's face it...your family is the only one I'll ever have. I don't want one, not full-time, anyway. I love my career. I love my freedom. I don't really want a wife, and I sure as hell don't want to be anybody's dad. But being an uncle—now that's perfect." He grinned, exposing those dimples that his niece Emma had inherited. "They are absolutely amazing, but I get all the glory and none of the work. Just the fun parts. So, let me do this for them and for you and Jayne."

"Gray, I can't just take your money."

"I'm not giving it to you. I'm giving it to Tori and Emma and...and whoever this new little one turns out to be. I was going to set up a college fund, but I think this will be better. And cheaper."

Josh didn't know what to say. He felt ashamed for having to ask his brother but was shocked by Gray's generosity. Of course forty thousand dollars didn't mean as much to Gray as it did to Josh and Jayne, but it wasn't exactly pocket change, either.

Neither one of them spoke as the white noise of the basketball game filled the void in the room. Josh took the last drink of his beer, allowing the tension to ease out of his body. "Gray...I don't know what to say."

"We're brothers, you don't have to say anything. We just take care of each other." Gray got up, headed to the bar and poured himself another drink. "Give me a week or so to get some funds transferred around and I'll have the money for you. And it's after nine o'clock—you better head home so teacher's not late for school tomorrow."

Josh smiled at his brother, amazed at how in a matter of minutes they could go from nearly getting into a physical fight to his brother saving his ass. He stood up. "Yeah, I'm actually pretty tired."

"Go home to bed, old man." Gray took a drink. "You know, there is one thing you could do for me."

"Name it."

"If that baby turns out to be a boy, and since I won't be having a son of my own...do you think you could work Gray in as a middle name or something? I mean, it is a pretty cool name."

Josh chuckled. "You got it."

As he headed out the door, he couldn't wait to get home to tell Jayne. She'd finally have the main floor laundry and walk-in closet she'd always dreamed of. If that wouldn't boost her spirits, nothing would.

****

The two weeks following Karen's IVF procedure were turning out to be the two longest weeks of her life. That's how long it would take to find out if IVF had worked. It had been ten days and she was going nuts. She spent every waking moment trying not to wonder if she was pregnant, which invariably made her think of nothing but whether or not she was pregnant. The more she tried to chill out and not think about it, the more obvious her fixation became.

She figured that Rick would be divorcing her soon...the mood swings were even getting on her nerves.

Only her dog Kramer would be left when this whole fertility business was done. No more friends, no more husband—just a spazzy fur ball that was obviously too stupid to understand what a pain in the ass he'd attached himself to.

Work was usually her reprieve from the troubles of life. Lately, though, there were troubles at the workplace as well.

As glamorous as Karen knew selling packaging supplies sounded, it really wasn't. The big money was in selling automation...new packaging equipment lines that would maximize production and increase efficiencies. Blah blah blah. Even Karen was sick of hearing herself talk about it. Or maybe it was just because she'd been doing it for ten years and the hormones were making it seem more annoying than usual.

Even though there was big money in selling equipment, the steady income came from selling consumable items like boxes, tape, shrink film, bags, etc. That required not only the knowledge it took to sell equipment but the ability to maintain the customer by providing great customer service, better products and going above and beyond the call of duty. That was something Karen prided herself on, and it accounted for the large stable of customers she'd had for years.

Lately, though, there was a big, long-time customer she was getting some weird vibes from. Something wasn't quite right. She had a suspicion that maybe they were looking at other suppliers, though she couldn't figure out why. Over the past few years, she had helped them go from a company that used entirely too much inefficient labor to one that she'd guided to streamline their processes and increase their productivity and profits along the way.

In addition, she'd been there whenever they'd needed it. Every time the operations manager wanted to run by some ideas—Karen was there to listen (regardless of whether the idea was valid or preposterous). If they weren't willing to buy new equipment, Karen spent her own time helping them find used equipment on eBay, which she didn't make a dime from. If they didn't order product in time, Karen was known to load up her car with boxes or stretch film to deliver what they needed herself before they ran out.

She was always there when they needed her and often when it went way beyond the call of duty.

So Karen decided to stop by the magazine distributor's facility unannounced and do a little snooping. She figured she was probably just being paranoid and would feel better once she put her concerns to rest. Why on earth would they be looking elsewhere after she had been so good to them?

When she walked in through the back of the warehouse, she was greeted with smiles and waves from the many employees she'd grown to know over the past few years. She took care of them, and they appreciated it. As always, it felt good to be valued.

As she turned the corner into the production area, she stopped in her tracks. There were two brand new, shiny machines—a stretch wrapper and a box erector—neither of which she'd sold to them. Her heart started pounding. Surely she was seeing things.

She continued to say hello to people she knew as she made her way to the supply racks, trying to act nonchalant when she had the urge to take off her heels and run. And, sure enough, there was a whole pallet full of shrink film from one of her competitors.

Motherfucker. I can't believe it.

Just then she saw Paul, the operations manager, speeding her way. He had a fake smile plastered on his face.

"Karen, good to see you," he said as he got closer. "I didn't know you were stopping by."

I bet you didn't, you son of a bitch. Karen mustered up all the strength she could to sound normal. "Hi, Paul. Just thought I'd stop by and see if you guys need anything."

"Well thanks…we're doing good for now." His demeanor could have been a video definition for the word uncomfortable.

"Yeah, it sure looks like you're doing okay. You've got some nice new equipment over there," she said, pointing to the new machines, one of which had just started stretch wrapping a pallet of boxes.

"Um, yeah, about that...." His voice trailed off as he broke away from her stare.

"What the hell, Paul?" Karen asked, unable to hold it in any longer. "Why on earth didn't you buy those from me? Or at least give me a chance to quote?"

"Well, these guys came in and...I don't know, my boss seemed to like them—"

"Paul," she said, her voice commanding he look at her. He did. "I have bent over backward for you guys. I've assisted you in buying used equipment that I didn't make a dime on, just to help you out. I've delivered product on the weekends when your people screwed up and ran out of stock."

"I know, Karen, I know." He looked down at his boots. "But these guys offered some really good pricing—"

"How do you know it was good pricing? You didn't even have me quote! I carry those same brands...in fact, we're their largest distributor in town. I could have gotten you a better deal, I'm sure."

"I just thought maybe I should mix it up a little bit, give another supplier a shot."

"Why? Am I missing something here? Have I done something wrong? Is our service lacking? Is our product not of good quality?"

"No, no...everything's been great."

"Then...why? I've worked so hard for you." Oh no. Crying Karen was lurking on the edges of Karen's hysteria. *No, don't cry. Don't do it. This is business. It's not personal. Do not cry.*

Paul shrugged his shoulders. "Karen, I don't know. I just thought I'd see what someone else had to offer."

In her overly stimulated hormonal state, Karen heard, *You aren't good enough. I don't like you anymore.*

Crying Karen took over.

"Paul, I don't understand. We've worked so well together...all the lunches...I thought we were partners in this. Friends."

Paul stared at her with horror on his face. "Um, Karen…don't cry. It's nothing personal—"

"But it is, Paul!" More tears, they were streaming down her cheeks. She noticed workers now stopped, staring at the normally together, efficient, businesslike Karen falling apart on their production floor. "You could have given me a last look. You could have been upfront with me and given me a chance to compete."

"I didn't say I was giving them all the business—"

Crying Karen was on a roll. "But you just spent sixty thousand dollars with them on equipment. You just took almost five thousand dollars out of my pocket! How is that not personal?"

"Maybe you should leave for now, calm down, and we can set up a meeting to talk about this." He still looked completely freaked out, but his voice had grown more firm.

"Good luck getting them to fix your machines—they have the worst service tech in town," Crying Karen said in one last fit of emotion before stomping toward the back entrance. She didn't dare look at anyone as she made her way around the maze of boxes, conveyors and pack stations. When she got outside, she couldn't climb into her car fast enough.

Barely able to see through her tears, she sped out of the parking lot, onto the street and pulled into a large Walmart parking lot a few blocks away. When she pulled into a parking spot, she went from whimpering to full-out, ugly-cry bawling. This was just too much.

She gave into the powerful emotions she was so unaccustomed to feeling—anger, hurt, betrayal, shame. Shame was the worst of it.

What had she just done?

She'd spent the past ten years building her reputation in the industry as a hard-as-nails, knowledgeable, fair competitor. She was well respected. Was.

Now she'd be the laughingstock of the packaging industry in St. Louis. Word would get around. Karen

Gordon had cried in the middle of a customer's plant. Cried like a baby because she lost a couple of orders.

How would she ever show her face there again? And even worse…she was more hurt by the customer's actions than by her own ridiculousness. Under normal circumstances, Karen could separate business and personal relationships. She'd never had a problem before. *You win some, you lose some.*

But today, something had snapped in her. Her feelings were hurt. No doubt about it. She felt like a friend had stabbed her in the back. Sure, the hormones likely had something to do with it. But maybe Karen wasn't as stoic and emotionless as she'd always liked to think. Maybe, in the end, she was actually just a woman after all. Not a robot. A woman with emotions that couldn't always be kept in check.

"Oh my God," she whispered, sitting back in her seat. What was she going to do now? Any other time, she would call Claudia or Jayne. She shook her head, knowing she didn't have that option now. She grabbed her phone and speed-dialed Rick.

"Hey, babe," he answered. "I'm about to go into a meeting. What's up?"

"Oh…I just needed to talk," she said, trying to sound normal.

"You sound strange. Is everything okay?"

"I just…I really screwed up at work."

"I'll be right there," she heard Rick holler at someone in his office. "Karen, can I call you back after my meeting?"

"Yeah, sure," she said, tears in her voice.

"Listen, I can skip my meeting—"

"No, it's okay. Just call me later."

"As soon as I'm done."

He hung up, and Karen felt so alone. She had to talk to someone. Someone that could make her feel like she hadn't just screwed up her whole career.

With a sigh, she dialed her mom. Her mom could be supportive when she wanted.

"Hello?"

"Hey, Mom, it's me." Karen bit her lip. "Mom, I really screwed something up." She relayed the events of the afternoon to her mom and felt embarrassed as she spoke the words out loud. Her mom was quiet the whole time. Once Karen was done, she broke her silence.

"Oh, honey, you most certainly did screw up. I don't know how you can ever go there again. I mean, you're a businesswoman. You can't go around crying in front of customers. Not to mention, sweetie, you don't look very good when you cry. If I were you, I'd hand that account over to someone else and see if they can repair the damage you've done."

Shocked by her mom's harsh words, Karen had an epiphany before she could even respond.

Her mom was doing to her what Karen had always done to her friends. Saying exactly what she thought, regardless of how it might hurt them.

The revelation almost took her breath away.

No wonder Claudia hadn't told her about Sam—Karen would have been brutal with her. And Jayne must have been terrified to let Karen know she was pregnant. How could she have not seen that? She was so busy spouting whatever came to mind that she'd never stopped to think of how those words came across. Some friend she had been.

The apple certainly didn't fall far from the tree.

"Karen, are you still there?" her mother asked.

"Yeah, Mom, I'm still here." Karen sighed. "Thanks for helping me."

"You're welcome, though there's nothing I can do to help you. You're on your own with this mess."

Don't I know it.

****

After composing herself in the Walmart parking lot, Karen headed toward home, her mind swirling with new thoughts of self-loathing. By the time she reached her neighborhood, she'd decided she was lucky her friends had ever stuck by her. Sure, she'd been loyal to them and supportive at times. But the flip side of that was probably not easy for them to deal with.

Driving down her street, she realized how much she was growing to love her new neighborhood. The fenced-in yards and manicured lawns that she once would have equated to small prisons now looked inviting and soothing to her. Instead of thinking the houses all looked alike in some military barracks sort of way, Karen now saw them as organized yet individualized with their own style.

Peggy, who lived a couple of houses down and across the street, waved at her as she drove by. Karen waved back with a smile. Just like Gabe and Anthony, she'd found a great neighbor in Peggy. She had a great sense of humor and was always lending a helping hand. The kind of neighbor everyone hopes for.

Instead of suburbia being the bland wasteland Karen had imagined, filled with boring, unimaginative, close-minded people…it just dawned on her in this moment of self-introspection that *she* had been the close-minded one.

Oh sure, Karen prided herself on being the epitome of open-mindedness, welcoming of all kinds of people. *But no, Karen, you've been a condescending bitch.* Somehow she'd gotten into her mind that being accepting of others only meant the ones she felt worthy of her acceptance. She had no problem with gay people or anyone's religious preference or the color of someone's skin. But she'd never hesitated to look down her nose at people she felt were too status quo. As if her life in the eclectic part of the city had made her something special. It just meant the parking was lousy and the crime rate was higher.

Here, in the place she and Rick had decided to nest, were people just like she'd lived by in the city. Some were boring as hell, some were weird, some annoying—sure. But there were also great people that were friendly, non-judgmental (something Karen was realizing she needed to work on), caring, and interesting. It wasn't where you lived that determined any of that, or how close you were to the trendy parts of town.

The suburbs were just a great place to live. The schools were good, the yards were large and the collective goal of the community was to raise families in harmony. How could Karen have ever found fault with that?

Josh and Jayne lived in the 'burbs, and they were two of the best people she knew. There was nothing dull or boring about them. Karen had assumed they were the exception. Now she knew differently.

She pulled into her driveway, smiling at the welcoming sight of what now truly felt like home. Maybe those hormones were acting like some sort of truth serum.

Karen just didn't know if she liked what it was revealing about herself.

Chapter Twelve

Claudia had somehow convinced herself to stop analyzing her relationship with Sam...what it meant, where it was going. For once in her life, she was trying to live without the image of a goal or finish line burned into her consciousness.

Sure, it wasn't easy for her. She was such a planner by nature. But she felt she owed it to herself to just be in the moment and see where it took her.

So far, things had been going quite well.

Instead of just stolen moments after Isabella went to bed, they'd gone the extra step and gotten a sitter a couple of times and gone out on a proper date. It was nice. There was a newness to it but grounded in the familiarity that can only come from being a couple for more than a decade. It was easy to fall for him all over again...he really was everything she'd ever wanted in a man. Well, except for the whole cheating on her thing.

But thinking about that wasn't part of living in the moment.

A part of her was glad she hadn't spoken to Karen in almost two weeks. The secret was out, so her affair with Sam no longer needed to be clandestine. It made things easier. And not having Karen's constant judgment was a relief.

But another part of her missed Karen. Claudia had talked to Jayne, but it really wasn't the same knowing the threesome was...well, not exactly a threesome at the moment. Of course Claudia knew the right thing to do was pick up the phone and apologize for keeping secrets from one of her best friends. It had been a petty thing to do, and certainly not something a true friend does to another.

Yet this little reprieve from Karen suited her new relationship with Sam. Maybe a little distance from Karen wasn't such a bad thing right now.

Of course Claudia knew it was just because Karen would speak the truth. Karen would be that voice of reason, reminding Claudia of why being with Sam was a bad idea.

Well, everybody needed a break from reality every now and then. This was Claudia's turn.

Sorry, Karen. I don't have time for your negativity right now, she thought as she rolled over in bed and snuggled up against Sam. The first rays of sunshine were starting to peek through the blinds and were splashed across his face. He stirred, smiling.

"I like this," he murmured, just barely opening his eyes as he pulled her closer to his naked body.

"What?"

"Waking up with you in the morning."

She liked it, too. He was normally fastidious about his appearance, but now his dark brown hair was disheveled and his beard was starting to show. He looked sexy as hell. Claudia cleared her throat. "It's been years since we've done this."

"Claud, it's been too long." He kissed her, brushing the hair from her face. "I've always thought you look the most beautiful when you wake up."

Claudia smiled at him with a bashful grin. "You're just saying that."

"No, it's true." His voice was firm. "No makeup, just you. Perfect."

She felt her cheeks grow warm. "You're not too shabby yourself, Mr. Knight." They kissed again and Claudia began to get aroused.

"What are we going to do about Izzy?" Sam looked at her with caution in his eyes. "I thought you didn't want her to get any ideas about us being together…."

"Well, I don't know." Claudia sat up, pulling the sheet over her chest. "She knows something is going on. We're together all the time now when we never used to be."

"Yeah, I know."

"Has she said anything to you?"

Sam ran his fingers through his hair, making it stick up even more. "She said to me the other day that she was glad we were friends now."

Claudia smiled. "That was sweet. How did you respond?"

"How could I? I just said I was happy too." Sam grabbed Claudia's hand. "We've been playing this game of being together again for months now. I want to make it permanent, Claud. I screwed everything up so badly. This is my chance to make it right, to make it last forever this time. I owe that to Isabella. I owe that to you."

Claudia swallowed. She could hear her heart pounding in her ears. Sure, she was enjoying their new life of being together. It's what she had always wanted but lost. Yet there was Karen, in the back of her mind: *Why would you ever trust him again, Claudia? What's gonna keep him from wanting out a few years down the road? The right piece of ass walks by, and suddenly he won't want to be monogamous anymore.*

Claudia put her hands over her ears. *Karen, shut up. Get out of my head. Leave me alone.*

"What, you don't want to hear that?" Sam asked, concern filling his eyes.

"No, it's not that." Claudia smiled at him. "I want to believe in a forever for us. It's what I've wanted since I was nineteen years old."

"Well, then…" Sam climbed out of bed, pulled on his boxer briefs, and reached for his pants. He pulled a small box out of the pocket and then climbed back into bed. "I was waiting for the right time for this. I don't know when the right time is… I just know I don't want to wait anymore. I know what I want. I hope you want it, too."

He opened the small blue leather box, revealing a beautiful Tacori diamond ring nestled inside. Claudia's first ring had been beautiful; this one was downright decadent. The oval cut center stone had to be at least three carats, and it was set in a band that was made to look like an heirloom from a long-ago era. Claudia gasped out loud.

"Claudia, will you marry me?"

"Sam..." The whisper came out as little more than a vocal tremble. She had not been expecting this at all. Her heart raced as she tried to understand the tumble of emotions cascading through her mind. She loved him, no doubt about it. She always had. And what would it mean for Isabella, having a complete family instead of living a life shuffled back and forth between two people that made bad choices she was forced to live with?

Looking a little deflated, Sam said, "If you don't know the answer right now, I can wait. I can wait as long as it takes."

Claudia took a deep breath. "Sam, I want to say yes." She looked at him with tears in her eyes. "I just...I don't know if I'm ready yet."

"Maybe this will help make up your mind," he said with a wink as he pulled the ring from the box. He placed it on her finger.

Wow. I could get used to this. "Sam, it's absolutely stunning. I love it."

He chuckled. "You can wear it while you think about it."

"So you think I'm that materialistic?" She grinned. "You just put a gorgeous bauble on my finger and I won't be able to part with it?"

"I'm kind of hoping it will be like a puppy, yeah." They both laughed, and Claudia leaned into him, staring at the ring. He put his arms around her and Claudia loved the feel of him surrounding her.

Isabella came running into the room. "Daddy! You're here!"

Claudia and Sam exchanged a glance and embarrassed smiles.

"Yes, Miss Isabella, I'm here," he said with a chuckle.

"Ooo, Mommy, what's that pretty ring?"

Claudia giggled. "Oh, something I'm thinking about

keeping."

"It's so pretty. You should definitely keep it."

"You think so?"

Isabella climbed into the bed, snuggling between her parents. Sam started tickling her. As Isabella's high-pitched giggles escalated in volume, the sound made Claudia's heart soar. She looked at the sparkling ring on her finger and over at Sam and Isabella, identical smiles lighting up their faces.

Everything felt perfect.

****

It had been a full twenty-four hours since Karen had colossally shamed herself in front of her customer. She was getting used to the idea of what she'd done…though she was trying to pretend that it was all a dream and everything would resume as normal on Monday morning.

Delusion seemed an appropriate choice.

By the time Rick had called her back after his meeting on Friday, she was calmed down and at home after the warm-and-fuzzy talk with her mom. If anything, she was more disturbed by hearing herself in her mother's diatribe and the realization that she'd been a close-minded snob. But she hadn't decided if she was going to mention any of that to Rick. So she told him she'd just talk to him when he got home from work.

Rick, being one of the few people on the planet who understood Karen and still liked her, knew how to make her feel better. He came home a little early and had bags full of their favorite Chinese food. Shrimp fried rice, crab Rangoon, egg drop soup. To Karen, that meant love.

While they ate, she told him what had happened at work and was able to get through it without having another meltdown. He listened, rubbed her back, nodded. He didn't exactly tell her everything would be okay, but he didn't leave her feeling worse like her mom had.

She felt heard and she knew he cared. But he was, after all, a man. There was no substitute for a girlfriend when your world is falling apart. Here she was desperate to find out if her last chance at being a biological mother had worked and she had thrown her professional reputation down the toilet. If there was ever a time she needed Claudia's calm, strong mothering and Jayne's hopeful demeanor—

It was now.

Instead, Karen went to bed early on Friday night. Her sleep was a bit restless, the kind that leaves you still feeling drained when you wake up the next morning. Nothing a black cup of coffee couldn't cure.

She kept telling herself everything was fine while she made a big breakfast, including her special pancakes—much to Rick's delight. While she cleaned the house, she played upbeat music to make sure Crying Karen didn't show up. The day was turning out to be beautiful...the type of moderate spring day that made you absolutely love St. Louis and wish there were more of. Feeling stir crazy, she made some iced tea, grabbed her e-reader and went out on the deck to enjoy the weather. Kramer was already outside, running around with abandon while Rick trimmed their trees and bushes with an artful flair. He looked kinda hot when he did yard work—an unexpected bonus of suburban living.

Kramer ran up to give Karen some sloppy kisses before taking off after a fuzzy bunny that had dared to invade his yard. The temperature was sixty-five degrees, there wasn't a cloud in the sky and a gentle breeze made the white blooms ripple on the Bradford pear trees lining the back of their yard.

Although it was the perfect opportunity to dig into the newest Claire Cook novel that she knew would make her laugh and lift her mood, she just couldn't concentrate. It wasn't just the worries at her job or the agonizing wait to find out if the IVF worked. No, the biggest ache in her hormonally ramped up heart was the absence of her girls.

Life was just unbearable without them.

Grabbing her phone and silently telling Crying Karen to *stay the fuck away*, Karen was careful as she typed the most important text message she'd ever crafted: *I've never told you guys this before, but I'm sorry. Neither of you did anything wrong; I brought this on myself. Please meet me for coffee, Picasso's 4:00?*

She hit send on the message and felt a sense of relief, which was immediately followed by agony. What if it was too late? What if they liked their lives without Karen in it?

Kramer ran up and put his paws on her lap, demanding affection. Karen whispered, "Well, little dude, I guess I'll at least have you, huh?"

****

Jayne and Josh had spent that Saturday morning meeting with an architect who was a friend of a friend. Jayne was beyond thrilled as they talked about the plans for the addition to their home. They were going to really gain a lot of much-needed space, but Josh was adamant that the addition reflect the historic age of the home. So there would be arched doorways, hardwood floors and wide crown moldings.

And a walk-in closet! Jayne thought Josh had never looked sexier than when he told her there would be a walk-in closet with a built-in shoe rack. She imagined him naked in the closet, in front of all of her shoes, wearing nothing but a strategically tied bow.

Now *that* was sexy.

The immense tension she'd felt since finding about baby number three was starting to dilute a bit. Of course adding space to the house wouldn't make changing more diapers any easier or suddenly make more hours appear in the day.

But it was something. Something that would make their lives easier and give a little more space in their home on those days that were overwhelming.

Thanks to Gray. He had a way of irritating people so much with his arrogance and sense of authority that when he made these wonderful, selfless gestures…well, they caught you completely off-guard. It didn't exactly negate the other irritations but went a long way to make his ego easier to live with. Deep down, Gray was a good man. He just made it difficult to remember that most days.

But not the day before. Jayne was already high on the I-love-my-brother-in-law freight train when she got a call from his administrative assistant late on Friday afternoon.

"Mr. Brandt would like to see you in his office if you have a few minutes."

Jayne rolled her eyes but grinned. "Please let Mr. Brandt know that I'll be right up."

When she reached his office a few minutes later, he was typing on his computer at lightning speed. Without looking away from his screen, he said, "Mrs. Brandt. Lovely to see you. Come on in."

"Can I shut the door so I can call you Gray?"

He grinned. "Nah, leave it open. I like it when you address me as your superior."

"If you weren't my walk-in-closet-benefactor, I would probably punch you right now."

His dimples appeared. "I know."

Jayne made herself comfortable in one of the high-backed leather chairs in front of his desk. "So what's up, *Mister* Brandt?"

"I've got a new project I'd like you to work on for me."

Jayne's heart sank. She barely had time to get her job done now...adding a new project would be a disaster. But he was being so generous to their family, there's no way she could tell him she had too much on her plate. Besides, he was her boss. She pretty much had to do what he said. Plastering a smile on her face, she said, "Great! What is it?"

"Check this out." He tossed a copy of the *St. Louis Post-Dispatch* newspaper toward her. It was turned to an article in the business section about employee perks of the best places to work in St. Louis. As Jayne scanned the article, Gray continued. "Look at that...the biggest employee perk is on-site daycare. If we want to compete with the big companies in town like Monsanto and Nestlé-Purina to lure and keep the best employees—we have to offer programs that matter to people. Reading this article, it sounds like this is one of the most valued employee benefits."

"Well, sure—any parent would love that."

"And the best part is that it won't cost us anything. The employees would pay for the daycare expenses, but since we're doing this as a service, not a profit center, it should cost less for the employees than a typical daycare provider."

"So Nixon Pharmaceutical is going to start an on-site daycare for employees?"

"That's the idea. I wanted to see what you thought of it first."

"Gray—that would be amazing! It would save parents so much time, and if it could save employees money on daycare expenses...well, that would just be icing on the cake."

He offered a cocky grin while he leaned back in his chair and put his feet on the desk. "That's kind of what I thought. I'm an idea guy. Go ahead, thank me."

Jayne giggled. "Thank you, Gray—I mean Mr. Brandt."

"You're welcome. But this is far from a done deal. Now that I know you're on board, I'm going to send an email to Christy in HR. I want her to head up this project, working closely with you. I'll give her a scope of what questions we need answered before I can take this to the board for review."

"So, realistically—if all goes well—when do you think this could really happen?" Jayne tried not to sound as excited as she felt. Inside, she was doing cartwheels and handsprings.

"Why are you in such a rush?" he asked with a wink, putting his feet down. "It's like you have some vested interest in this."

"No, not at all." She grinned. *Just the three hundred and fifty dollars I'm already spending each week on daycare, not to mention the additional two hundred plus I'm looking at for the new baby.*

"Well, then—chop, chop. The sooner you and Christy do the fact-finding for me, the sooner we can hopefully move forward with starting a daycare facility here."

"You don't have to tell me twice." Jayne stood up, and her voice faltered as she said, "I can't thank you enough for all you've done for us."

Gray shook his head, dismissing her. "Jayne, forget about it—"

"No, please let me say this." Her eyes welled with tears. "Between the promotion, the house addition and now this... You are just too much."

He shrugged. "It's not all me, Jaynie. You earned that promotion. And this daycare idea—it makes sense for Nixon. I want the best talent in town, and I want them to stay a long time. Offering an employee benefit like this just makes sense." He leaned forward. "And if I can help my family in the process, then it's like you said—icing on the cake."

"Well, thanks for baking so many cakes."

"Now you *know* I can't cook." He turned back to his computer, signaling he was done with her. "I'm emailing Christy now—she'll be getting with you on Monday."

"I look forward to working with her."

"Good. Now enjoy your weekend and give my nieces kisses from Uncle Gray."

"I will."

"If I have time on Sunday I'd like to take Tori to see that new Disney movie. But you know I can't handle Emma too."

She laughed out loud. "We can barely handle the two of them."

Gray chuckled as he started typing. "You better hope that kid in your belly is one laid-back baby."

"Maybe it'll take after its dad."

"You better hope so."

Jayne practically skipped all the way back to her desk. Wow, if they could spend less on daycare and have her babies right there with her...she was starting to see a light at the end of the tunnel.

Finally.

And now that they'd met with the architect, it was all starting to seem more real. Their time frame was to have all the work done by the end of August, which was a full two months before the baby was due in early-November. That would give Jayne plenty of time to get everything organized and settled in. And maybe she and Josh could bring to life that vision she'd had of him with the bow in the closet.

As things were starting to fall into place, there were at least a half-dozen times in the past couple of weeks when Jayne almost picked up the phone to call Karen. But she knew she better not. Sure, Jayne was upset about some of the harsh things Karen had said that night at the party. But deep down, she knew Karen was just speaking from hurt, and the hormones weren't helping either.

Jayne knew Karen owed her an apology; after all, Jayne hadn't really done anything wrong. But for Karen to apologize, hell would have to freeze over. Jayne didn't need an apology…she just needed her friend back.

But she was afraid to call Karen because of the guilt she felt over getting pregnant without even trying. What could Jayne possibly say to Karen to make that situation better? Karen must have been devastated. Jayne wanted to hug her and tell her she was so, so sorry that life wasn't fair and she's sorry if this new event in her life was hurting her friend. But maybe the pain was so raw and fresh…maybe Karen didn't want anything to do with her anymore.

So Jayne did her best to not think about Karen as she tried to make sense of this new, unexpected version of her own life. Now that things were looking better, she hoped Karen would come around soon. Although Jayne had chatted with Claudia, she sure missed Karen's sharp wit and unfiltered doses of reality. She could really use that now.

Jayne and Josh were sitting at the kitchen table, chatting, while looking at the initial sketches the architect had made. The girls were in the family room playing and watching *Dora the Explorer*. As Jayne talked with animation about the details of the addition, she looked up to see Josh staring at her, a huge grin on his face.

"What?" she asked, her face burning warm.

He tenderly touched her cheek. "I just missed this so much."

"Missed what?"

"Seeing you happy and bubbly."

Jayne grabbed his hand and kissed it. "I'm sorry I haven't been myself. And I know things aren't going to be perfect—"

"Far from it," he said with a chuckle.

"But you've worked so hard coming up with ways to make it better for us." She squeezed his hand. "I think it's all going to work out." She actually believed her optimism. It felt good to be hopeful again.

"I think so too." His intense green eyes shone with relief. "I love you, Jayne."

"I love you, Josh."

Emma went running down the hallway past them.

"Emma, what are you doing?" Jayne asked, her mother radar on high alert.

"I goin' potty!" She dashed into the bathroom. They had been trying to potty train her the past few weeks, but with little luck.

Jayne stood up. "Do you need help?"

"No Mommy! I do potty all by myself."

Jayne and Josh grinned at each other. "Okay, sweetie. Let me know when you're done." If they could get Emma potty trained before the baby came, that would mean only one child in diapers. *Come on Emma, you can do it!*

Atticus, their chocolate lab mix, sauntered down the hallway, following Emma. Jayne loved how Atticus treated the girls like his own: always following them and keeping a watchful eye. Little did the old dog know there would soon be a new one to watch over.

"So…" Josh said, taking hold of Jayne's hand and pulling her onto his lap. "Where were we?"

"You were saying how much you loved me."

"Oh, yes, I was." His naughty grin always made her smile in return. "So I was thinking…why don't you go lie down on the couch, put your feet up and take a nap? And I'll make a batch of my special meat marinade and get some steaks soaking so I can grill out tonight."

"You had me at steaks."

"I'll grill some veggies, too. Maybe some zucchini and cauliflower?"

"Yes and yes."

"Mommy!" Emma yelled with excitement, running naked out of the bathroom. "I go poop in the potty! Come see!"

Jayne hopped off Josh's lap, and they all rushed down the hallway. When they got to the bathroom, Jayne was confused. She looked in the little pink training potty...but it was empty.

"Did you go in the big potty?"

Emma shoved her way through the door. "No, I go'd in the pink potty." The toddler scrunched up her face. "Where is my poopies?"

Jayne looked at Josh with confusion. "Emma, are you sure you went?"

"My poopies was in there!" Emma, now totally distraught, pointed to the training toilet.

At the same moment, Jayne and Josh noticed Atticus sitting in the corner of the bathroom, licking his lips.

"Oh my God," Josh said, shaking his head. "Emma, was Atticus in here when you were using the potty?"

"Um...yeah. He watched me on the potty."

"And when you came to tell us you went potty, was Atticus still in here?"

"He was smelling my poopies."

Jayne couldn't decide if she should laugh or cry. "Sweetie, I think he did more than just smell them."

"At'cus took my poopies?"

Jayne and Josh exchanged a glance.

Emma crossed her arms. "Bad dog, At'cus! Those was my poopies!" The dog laid down on the tile floor, looking very unconcerned.

So maybe things were going to be manageable. That didn't mean they were ever going to be easy.

As Jayne headed to the kitchen to grab some heavy-duty cleaning supplies, she heard her phone chime with a text message. She picked it up, read the message from Karen and smiled as tears came to her eyes.

"Hey, Josh?" She'd left him in the bathroom with Emma on bottom-wiping duty.

"Yeah?" he hollered back.

"Instead of taking a nap, do you care if I go meet the girls for coffee?"

There was a pause, and she heard Josh walking toward her down the hallway. "You mean Karen too?" he asked, poking his head in the kitchen.

"Yeah. She just sent a great text and wants to meet at Picasso's."

Josh smiled; she knew he could see the tears. "It's about time you guys patched things up. Sure, take all the time you need. Atticus and I have everything under control."

Atticus sauntered into the kitchen, tail wagging, not sure why his name had been called but happy to be there. Jayne giggled. "I'm sure you do."

****

Claudia couldn't stop looking at the amazing ring on her finger. She'd been staring at it all day, trying to get a feel for it. Did it feel right? Did wearing a wedding ring suit her anymore?

Although she'd been secretly seeing Sam again for more than three months, things now seemed to be moving faster than she'd expected. Under any normal circumstances, Claudia would never consider marrying anyone she'd only been dating for three months.

But there was nothing normal about this.

When the three of them had gone to the Soulard Farmer's Market that morning, she felt like wearing the ring was a chance to try it out...see how it felt to be a wife again. Sure, they looked like a family. The ring everything appear legit.

So why did it feel so strange to Claudia?

Maybe it was because they were living the life she always thought they would, but it was an ideal she'd given up on. The past six years had shattered those dreams, and it was hard to slip a ring on her finger and expect her heart and mind to pick up where it had left off before she'd found another woman in her bed with Sam.

People change, don't they? I mean, it's possible, right? That was the million-dollar question. She already knew that she and Sam were compatible. Until he'd decided he didn't want to be monogamous, they had a great marriage. They were good friends, worked well on projects together, valued each other's opinions. They fit together like puzzle pieces. Always had.

So what it all boiled down to was whether their divorce was a colossal mistake on his part or a sign of a character flaw that would rear its ugly head again.

As they made their way through the market, there was no doubt what reconciling with Sam would do for Isabella. She'd never known a life where her parents were together, a unit. Now that it was happening…the little girl positively glowed. Her two favorite people, no longer separate entities. It was like Christmas and Halloween all rolled into one.

The ring continued to catch her eye after they got back home. Isabella went outside to play in the yard while Sam helped put the groceries away. He was going to grill the salmon they'd bought for dinner and Claudia would do the rest. It was nice to be cooking for another adult again—Isabella certainly hadn't acquired the most sophisticated palate yet.

Sam had some work to do, but instead of hiding in the office like he used to when they were married, he brought his briefcase into the kitchen and worked at the big farmhouse table they'd bought at an antique store in Hannibal while they were engaged all those years before. The immense sparkling diamond caught Claudia's eye when she pulled down her *Better Homes and Gardens Cookbook*. She remembered how much Sam loved carrot cake, and today seemed special, so she thought she'd make a cake.

They didn't talk much while he worked on his laptop and she puttered around the kitchen. She'd sometimes catch him watching her, and he'd smile when their eyes met. At one point, he caught her looking at the ring.

"Are you getting used to the feel of it yet?" he asked, his eyebrows raised. "Is the puppy too irresistible to return?" His pleading expression made him look vulnerable. And adorable.

She gave in with a smile. "I'm still considering it."

"It looks good on you."

It really does. "I'm just trying it out."

He was quiet for a moment. "No pressure, Claud. I don't need an answer until you're ready."

Her heart did a little flip…she thought maybe she was ready. As she started putting carrots through the food processor, she let her mind pretend he'd never left. He'd always been hers. They'd always been a family. That felt perfect. The ring was right.

"I'm gonna take a break and stretch my legs." Sam stood up. "Think I'll see if Izzy wants to play catch. Why don't you come out with us?"

"Well I would, but this carrot cake isn't going to make itself."

"You're making carrot cake?"

Claudia chuckled at the excitement on his face. "Yes, I am. I figure if you're going to dangle this big of a ring in front of me, the least I can do is make you some dessert."

He walked over, put his arms around her and kissed her neck, his lips just grazing her flesh. "I'd choose your carrot cake over a diamond any day."

She swallowed, feeling a now familiar stirring inside. "I thought you might."

"Then maybe later we could have dessert in bed…."

"Maybe." She pulled away, surprised at how much passion still existed between them.

There was desire in his eyes as he stepped back. "I better get out of this kitchen while I still have the willpower."

He went out the back door, Claudia taking the opportunity to admire his firm, round bottom as he walked away. Age hadn't hurt him a bit.

As she mixed up the cake batter, she felt full in a way she hadn't in so long. The warmth of desire he had aroused with just a kiss on her neck still lingered, and the overwhelming proposal from earlier in the day left her in a fragile yet hopeful emotional state. Pretending to be a real family that day had felt so right.

And if you just say yes, it can be like that forever.

Sure, some people wouldn't understand, but it certainly wasn't like they were the first people to remarry again. Lots of people regretted divorcing. Claudia wasn't about to give up on the dreams she'd had all these years just to go along with what other people thought. Sure, she was a *good girl* and seldom colored outside the lines. But this was her life. No one could tell her what to do.

She was going to marry Sam. And this time, since he'd seen how empty life was without her, it would be different. This time really would be forever.

The moment she made up her mind, she felt like she was going to explode. She had to tell Sam. She had to tell him yes. *Yes, Sam, I will marry you.*

She raced to the back door. There was Isabella, with her pink ball glove and pink ball, playing catch with her daddy. "Sam! Come in when you get a minute. I need to tell you something." The grin on Claudia's face was enormous; it almost hurt.

He smiled back at her. "I'll be there in a minute."

Just then, Sam's phone beeped with a new text message. But to Claudia, it sounded like a bomb going off as her heart sank.

In that split second, she realized a truth she couldn't escape: She could never trust Sam.

The beep of that text message sent a shiver of fear through her in an instant. It didn't matter who it was from—it was a sign she would always be wondering. Every time his phone rang or he got a text or he worked late...was there someone else? If a new girl started at the office, was she a potential threat? If there was a charge on their credit card she didn't know about—was it a sign of something bad? If he bought a new cologne, was it for Claudia? Or someone else?

Maybe he had changed, but the fact that something as simple as the beep of a text message caused her to break out into a sweat told Claudia she would never be able to live with finding out if he'd changed or not. It didn't matter if he really was ready to be monogamous. Because she wasn't ready to take a chance on him again.

She'd done that once, and it hadn't turned out so well.

Claudia knew she deserved a life not spent looking over her shoulder. A life not spent wondering how long she would be enough for him this time. She deserved trust…something she didn't think she could ever truly have with Sam again.

Tears slid down her face as she slipped the ring off her finger. The sound of Sam's footsteps approaching the door was interrupted by her own phone chiming with a text. The back door opened. As Claudia read the message from Karen, she began to smile through her tears.

Chapter Thirteen

Seven Months Later....

Claudia was so excited to have an excuse to entertain. It was early November, so with the holidays approaching she would soon have plenty of reasons to throw parties. But it had been Easter since she'd had anyone over for a celebration. This baby shower was the perfect happy occasion to gather friends.

Isabella was at Sam's for the weekend, so Claudia was able to focus all of her attention on the baby shower. She'd been planning for months and was thrilled the day was finally here. The weather was cooperating; it was sixty degrees out, mild for fall in St. Louis. The sun was shining as the last of the colored leaves clung to the trees.

When Sam picked Isabella up the night before, his demeanor was the same as it had been for the past few months—courteous but distant. Funny how he had been desperate to be friends and have a good relationship with Claudia when he'd left her years ago, but when she turned down his proposal and ended their tryst...he was no longer concerned with being friends. When the tables were turned, and he was the one being rejected, he wasn't so gracious and understanding.

Oh, he wasn't being a jerk about it. He just made it clear that if he couldn't have all of Claudia, he didn't want much to do with her.

She was okay with that—it was easier that way.

So she threw herself back into the life she'd been living before she went down the path of considering getting together with Sam again. A life centered on Isabella and enjoying her own friends. Her very pregnant friends.

"So have you come up with a name for the little guy in

your belly?" Claudia asked Jayne a couple of months earlier as the three of them enjoyed lunch on the beautiful patio at McGurk's.

"We sure have." Jayne grinned as she leaned in, as if sharing a huge secret. "Nicholas Gray Brandt."

"Aw, that's sweet."

"I can't believe you didn't want to be surprised by the sex," Karen said, rubbing her belly. "You're usually so into that stuff."

Jayne chuckled. "Well, yeah, but everything about this baby was a surprise, so we felt like we didn't need any more."

"And it's so great it's going to be a boy," Claudia said, enjoying a sip of the only alcoholic beverage at the table.

"It will be our only son, that's for sure."

"You never know," Karen said with a wink, "the Brandts seem to be a pretty fertile bunch."

"That's why I drove Josh myself to the urologist last week to get his vasectomy." They all shared a laugh. "So Nicholas will definitely be our last."

"Now if you get pregnant, you've got some explaining to do."

Jayne blushed. "You bet I do."

"Why didn't you want to know the sex?" Claudia asked Karen. "You're the opposite of Jayne; you don't normally go for surprises."

"Oh, hell, I figured that since absolutely everything about this baby's conception was so calculated and controlled, I ought to leave something up to chance."

"Well I, for one, hope to God you don't have a girl. I cannot even begin to imagine watching you with an irrational, emotional daughter."

Jayne giggled. "I never thought of that, but you're right, Claud."

Karen snorted. "Very funny you two. I can handle whatever this baby brings, trust me."

"I'll remember you said that," Jayne said, a smirk on her face.

Their food arrived, and as they started eating, Karen nudged Claudia. "I've got a job for you, if you want it."

Claudia had no idea what she had in mind. "What?"

"I don't want to register for all the baby junk we need. I was hoping you would do it for me."

"You mean you don't even want to be there when I register you?" Claudia asked in shock.

Karen shoveled in another bite of her Spinach-Artichoke Chicken Breast. Claudia was amused at how the usually controlled Karen seemed to be eating like there was no tomorrow.

"Hell no. Rick and I stopped into Babies R Us last week to register, and it was so overwhelming I thought it was going to induce labor right there in the store. So if you want to do it, the job's yours. I trust you implicitly."

Claudia beamed with pride and also utter excitement. She loved stuff like this. "You will not regret handing this over to me."

"I know. That's why I'm doing it." This time a helping of Yukon mashed potatoes went in.

Jayne stared wide-eyed at Karen. "How can you not pick out your own baby stuff? I mean, there are so many different things you have to decide—"

"Exactly. Too much. That's why I don't want to do it." More chicken. "Not everyone gets into this crap like you two do. I just want this baby, but I don't have the urge to shop for all the minutia it requires. Claudia is a mom extraordinaire—she's got this. Not my problem anymore."

Shaking her head, Jayne sighed. "It's like you're from another planet sometimes."

Karen shrugged. "That's possible."

And so Claudia got to spend hours and hours on her weekends without Isabella, picking out the best and latest in infant supplies. Car seats, high chairs, bottles, monitors...the list was endless and an absolute joy for Claudia to immerse herself in. She was proud of the registry lists she created for Karen. Her research ensured the products were safe and effective, and all in good taste.

It made her want a baby all over again. And, who knew? Maybe she'd have another one someday. Although the rekindled relationship with Sam ultimately wasn't right for Claudia, it did make her realize something.

She didn't want to be alone forever.

And in an odd way, it gave her the confidence to think about really throwing herself back out there again. She felt stronger after finally putting an end to the dreams of Sam she'd harbored since she was in college. Telling him no and walking away was her way of letting go. She was done with all of that. Maybe that's all she needed to finally move on.

So she was keeping her eyes open when she was at the market or picking Isabella up from school. There were a couple of single dads she was starting to flirt with. At work there were a few clients who had always shown interest; she was warmer with them and laughed louder at their jokes. No, she hadn't been on any dates, but she knew if someone interesting asked—she'd say yes. And she'd even look forward to it.

In the meantime, between Karen and Jayne's babies-to-be, Claudia knew she wouldn't have to worry about getting her baby fix. She'd be able to kiss and hug and love on their little ones while she still imagined someday having another of her own.

So after all the planning and registering, the big day had arrived. As she always did right before a party began, Claudia took a moment to survey what she'd created.

It all started with the theme on the invitations, which she had designed and printed from one of her favorite stationary websites. Since they didn't know the sex of the baby, she chose an adorable contemporary pattern with ducks, giraffes and bears in lime green on a chocolate-colored background with bright orange accents. She continued with that theme in the party's décor.

After deciding on a lunchtime shower with a simple sit down meal of chicken and tuna salad on brioche, served alongside a fruit salad and homemade chips (yes, she made them herself), she made sure the linens and chiffon bows on each chair matched the theme. At each place setting was a gift for each guest: a small Mason jar holding three brilliant orange roses with a small lime ribbon tied around the lip. Each jar held a place card on which Claudia had written each guest's name in calligraphy with great care. In the bottom of each jar was a packet of seeds for the intense orange roses so each guest could plant their own in the spring.

Of course she had made the cake herself...the most daunting part of the party for her. But she was pleased with the outcome; she only hoped it tasted as sweet as it looked.

Instead of her usual punch, she decided to make it more casual to suit Karen with glass-bottled sodas she chilled in a large metal ice-filled tub. Of course the soda had to match the theme, so she bought the color appropriate sodas of Root Beer, Orange Cream and Key Lime from the local Fitz's Bottling Company.

She knew Karen wouldn't want it too fussy, so although instinct told her to do more decorating, she was pretty sure Karen would be rolling her eyes as it was. So she stopped there. And as the doorbell rang, Claudia thought it all looked perfect.

When she opened the door, Karen was there, looking every bit like a glowing expectant mother.

"The guest of honor is here," she said, stepping inside, giving Claudia a hug. "I wore a brown dress so I'd match my own party. I thought you'd approve."

Claudia laughed. "Of course I approve. And brown looks good on you."

"I know. I would have said screw your color scheme if it hadn't worked for me." They both laughed, and Claudia noticed how pretty the brown wrap dress looked as it draped over Karen's swollen belly and complemented her blonde pixie cut with darker lowlights. Her hazel eyes seemed to pop and her expression relayed more excitement than Karen normally allowed.

"Did you drive yourself?"

"No, Rick dropped me off and he'll be coming back to

get me with his SUV so we can carry home all the gifts."

"Oh, didn't I tell you? I asked people not to bring gifts."

"Ha. I only show up for these things if there are gifts." Karen turned to look into the living room. "Oh, Claudia…it looks so pretty."

"It's not too much?"

"Well, of course it's too much. It's a party by Claudia Knight aka our Midwestern Martha Stewart." Karen put her arm around Claudia. "But I love it. It's just right."

Claudia felt relief and pride. "I'm glad. I really wanted to do more, but I had your voice nagging me in the back of my mind and decided I better stop."

"See, all my negativity paid off."

"It did."

"And look at the soda," Karen said, walking over to the tub brimming with ice and bottles. "Even the soda matches. You know you have a problem, right?"

Claudia chuckled. "Yes. Maybe there's a twelve-step program I could join."

"I hope so. 'My name is Claudia and I am addicted to entertaining.'"

"Shut up." They were both giggling when the doorbell rang again.

When Claudia opened the door, she was delighted to see Gabe and Anthony on her porch.

"I'm so sorry we're here a couple of minutes early," Anthony said, stepping inside. "But we thought it would take longer to get here."

Claudia smiled graciously. "That's okay—"

"Oh my God," Gabe said, adjusting his glasses as he walked inside. "Your house is amazing and look at how you've decorated for the party!"

"Exquisite," Anthony said, shaking his head. "I mean, Gabe, you throw fabulous parties but have you ever seen such lovely décor for a baby shower? Tasteful, charming, understated."

In agreement, Gabe nodded with vigor. "You're

absolutely right. Bravo, Claudia."

She could feel she was blushing when she said, "Oh, you guys are too kind. I just love throwing parties... I tend to go a little overboard."

Karen piped up from the dining room, "She's only serving sodas that match the theme."

"How clever!" Anthony said. "Karen, you look beautiful. Are you sure that baby's not going to pop out today?"

They all hugged and Karen moaned. "If it wants to come out today, I'm fine with that. But according to the doctor, we've still got four weeks to go."

"Are you sure there aren't twins in there?" Gabe asked.

"Thank God, no. But unfortunately I think a lot of this is ice cream and pasta. I've kind of been out of control."

"Not to worry," Gabe said, putting his arm around her and guiding her to the sofa. They took a seat. "Once the baby comes and you're feeling stir-crazy and want to get out, I've got some great indoor spots we can go with strollers to get in some power walking. And if you breastfeed, I hear the pounds just melt off."

"Well good, because the only thing melting right now is all the cheese I'm eating."

Claudia ran to grab the door again, and over the next fifteen minutes was on constant door duty and taking guests' jackets. In all there would be sixteen people, between Karen's coworkers, friends, mother and sister-in-law. Most everyone had arrived when Claudia realized Jayne wasn't there yet.

Just then, the door opened, and the very pregnant version of Jayne came in.

"Claudia, I'm so sorry I'm late," she said quietly, trying to sneak in. As if someone that looked like she had swallowed an oversized basketball could walk in unnoticed. But she looked adorable. Her auburn hair and pale skin still gave her that young girl quality she would probably never outgrow. And her big doe eyes and broad smile lit up any room, including this one.

"And I thought Karen was about to pop!" Anthony hollered from the living room. "Jayne, you look like you should already be in the hospital."

Jayne giggled. "Any day now, Anthony. Any day."

"Let me take your jacket," Claudia said, helping Jayne. "And you're just in time."

"Good." Jayne sighed. "I haven't been feeling so great today. I think I'm just worn out."

"Well, all that's required of you here is to eat and relax."

"Two of my favorite things."

Soon they were all seated at the tables, eating, chatting and sharing a lot of laughs. As always with Claudia's parties, it was a great success. This was her favorite part of any event…once things were underway and she got to enjoy the sights and sounds of her guests having fun. It's why she went to all the trouble to create the right environment. So everyone could celebrate what was good about life, even if just for a little while.

She was about to get up and start gathering trash when Anthony grabbed her arm. "So, Claudia, do you remember a few months ago when we mentioned that guy to you…the divorced man, in finance, totally handsome?"

"Yes, I do remember that."

"Well, we saw him last weekend, and he's still single. And he's like a car with low miles, a great engine under the hood and no door dings—he won't last long out there."

Gabe chimed in. "He's right."

Claudia loved their banter. Feeling a burst of confidence, she said with a grin, "Have him call me."

Anthony looked surprised. "Really?"

"Sure. I look forward to hearing from him. If he's all he's cracked up to be, I'd be crazy not to give him a shot."

"You will not regret this." He looked so excited, as if he was cupid himself and had just made the love match of the century. "You two will be perfect for each other. I already told him about you, but I warned him that you might be hesitant…so he'll be thrilled when I give him your number."

"We even showed him your picture on Facebook," Gabe said. "That really piqued his interest."

"Then you have to show me his picture," she said with a pout. "Fair's fair."

Anthony whipped out his phone and had the picture in front of her within thirty seconds. Wow, they were right. He was the cat's meow. And Claudia was ready to come out and play.

"Um, Claudia?" Jayne said in a hushed tone, walking into the room from the bathroom. Claudia looked up to see that her pale face had turned white as a sheet and her eyes were full of fear.

"What's the matter?" Claudia asked, rushing to her side, trying not to make a scene.

Jayne whispered in her ear. "I think my water just broke."

"You think?"

"Okay, it did," Jayne said with more insistence. "I've got one of your hand towels between my legs. Not your nice embroidered ones, the regular ones from under the cabinet."

"Jayne, I don't care about my towels. Oh God…do you want to lie down upstairs and wait for Josh to come get you?"

Jayne shook her head with a look of panic on her face. "I can't wait for him to get here—that's at least a forty-minute drive, plus he's got the kids with him. This is my third baby and the last one was born within four hours of my water breaking. This little guy might just fall out."

"Okay, then we'll get you to the hospital right away."

Karen had seen the two of them talking in hushed tones and knew her friends enough to know that something was up. She wasted no time approaching them. "What's going on? What's wrong?"

"My water broke."

"Holy shit!" Karen's voice was probably louder than she intended. All party conversation stopped as everyone turned to look at them.

Jayne looked thoroughly embarrassed as she offered a sheepish grin. "My water broke," she announced to the other thirteen guests. She turned to Karen. "I'm so sorry, Karen. This is your day, I didn't mean for this to happen—"

"Oh, jeez, Jayne—like I give a rat's ass. You're going to have a baby. Today. We've got to get you out of here."

"I'll drive you." Anthony jumped up. "We just need to put some plastic or towels or whatever down in my car first. Then Gabe can catch a ride home with Karen, right?"

"Of course," Karen said. She looked torn. "I wish I could take you myself—"

"No, no," Jayne protested. "Enjoy your shower. Claudia went to so much trouble to give you such a lovely party…I don't want to ruin everything."

"As soon as it's over," Claudia said, "I'm going straight to the hospital. Mercy, right?"

"Yes," Jayne said, and the grimace on her face told Claudia she was having a contraction.

"How long have you been having contractions?"

"Well…" Jayne looked embarrassed. "Now that I think of it, I think that's why I haven't felt good all day. I think I started having contractions early this morning, but I thought they were just Braxton Hicks. They're only about four to five minutes apart now."

"Get some plastic!" Anthony hollered, grabbing his jacket out of the closet and throwing it on. "Which one is yours, sweetie?"

Claudia grabbed more towels from the bathroom while Jayne got on her jacket. She helped get Jayne settled in Anthony's car and waved while they drove away. Jayne was on her cell phone with Josh as Anthony sped down the street.

When she rejoined the shower, Claudia was distracted. She was doing her best to be a good hostess and give Karen the party she deserved, but she was a bundle of nerves, worried about Jayne.

She could tell Karen felt the same way as she ripped

through the presents at lightning speed. She'd already called Rick and told him to head over so they could leave as soon as possible. Between Karen and Claudia, they managed to get all the guests out of the house within an hour, and that included opening gifts, eating cake and even playing an obligatory shower game.

After the last person left—Karen's mom—Karen shut the door behind her and groaned. It was just Gabe, Claudia, Rick and Karen. "I thought she'd never quit talking and get out of here."

"Well, we kind of did rush everyone out," Claudia said, though she too was glad it was over so she could head to the hospital. "You know, you're eight months pregnant and if you're tired, I'm sure Jayne would totally understand if you went home—"

"Are you kidding me? I was there when Isabella was born, and when Tori and Emma were born. And they were both in the middle of the night. I am *not* missing out on the entrance of Nicholas Brandt. You know how good-looking Brandt boys are."

Claudia laughed. "That's true."

"And Anthony's still at the hospital," Gabe said, "so I can ride there with you and he'll take me home."

"Perfect," Rick said. "I've got the car all loaded up— your loot barely fit in there."

"By the way, Claud," Karen said, "you registered me for some great stuff."

"You bet I did."

"So we're ready to go then? Throw on coats and head to see the third and final Brandt baby enter the world?"

"Yep, I'll clean this up when I get home," Claudia said, grabbing her phone and keys off the counter. Claudia was the last one out.

She stopped and took one last look around. This was one of the craziest parties she'd ever thrown, but it had still been good. And she'd even managed to set the ball rolling for a hot blind date coming up soon.

As she headed out the door, she watched Rick help the

obviously unbalanced Karen into his car and smiled. Years ago she would have never dreamed Karen would want to be a mom. And then when she wanted it so badly and it wasn't happening...Claudia felt helpless. She didn't know how to make it right.

Then watching Jayne become so discouraged after getting what she thought she'd always wanted was heartbreaking, too. The giggle in Jayne's voice and spring in her step seemed to disappear for a while. But over the past several months, it was slowly coming back. Jayne was coming back.

Seeing them both there today, it felt right again. Like they'd all managed to get where they were meant to be and even learn a little along the way. And now there would be two new babies. If that didn't bring hope and joy, what did? Claudia's friends had so much to look forward to.

And after finally letting go of a man and a dream she'd allowed her heart to hang onto for far too many years...Claudia felt more hopeful about the future than she had in years. She locked the door behind her.

Who knows what might be in store?

THE END

ACKNOWLEDGEMENTS

Loads of thanks and gratitude to:

The motley crew at Omega Packaging for ensuring there's never a dull moment at the day job.

Cindy Klatt for your massive amount of support, encouragement, friendship and belief in me. Who knew sneaking me out of class would have turned into a 30-year friendship?

Dana Hilyard for your support and mastery at the carpool—I'll never forget spending the coldest night of my life with you. Greer Schnider for your My Little Pony expertise. Diana Spradling for your prayers and laughs; so lucky to know a cheerful spirit like you.

The crazy gang at Turquoise Morning Press for always being there to cheer me on or give expert insight. So glad to have found a great literary home. Jen Anderson—it's nice to have a local TMP buddy. And thank you, Kim, for all you do.

Judy Alter for sharing your wisdom, encouragement and guidance. I'm grateful to have such a collaborative editor to bring out my best.

The friends that have humbled me with your love and support: Christie Ashabranner, Sarah Bernard, Mary Jane Gilliatt, Robin Hamilton, Julie Heintzelman, Hollie Henderson, Jane Humbarger, Missy Humbarger, Kathy Kelley, Terri McCollum, Mike and Audrey Munsch, Dan and Angie Painter, Sherry Rosenberger, Sean Shelton, Sharon Spearman, Sue and Darril Swaller, Craig Taggart, Amy Wood, and Peggy Woodward.

Gordon Gilliatt for your love and the gift of your son.

LouAnn Schnider for being the closest thing to an angel here on Earth.

The entire Schnider clan—Troy, Kelly, Merrick, Greer and Marlowe—for filling me with love and laughter. There's nothing better than family.

My furry loves: Piper, RJ and Rosie. For giving the kind of love, acceptance and silliness you just can't find from a human. You're worth the bed space you steal every night.

The three most amazing friends of my life...Angie Linan, Kara Mathes and Leigh Cook. You're all delightfully strange and wonderful in your own ways. Couldn't do any of this without you—glad to have you beside me for this ride.

Tressa, Emily and Nate for comic relief and reminding me why any of this matters. I hope I've made you proud.

Jay for tucking me in, bringing me things "while you're up" and making me feel more beautiful and loved than I ever deserved. You're number one. And I mean that in a good way.

Love in Sight by Holly Gilliatt

Looking for love is easier if you can see where you're going.

Praise for *Love in Sight*

"I felt that this story was completely believable, as were the characters. ...I highly recommend it!"—**Diana Coyle at Night Owl Reviews**, 4.5 Stars *Night Owl Top Pick*

"This was such a heartwarming and emotional read for me. ...Characters that felt so real...and had me so involved in them and their story from the very beginning. Didn't want to see it end."—**Mariann at Belle's Book Bag**, 5 Stars

"The author provides a unique insight into the characters and their many dimensions. ...It is a story of finding out who you are, what you want and if you are willing to make the adjustments necessary to live your happy ever after."— **Debbie at Literati Book Reviews**, 4 Stars

"This book was incredible. I'm still thinking about it even though I finished it several days ago. ...I highly recommend to everyone and if I could give this book more than 5 stars, I would."—**Julie at Read Your Writes Book Reviews**, 5 Stars

Books by Holly Gilliatt:

'Til St. Patrick's Day (Book 1 in the St. Louis Sisters Series)

Love in Sight

Dreams, Interrupted (Book 2 in the St. Louis Sisters Series)

ABOUT HOLLY GILLIATT

A self-confessed music, movie and accessories junkie, Holly Gilliatt's passion has always been writing. Give her an algebra quiz and she'll curl up in the fetal position. But throw a test requiring all essay answers her way and she's in heaven. Between the day job, husband, three kids at home, two dogs and a cat—it's not easy to find time to write. So she sacrifices the laundry pile to spin her tales of laughter, friendship and love. This is her third published novel. She's proud to call the St. Louis area her home.

www.hollygilliatt.com

If you enjoyed Holly Gilliatt's *Dreams, Interrupted*, please consider telling others and writing a review.

You might also enjoy these women's fiction authors published by Turquoise Morning Press:

Grace Greene, author of *Beach Winds*
Margaret Ethridge, author of *Commitment*
Jennifer Johnson, author of *Rescuing Riley*

Turquoise Morning Press
Romantically Yours!
www.turquoisemorningpress.com

Made in the USA
Lexington, KY
18 January 2015